MW01258993

ADRIAN'S UNDEAD DIARY

Chris Philbrook

Book Two

ALONE NO MORE

Adrian's Undead Diary: Alone No More
Copyright © 2010 Christopher Philbrook

All rights reserved. No part of this book may be
reproduced or transmitted in any form or by any
means, electronic or mechanical, including
photocopying, recording, or any information storage
and retrieval system, without prior written permission
of the author. Your support of author's rights is
appreciated.

Published in the United States of America

First Publishing Date December, 2010

All characters in this compilation are fictitious. Any
resemblance to actual persons, living or dead, is
purely coincidental.

Cover design and interior layout by Alan MacRaffen

For my friends, who are too numerous to list here,
and far too important to me to forget.

Also, a massive debt of gratitude goes out to the AUD community
as a whole,
without whom there would be no books to read.

-Chris

Also by Chris Philbrook:

<u>Elmoryn - The Kinless Trilogy</u>
Book One: Wrath of the Orphans

Coming Soon:
Book Two: The Motive for Massacre
Book Three

<u>Adrian's Undead Diary</u>
Book One: Dark Recollections
Book Two: Alone No More

Coming Soon:
Book Three: Midnight
Book Four: The Failed Coward
Book Five
Book Six
Book Seven
Book Eight

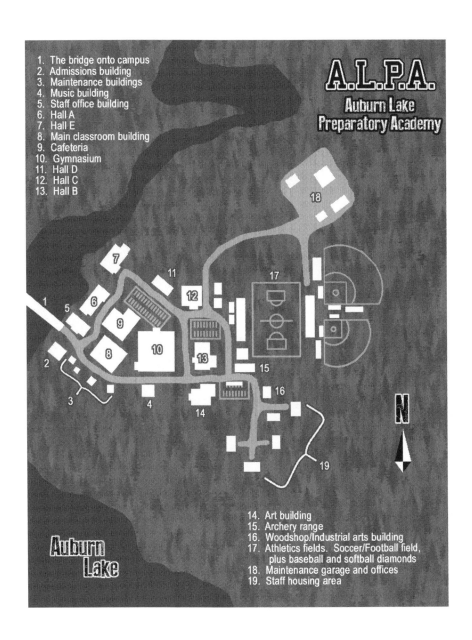

1. The bridge onto campus
2. Admissions building
3. Maintenance buildings
4. Music building
5. Staff office building
6. Hall A
7. Hall E
8. Main classroom building
9. Cafeteria
10. Gymnasium
11. Hall D
12. Hall C
13. Hall B

A.L.P.A.
Auburn Lake
Preparatory Academy

Auburn Lake

14. Art building
15. Archery range
16. Woodshop/Industrial arts building
17. Athletics fields. Soccer/Football field,
    plus baseball and softball diamonds
18. Maintenance garage and offices
19. Staff housing area

TABLE OF CONTENTS:

One Mistake:
The Last Stand of Hall B

"I'm telling you Deb, he just wants to fuck you." The 17 year old brunette said to her bunkmate a couple feet above her. Their bedroom was dark, but their conversation animated.

"Kim, I know he's a retard. That's fine, I just want to fuck him too. I can't stand him, but he's pretty fucking hot." Deb said as she stared intensely at the posters of athletic men stuck to the ceiling just above her top bunk. "Plus it's not like he's smart enough to have his feelings hurt after we hook up."

"Ha. Slut." Kim snickered.

"You girls talking about me again?" A man's whisper came from the door that was just ajar at the head of their bunk. Both girls nearly leapt out of their beds, shame, shock, and a stifled laugh all readily apparent on their bright red faces. Standing with his grinning face just inside the dorm room was Adrian, one of the school staff at the prep academy the two girls attended.

"Mr. Ring, you shouldn't sneak up on us like that." Kim said in a scolding fashion at the staff member. She kind of liked him, he was tall, dark, mysterious, pretty funny, and you could always see a little peek here and there of some tattoos. She might stray from her normal bounds for him some night, if she thought he'd go for it.

CHRIS PHILBROOK

Deb in the bunk above her added to the diatribe, "Yeah Mr. Ring. Seriously, it's late, and this is clearly girls only time." The thin blonde twirled her hair in a largely adolescent attempt to look sexy.

Adrian laughed in a hushed tone, careful not to wake up the girls sleeping in the other bunks in the room, and said back, "First, it's Adrian, not Mr. Ring, Deb. I'm not your teacher. And secondly girls, if it's this late, and its girls only time, I shouldn't be able to hear about your attempted sexual conquests in the kitchen downstairs, right? Volume ladies. It's a school night."

That hushed both of the girls. With no witty comeback coming to their minds both girls let out simultaneous sighs, and laid back down in their beds. They were defeated by logic.

"FYI Deb, he's dirty. You might catch something. Date one of the nerds. They'll get more handsome soon enough, they're probably clean, and they'll also appreciate you a lot more." Adrian said with a smile and a wink, and pulled the door shut.

Both girls sighed again, sick of the same old lecture. After a minute of silence, they both let out muffled giggles. Kim reached over and grabbed the remote to small TV on the bureau next to their bed and thumbed through the channels. Every channel was filled with the same old shit she thought. It was always shitty reality TV, infomercials about getting rich quick, and 24 hour news channels at this hour. She lingered on a news report of multiple homicides reported all over the world in what looked to be another coordinated terrorism attack, but decided it was the same shit as it was always ways, and hit the power button. The TV blinked off with a static snap of protest, and went black.

"Goodnight whore," Kim said as she rolled over onto her stomach.

Deb replied in a half asleep mumble, "Goodnight skank."

ALONE NO MORE

*****

The two girls woke up at 7am just like they always did for school days. It was a Wednesday, and just like every other Wednesday at the school they had classes first thing in the morning. Tough classes. Classes like AP Calculus, AP History, AP Chemistry, and AP Physics. The school they attended was an exceedingly expensive private preparatory high school, and only the best and brightest were allowed to attend. Although in Deb's case, having a lot of money could get you around the best and brightest part.

Both girls spent their early morning putting themselves together. They woke up a little earlier than the rest of the girls to ensure they'd have plenty of hot water, and had plenty of mirror time in the bathroom. Both girls were interested in several different guys on campus, and didn't want to miss a day of looking good when they were on the prowl. God forbid a guy passed on them because one of them didn't straighten their hair that day.

Once Kim and Deb got their appearances perfect, they headed downstairs and sat at the dining room table. Adrian sat at the table in front of his laptop, brow furrowed in an amused, but also vaguely concerned expression.

"Something funny Adrian?" Kim asked him.

"Well Kim," he scrolled his mouse wheel, "weird news reports online all night. Lots of random attacks all over the world. Some places are saying the attacks are being perpetrated by zooooooommbieessss." He drew the last word out and made a blank drooling stare. It was a very good zombie face. He shrugged, and closed the laptop, gathering his stuff to head out.

"Yeah sure. Probably another stunt for some TV show," Deb said as she peeled an orange, her normal morning breakfast.

"Something like that." Adrian tucked his computer away in its case, dumped out his cup of coffee in the sink, and double checked he hadn't left anything. "Remember girls,"

11

he looked at the two of them, panning a dead serious expression. "Shoot them in the head. It's the only way to kill them." He held his expression for a second then slowly busted out into a sly grin.

The two girls mocked him for being a mega nerd as he made his way out the back kitchen door, waving as he clicked it shut behind him.

"I like him." Kim said to Deb.

Deb delicately chewed her orange slice, and replied after she swallowed the pulp, "He's cool. I heard his girlfriend is cool too. She came to pick him up a week ago when his car was getting fixed or something."

"Girlfriend huh?" Kim's mind started racing at the thrill of the hunt. Maybe she'd try to press the issue with Mr. Ring some night. Kim started peeling her own orange, starting her devious plan for seduction.

"Slut." Deb said.

"Yep." Kim replied as she starting eating her orange.

Turns out it never mattered, they never saw him again.

*****

The two oversexed teenage vixens (or so they thought themselves to be) made their way to the campus cafeteria to socialize before they had to go to class. Neither of them ate at the cafeteria of course. They simply moved table to table, making their rounds to all the boys they wanted to give a little attention to. Just like any school, it was a popularity contest at Auburn Lake Prep. Almost everyone was smart there, and there were a lot of good looking kids as well, so it came down to money, or popularity. The two girls made sure they laid some seeds with several boys before the bell rang and everyone was summoned off to their first classes.

Kim and Deb both had AP Calc as their morning class. Mr. Dalembert taught it, and if you could find a nerdier, drier person, you should be searching for Bin Laden Kim felt. Both girls would rather sit at home with their parents, getting lectured about curfew times than sit through one more of his classes, but such was life. They shuffled themselves into their desks, fetched their scientific calculators and their books from their bags, and settled in for the long haul. Two hours of pure, mathematical agony.

The class went exactly as both of them had expected. Well, not entirely as expected. Mr. Dalembert had a strict no cell phone policy in his class. He fully expected everyone in the class to focus themselves entirely to the shrine of trigonometry, geometry, algebra and calculus when he was on his pulpit. No exceptions were allowed. In fact his rule carried a stiff penalty. Every time a student was caught with their cell phone out in class, their semester grade went down one full point. It didn't take many grade deductions to show up on their reports for the kids to find out mommy and daddy were pissed. It was an effective system.

That's why there was a stunned silence when Mr. Dalembert called out to Pete at the back of the room towards the end of class, "Peter, is that a phone in your hand?" Mr. Dalembert's long, hawkish face was even more avian as his eyebrows cocked up in his overdone look of shock.

Peter, or Pete as he preferred, was the resident math genius. His eyeglasses were a little too thick, the frames a little too large, and his jet black hair was always mussy, and not in the trendy emo way. Pete was awkward, too skinny, and was for sure a social outcast from girls like Kim and Deb. In fact, both girls had bet last year that he was still a virgin, despite being a senior.

"Mr. Dalembert, I'm sorry sir. I just... It's just..." He replied without looking up an inch from his phone. It was a very expensive phone. Internet, email, super high def camera, you name it, it did it. At least Pete couldn't be picked on for having second rate gadgets.

"Peter it's just that you lost a point off your grade. I expected better of you, really." Mr. Dalembert took out his dreaded red pen and marked down a check in his grade book. Everyone knew it was next to Peter's name.

"I think you should turn on the TV Mr. Dalembert. Something serious is happening." Pete finally looked up, his young, awkward expression showing a little confusion, and a little fear. Everyone else in the classroom was looking back and forth between the student and teacher, waiting to see how the weird power struggle played out. Something in Pete's face must've been sincere though, because after a few seconds of looking at him, Mr. Dalembert went over to the TV that hung suspended in the corner of the classroom, and he turned it on with the remote.

Kim and Deb exchanged slightly excited glances at one another. When the television went on, it meant study stopped abruptly, and that meant a break from the droning of numbers and formulas.

"Go to one of the news networks," Pete finally sat his phone down on the desk and started walking slowly to the front of the classroom. He looked almost afraid of what the TV might show. Kids from the back of the classroom started to get up, joining Pete slowly in the front, trying to get a good look at whatever it was that had him spooked.

The teacher flipped through a few dozen stations before arriving at one of the more reputable news networks. They were on commercial though, and Mr. Dalembert gave a disappointed look at Pete. "Peter if whatever it is that's got you worried were serious, they would not go to commercial. This had better be good mister." He returned his gaze to the television after his dressing down of the kid.

"It will be. Well, I don't think it'll be good, but I think it's legitimate." Pete never took his eyes off the screen.

After a few minutes of incessant commercial rambling about various medications that apparently everyone should know they needed, the female anchor finally appeared again, and Pete leaned in to hear. She talked for several second with the caption *Worldwide Murders* over her shoulder, and a picture of police lights flashing. The volume was too low though, and a chorus of "turn it up" sprouted. Mr. Dalembert obliged them after fumbling with the remote for a second. Eventually the anchor's voice carried over the growing din in the classroom, and everyone fell silent to listen. The television had won.

"Reports are mixed, and we are trying to verify them at this hour, but what we can tell you is that multiple of our bureaus are saying that there has been a seemingly random, dramatic spike in personal attacks all across the world. We are hearing that the majority of these attacks appear to be assaults committed by either a drugged, or ill group of citizens. They are characterized by muted flesh tones, a general appearance of disorientation, and an immediate need to attack others, including animals. Now we aren't sure exactly what of those reports is fully true or not, but that's what's coming in from over 20 of our bureaus across the world, including here in the United States." As she talked the image over her shoulder changed to a collage of photographs. Each picture was a snapshot of people wandering, covered in blood, wounded, injured, and scared. The pictures were of white people, black people, Asian people, all people. Some of the pictures even showed the purported attackers. They were blank faced, covered in dried blood, walking as if on autopilot. In almost every shot they were moving directly towards the person taking the shot. Many of these attackers snapped their jaws closed repeatedly, as if they were trying to take bites out of their intended victims long before they reached them. It made for a very unsettling collection of images.

Pete swallowed hard, and looked around the classroom before opening his mouth, "those are zombies."

The entirety of the classroom erupted in nervous laughter at him, and his ridiculous statement. Mr. Dalembert turned the volume on the television down as the class slowly winded down its response to Pete. The teacher just shook his head, finally clicking the television off.

"Everyone back to their seats please." Mr. Dalembert put the remote away in his desk and continued to laugh under his breath, still shaking his head in amusement. The class made their way slowly back to their chairs as they all took turns making fun of poor Pete. All of the mockery, all the ridicule was lost on him though. He pleaded the seriousness of the matter to everyone, even the people who were making fun of him to his face. Deb and Kim were about to stand up and take Pete's side, if only to prevent him from becoming a homicidal classmate later when Mr. Dalembert broke in.

"Enough." His tone said everything that needed to be said. The class fell silent as he slowly raised the dreaded red pen again. He waited a full ten seconds before he put the cap back on it, and sat it down on his desk. "Peter, thank you for bringing this odd situation to our attention. However, we still have an hour of calculus left this morning, and there have been no reports of anything strange happening near here that I am aware of. Thus, our calculations go on." He snickered at his own bad joke as he turned to the marker board behind him.

"Mr. Dalembert, if we wait an hour, it might be too late for us." Pete said in a deadpan voice from his seat at the back of the classroom. Kim and Deb both looked at him at the same time. He looked serious, and scared. Really scared.

That scared the girls very much.

*****

It wasn't until the girl's second period class that they started to notice that something was very, very wrong on campus. The school sounded a special alarm that only happened once in a blue moon. All the classroom doors were shut, and all the windows closed. Curtains were drawn down to obstruct the view into, and out of each room, and the teachers all changed their demeanors. They seemed more nervous, more withdrawn and cautious. They kept teaching, but many of them did so keeping their classroom doors in front of them. The school called it a "code blue" situation. The kids called it "lockdown." It had happened just once earlier around Christmas time when a student brought a handgun onto campus.

During the rest of second period there were more short alarms sounded. Most of them neither girl knew anything about. From where they were sitting, they could see people running around outside. Some were arguing, some getting aggressive, many yelling and screaming. Over what, they didn't know. Deb and Kim could almost feel the sanity slowly slipping away from the world as things progressively got weirder. When the period bell rang, they were escorted by staff to their next classrooms.

It was 3rd period, sometime around 1:30 in the afternoon when they started to see the cars come for kids. At first it was just one or two, but within half an hour, there was no place to park on campus.

It wasn't long after the kids started to leave that Kim's cell phone buzzed in her trendy little purse. She was afraid her current teacher would notice. Dr. Potter was the biggest teacher on campus, easily 300 pounds and growing one granola bar at a time. She knew he was quick to point out and ridicule a bad student, and she didn't want to be the one who got his wrath. She fished it out and kept it below the edge of her desk, out of Dr. Potter's eyes. He didn't have a red pen rule, but he was already steaming at having to stop two straight period's worth of classes so much over what he deemed to be "foolishness." She didn't want to risk the big man's ire.

It was a text message from her mother.

Kim, there is some very weird stuff going on. We are on our way to get you, but we won't be there until at least 8pm.

Okay. Should I be worried? She texted back quickly.

If you are on campus, you are probably fine. Your father is scared though. The hospital tried to call him in to help, but he decided to come get you first. He has his bat

17

Kim. Her mother wrote back.

Wow. The bat. The same bat he chased Darren off the porch with last summer? Lol.

Lol Yeah. Same bat. He's scared babe. So am I. Stay safe. Lock yourself inside if you see sick people, or people fighting. This thing seems to be spreading. See you in a few hours, love u.

Kim thought about it for a second then sent the final text back: **luv u 2.**

Kim slipped her phone discreetly back into her purse and looked over at Deb. Deb had been watching the whole time, and when they finally looked at each other, she raised her eyebrows, questioning Kim what was up. Kim leaned over subtly and whispered to her, "My mom and dad are on their way. Guess this is pretty bad." Deb grimaced and made a lemon face in response.

During fourth period, at about 3:30 pm or so, Dr. Potter their classics professor had to stop class half a dozen additional times to excuse a student to leave. Both Deb and Kim started to get that grinding, nagging pang deep down in their stomachs. The feeling of dread. Kim had the same feeling years ago when her mom sat the family down, and told them about her breast cancer. She knew something was wrong then, and she knew something was seriously wrong now. At least her mom had beaten the cancer. Hopefully this would end the same way too.

Deb looked fully concerned for the first time since watching Pete make his prophetic style announcement in first period. She went for her own purse and got her phone out. Kim knew she'd be trying to track down what her parents were doing. Deb's parents lived fairly nearby, only an hour or so away by car. She might be able to go home soon and figure out what was happening from there. It was then that Kim realized that almost everyone else in the classroom was on their cell phones as well as her friend. Each kid was locked on to the text message they were sending, and in the front of the classroom Dr. Potter stood, fists planted firmly on his wide hips, watching in frustration. She watched him take the whole scene in for some time, but they were both interrupted when the class phone rang on the wall. Everyone stopped typing in unison as he walked over and answered it. After a few seconds of listening, he nodded and hung it up again.

"Mike, Sarah, Christian, and Emma, you are summoned to the admissions building. I bid you good day." He made a grandiose gesture as he pulled the classroom doors open. The four students gathered their things quickly, and left the room almost at a sprint. Dr. Potter closed the door, and turned to address his class again. He stopped just short of saying something, hand still resting on the door handle, when he pulled the door open again.

"Class is dismissed. I suggest you return to your dorms or go to the staff administration buildings to consult your advisors as to what to do. I will not teach three students." He made another grandiose, mocking bowing motion, beckoning the three remaining students. Kim, Deb, and Kyle, the three teens left, exchanged one last set of glances, and took off out the door. As they went down the hall they could hear yelling coming from Mrs. Goodell's room across the hall. It sounded heated. Kim and Deb slowed, trying to listen, but it was clear it was not going to work. There were too many voices coming from the inside to pick anything out. The two of them turned and headed down the school house steps as fast as they could go. For once, Kim and Deb were glad they didn't wear heels.

Kim and Deb went out the glass doors of the school building just as they were shutting from when Kyle blew through them. He didn't wait one moment for them. Both girls gave him dirty looks as he rounded the sidewalk heading to the boy's upper class dorm, Dormitory C.

Deb spoke first as they came to a stop on the sidewalk in front of the school, "So I am totally and completely fucking confused here." She pulled out her phone and dialed it once more as she finished her sentence.

Kim sighed once deeply and took in the summer sunshine. She opened her eyes with a start when she heard a loud crunching noise coming from down the street. They both looked at the source of the noise, and saw two cars locked together in a fairly good fender bender. The cars were damaged pretty good, but no one looked hurt. The girls went back to their conversation after having their "people are such dumbasses" look.

"Me too. My mom and dad are on their way but won't be here for at least 7 or 8 hours. You get a hold of your mom or dad yet?" She looked expectantly as Deb listened into her phone, waiting for an answer.

Deb listened for a few seconds, and then hung up, "it's busy. All circuits are busy." They moved over and sat down on a nice stone bench right next to the perfectly trimmed hedges in front of the school. Engraved on the bench in an ornate script was; A gift from Andrew and Michelle, class of '83. This expensive detail was lost on them though. Their minds were elsewhere.

They sat there for some time one butt firmly planted on Andrew, the other on Michelle, waiting for the other to speak, waiting for a plan to form, but neither said anything. Finally Deb spoke up, "I'm fucking starved. You hungry?"

"Are you shitting me? All I ate today was an orange." Kim looked at her like she could not have asked a more stupid question.

"Let's hit the cafeteria then. I'm not skipping lunch today." She got up and dragged Kim along with her.

*****

The campus cafeteria was only maybe a hundred feet down the private school street. They walked holding hands the entire distance. This wasn't all that unusual for them, but today they were holding hands not out of friendship, but for mutual reinforcement. Together they were strong, apart they were vulnerable. Holding hands just made sure they wouldn't be separated.

Inside the double glass doors the cafeteria was nearly empty. Long row tables with built in round plastic seats lined the long room like bright blue Formica coffins. With few students inside, the hollow concrete cafeteria had an eerie echo to it, like an academic mausoleum. The girls were instantly unsure of their choice to come here. They were beckoned by the sole group of kids sitting in the center table though, and the thought of being wanted appealed to both of them, and they hurried over.

Twelve girls all sat around a laptop in the middle of the room. The girls were almost the entirety of the soccer team for the school. Teams are hard to break up apparently. Deb and Kim were friendly with most of them, and a few of their acquaintances greeted them absently. One of them, one of the co-captains Kim thought was the one operating the laptop.

Over the next hour and a half they figured out that the girls had come from Phys. Ed., which explained why they were dressed almost entirely in shorts and tee shirts, or tank tops and athletic pants. They had gathered here because the campus wireless signal was strong in the cafeteria, and they were starving as well. Kim and Deb helped themselves to the giant tub of salad at the salad bar while they all eagerly searched for information online.

More of the picture was coming into focus. When the girls had finished their third or fourth bowl of salad (who was counting today anyway? Everyone knows there are no calories during a crisis) they had come to the realization that this problem was not far away at all. They'd also figured out this was beyond just being a problem.

Outbreaks had occurred all over the world. People suddenly attacking each other for no reason. It seemed to start near hospitals, nursing homes, ghettos, crack houses, and warzones. Anywhere people were sick or injured, it seemed to fester fastest. Anyone bitten by the sick contracted the same strange illness within minutes. At first it wasn't anywhere in America, which seemed like good news, but the more the girls searched, and the longer they took to do it, more information came to light that it had in fact taken root in America. Quickly.

Boston, Dallas, Seattle, Detroit, New York City, San Diego, Tampa, Memphis, Charleston, Akron, Minneapolis, Chicago, Houston, New Orleans, and even Billings Montana had all reported large cases of these attacks. Some of these girls sitting right here at this table were from some of those cities and regions. It seemed like the harder they searched, the more reports they could find. And they did not like what they found.

The attacks were gory, horrific. So many people were biting, ripping the flesh of their victims apart, and leaving ragged, infected wounds behind. People ripped limb from limb, some disemboweled, many partially eaten. The pictures made their stomachs turn so badly most of them wound up vomiting the salads they'd just eaten. Kim and Deb had to move away and sit at another table. Soon enough, some of the girls started to cry. The ones from the regions reporting serious attacks all immediately started to think the worst. For them, going home was likely impossible until this all settled down.

"The FAA and TSA just announced all flights are canceled." The team co-captain said in between blowing her nose from crying. "Says here some of the flights that are in bound from other countries are being turned away, and some of them likely can't find a place to land. Some will probably crash." She barely got the word crash out before inhaling sharply, starting a trembling sob. That got them all going again.

"My little sister and my family are in Manhattan this week, visiting my aunt." One girl said.

"My dad is in San Diego."

"My brother lives in Redmond, near Seattle."

The stories went on. Everyone here knew someone near one of the major outbreaks of violence. Locally the stories were just as bad. The state police were sealing off the borders, trying to keep anyone infected out, or trying to prevent any possible terrorists trying to spread it from moving freely. What scared them the most of anything though, was the simple fact that NO ONE really seemed to know what was happening. No one.

That was when they heard the loud crash outside. This was much louder than the fender bender they'd heard earlier. Kim and Deb looked up from their tissues, eyes red, makeup long since ruined. Commotion could be heard down the street, and in a single, simultaneous action, the entire pack of teens jumped to their feet and ran out to see the source of the noise.

After jogging back down past the school building they saw what it was. A small car, something expensive Kim noted, had driven right into the side of the school building. Somehow it had jumped the curb, gone over another one of those engraved granite benches, and come to a rest nearly upside down against the side of the building. The grass, mulch and hedges were all trashed from the off course vehicle. Dozens of staff, parents, and students all stood watching as some bystanders rushed in to give aid to whoever was in the small luxury car. The teammates all yelled out to their coach as he sprinted in, squeezing himself right under the wreck to get at the driver. He was fairly young still, and quite athletic. He made the squeeze in under the car like a professional athlete. Another staff member and a few parents saw him, and acted immediately as well to help. They moved to the passenger side and started to extricate that person.

It took only perhaps fifteen minutes, but eventually they had three people out and on the ground. Unconsciously the girls had moved closer to the accident to get a better look.

Despite their earlier stomach turning experience with the news, they found themselves compelled to see what was happening right in front of them. Everyone turns and looks at the car accident when they drive by, after all.

The driver was the worst off by far. His arm had been caught between the car and something stronger than it, and had been shredded into pulp. His bloody pink exposed arm bones were cracked in multiple places, and it splayed out at a strange, impossible angle. His blood pumped freely out of the elbow area into the grass. His skin color drained in minutes, and he clearly and quickly faded into a still oblivion. The two other passengers were bad as well. The back seat held one of their fellow students. A freshman Kim thought, one of the members of the so-called Lollipop Guild Deb and Kim dubbed them. It seemed like every year the freshman got smaller and younger.

The student had very labored breathing, and couldn't focus on the people helping him. The coach muttered something about shock, and internal injuries. The front seat passenger was clearly the mother. She was the best off of all, and she still had broken legs. The front of their car had crumpled just enough to fold her knees backward, cracking the kneecaps, making them useless. She barked out scream after scream every time someone touched her, or moved her. They tended to her legs and her son for some time, trying to comfort, trying to treat. She started to quiet down when she fully saw her son's struggles. She went silent when she saw her husband with the severed arm stand.

No one noticed him until it had already happened. Everyone in the crowd was completely fixated on the fate of the son and his wheezing, struggling coughs. The dilated eyes of the child held everyone's focus just long enough for the father to rise inhumanly to his feet once more, and dive down on top of the coach.

Coach was wearing a grey school sweatshirt with a hood on it. He had been crouched down trying to render first aid to the boy when the father attacked him. Kim and Deb watched in horror as the recently dead driver of the car grabbed the sweatshirt hood with a vicious yank, throwing the coach on his back. The dad plunged his mouth downward with a silent snarl, and ripped a gouge out of the prone coach's shoulder, right where it met the neck.

The soccer coach screamed out in pain and slugged the driver in the face. He struck him so hard his body was thrown almost entirely onto the severely injured son. Using his shattered forearm like a crutch, the dead father raised him body to a half sitting position. Everyone gathered around had started to back away, either silent in shock, or screaming in confusion and panic. The zombie of the dead dad slowly looked around at the circle of people, his eyes milky white and vacant, yet filled with a strange, almost supernatural malice.

He had propped himself up enough to get to his knees when his son behind him made another wet, wheezy gasp. His head snapped around hungrily at his very own child, and he launched his whole body at the kid. People started running at full speed as the undead dad chewed his way into the stomach cavity of his own flesh and blood. The son's breathing labored further, and his eyes rolled into his skull as he fully succumbed to his agony. The screams of mortal horror from the mother were soul rending. She watched on helplessly, just a few feet away as her own husband ate her only son alive.

The girls jumped into action, strangely unified by the horrible scene unfolding in front of them. The entire team of soccer players rushed forward to aid their fallen coach. He had been slowly crawling on his back, trying to get away from the cannibal mauling the child in front of him. The girls got the coach to his feet just as the father was turning his attention to his helpless wife. Coach held a hand firmly over the deep bite wound on his neck, trying to stop the steady ebb of his blood. It wasn't working. His sweatshirt sleeve was already dark brown all the way to his elbows. He would bleed out soon if they didn't get him medical attention.

Leaning heavily on the two largest and oldest of the soccer players they managed to get him slowly past the school building, and around the corner of the cafeteria, over a hundred feet away. He collapsed on the ground, taking one of the girls with him, falling in a pile of limbs, bruises and blood smears. He rolled onto his back and started to direct the girls.

"Plug it, stick a shirt in the hole, put pressure on." He got the words out barely through force of will. One of the girls had an extra shirt on and she stripped it off immediately. It was warm that day, she wouldn't be cold. The girl nearest his neck rolled it up into a ball and pressed it into the holes from the attack. It looked like a solid tug on the bite wound could pull out a chunk of pink flesh the size of a plum. The bleeding slowed somewhat, but the coach was starting to slip into the glorious haze of shock. Some of the girls started to cry out again, begging him to stay with them.

Kim and Deb decided they needed to get help. Real, actual medical help for the Coach. The school nurse was located in the office building near admissions, but that would mean going over past where the accident had happened. It would be stomach turning at the very least, and potentially even deadly. Gritting their collective teeth, they went anyway.

The nurses' office was on the other side of the car accident. Taking a wide circle the two of them jogged quickly across the street and around the corner. They slowed and watched the disgusting scene at the accident continue to play out. The father was still murdering his wife when they slipped by. The son, who had died at his father's hands not five minutes earlier, was twitching on the ground. The girls didn't know if he was still alive or not, but they couldn't risk getting closer to the murderous dad to find out. The mother's body jerked reflexively as the father gnawed at her chest and throat. After a few moments of watching, the two girls froze. The dad had stopped eating, and was slowly rising to his feet. From far down the campus street another argument could be heard, and the father's attention went that way, towards the sound. He started a slow gait down the street, his legs propelling him forward almost as if he were on stilts. Their movement was no longer fluid and human, but artificial, and pure evil.

The girls stayed still until he was well away from them and the accident, then they bolted into the staff office building. The nurses' office was less of a clinic setting, and more of a straight office. There was a plain vinyl couch that served as medical bed, and a handful of sterile stainless steel rolling cabinets. Otherwise it was the same as all the other offices in the building. Deb and Kim burst into the office, bleating out the details of what was going on outside. It was a few seconds before they realized the office was empty, and they were talking to no one.

"Are you shitting me?" Deb blurted out.

"Wow. Where the hell is Nurse Daniels? Of all the frigging days." Kim wandered into the office and started rifling through drawers, looking for bandages and medical supplies. Deb joined her after a second, and within a few minutes they'd gathered what they thought was enough supplies to save the Coach. They left the building at a jog and headed back to where they had left the group. When they passed the accident scene the father was long gone, and his son had joined him. The only body still lying in the destroyed greenery was the mother. As they walked past her, she began to twitch as well. When Deb and Kim got back to the area where Coach had collapsed, everyone was gone. All that remained behind was a dark red smudge on the grass where Coach had been bleeding. The two bunkmates rolled their eyes almost in unison. Abandoned yet again.

Deb pointed at a spot of blood on the sidewalk leading into the cafeteria, "Dude, inside."

Kim and Deb took off and pulled open the glass doors into the cafeteria. Laying on one of the blue tables was the Coach. He was still alive, but in clear pain. He was tilted to the side just enough so he could drink some water from a bottle one of his players held to his mouth for him. He coughed when he drank too much, and slumped onto his back again, exhausted.

"Here!" Deb said as they rushed over to the table. The inexperienced medical practitioners went to work, doing the best they could. They applied ointments, bandages, and tape in alternating levels. None of them knew what to do really, and the Coach was in no position to give them any advice. It was all he could do to grit his teeth against the pain. Some of the girls who were emotionally drained than others simply sat watching, tears slowly running down their dirty cheeks.

"What're we going to do?" Kim asked the group after they finished getting the Coach bandaged up. It seemed to be working, his pain seemed to be abated, and the bleeding had stopped.

"I don't know." Was the most common response to her question.

Coach cleared his throat with effort and spoke softly, "Get somewhere safe and lock your selves in."

The girls all seemed to agree with him, and a dozen plans all began coming out in a cacophony of girl voices. After just a few seconds arguments began to spring up between the teammates. Coach sat there, eyes closed, listening to the immature girls threaten one another over different plans. After a minute or two he opened his eyes, and rolled his head to the side with a wince to face his young co-captain. She looked around helplessly as her friends tore into each other with insults and petty grievances. She looked down at him and made eye contact. He didn't say anything, but the simple act of meeting her gaze reminded her of who was in charge there.

"Shut the fuck up!" She yelled. She was young, only 18, but in her voice at that moment was the strength she needed to quiet her confused and scared friends. Awkwardly they shut their mouths for her, and started to stare away, or down at their feet. "This is no time to argue. Three people just died outdoors, Coach is really hurt, and we're not safe here. We need to get to real safety. Has anyone called 911 yet?"

Several of the girls all replied that they had tried. All said the same thing as well. All circuits busy. That took a lot of wind out of the sails in the room. No help would come for them. They had to help themselves.

"Coach, what do you think we should do? Where should we go?" The captain leaned down to him so he could hear easier, and make himself heard easier as well.

Coach furrowed his brow in a mixture of exhaustion and thought. He thought for a minute and finally said, "Get to a dorm. Lock yourselves in a room. Block the door off. Pick a room upstairs so they can't smash the window to get in. Keep trying 911 until someone answers. Wait for help."

They all nodded in agreement. It was a simple plan. It could work. After a few seconds of letting it sink in, the captain started speaking again, "Okay, do we know where the crazy dude is?"

Deb answered her, "He killed his wife, then headed down towards the athletics field area. It should be clear. His son is gone too. Don't know where he went."

"Cool, I guess. If we get Coach up, we can shuffle him over to Hall B and get him upstairs. We can shut ourselves in and wait this out. The cops'll be here soon. They gotta be." Once again everyone nodded in agreement with their captain. Even Deb and Kim were onboard with her leadership, and they both fucking hated girls.

"Close, but not quite," Coach muttered.

"What?" The captain asked him, confused.

"Leave me here. I don't think I'm going to be safe to be around soon." He let a long breath out after saying his statement.

"Not cool Coach. We aren't leaving you here." The captain shook her head dismissively at her mentor.

"Look Jenny. That crazy dude, the dad? He was dead. Gone. No pulse. And he sat back up and attacked me. Then he killed his son, and Deb said he also killed his wife. Deb also just said his son is now gone, and we all saw what happened to him. I saw one of the news reports earlier. It said that they think the bites infect. He bit me. So there's no sense at all in bringing me with you because if I am infected, I will bite you guys too. You can't risk it." He made so much sense it kind of hurt the girl's feelings. He wasn't abandoning them. He was making sure he wasn't a threat to them.

More tears flowed freely as they wrapped their heads around the situation. Finally Coach broke the sound of quiet sobbing, "If I am not infected, I will be safe here. I'm not bleeding anymore I don't think, and I have water. I can hide in here." He winced again as he looked around the cafeteria and kitchen. The girls all nodded separately at him. They wouldn't disagree with him anyway, it wasn't in their nature to challenge the Coach.

Deb and Kim didn't care anymore. The longer they waited the worse things would be when they finally did leave, and Kim played the role of asshole, "Look we have to go right now. If he's out there biting more people, at this rate the whole state will be infected by the time we get to Hall B." She said it as nicely as she could, but there were many looks of venom coming her way when she finished. They didn't want to be rushed.

Coach nodded at Kim, and reached up to hug his captain. They embraced warmly, if delicately, and he let her go. He smiled. Each of his girls came to him, and he embraced them the same way. Each was like a daughter to him, and he was their father away from home for them. This goodbye was painful on many levels for everyone. Everyone except Deb and Kim. They felt some of the pain of the group, but they weren't emotionally as invested in the Coach. They just wanted to survive.

Soon after the girls made their final plan, and slipped out of the back entrance of the cafeteria, through the kitchen. That door led almost directly in a line to Hall B, and would offer them as straight a route as could be found. Two of the girls got their Dorm keys ready so there was less a chance of fumbling a key at the last second. Once they were ready, they took off running.

All the girls were young and athletic, some more than others, but they reached the front door of Hall B in less than thirty seconds. The lead girl had her key up and ready when they started piling up on the doorsteps, and like planned, she had the door open in a jiffy. The girls all raced inside, log jamming briefly, but without injury. They slammed the door shut and it locked behind them. Panting, the group caught their breath.

"Okay. Let's figure out what to do," the captain said after they'd gathered themselves.

And that's what they did. The girls moved food and water up into the room they chose. All the furniture was double checked to be adequate, and they got all their clothes and major possessions moved around so they wouldn't need anything during the wait for help. In all, it took them only twenty minutes to get things ready, which under any other circumstance would have been a miracle of preparation time for teenage girls.

"Look outside!" Deb was standing at the back of the dorm, in the kitchen. She was pointing at three other girls outside, running at top speed towards them. They had the son chasing them. The dead son. The very son that they themselves had seen murdered by the father earlier. He moved just like his father had. The boy was rigid, stilted, obsessed. His stomach had a jagged tear in it, and his pink and purple insides pressed out of the hole. Only the shredded wrapping of his shirt kept them from falling out on the ground on front of him.

The girls screamed bloody murder as they ran from him. Deb opened the kitchen door and the three of them blasted their way in so fast the back door smashed against the counter next to it. Deb shoved the door shut and it locked immediately. The three new girls were hysterical, covered in scratches and bloodstains from defending themselves.

"Upstairs, get upstairs now!" Kim hollered as the son

31

continued his inexorable march directly at them. Like a flock of panicked birds they took flight, screaming their way up the stairs and into the dorm room they'd gotten ready. Once the door was shut they pushed a set of bunk beds in front of the door as added fortification. It happened to be the bunk beds that Kim and Deb shared, which was a bit of a bummer for the two of them when they realized their sleeping situation had been used as a barricade.

It was sometime before they were all calm again. Once they were, they heard the tale of the three new arrivals. The three had been going from one of the fields down in the back of campus to their dorm here when they saw the young student approaching. It didn't take a doctor to know something was wrong. At first, as could be expected, they tried to render aid, but once they got close enough to help, he pounced on them. Between the three of them they managed to get him off of them and down to the ground. They pleaded with him to stop, but he kept on coming at them. Eventually they started running away, and made their escape to Hall B. He followed them slowly, but his endurance was unending. They had to stop to catch their breath, and he did not. But they were safe now.

Time passed very slowly at first for the girls in the room. They took turns looking out the window to see what was going on outside. Every time a new person walked by they reported to the room.

"Another kid, running away."

"Another kid. Dead, still walking around."

"Adult dead guy chasing teacher." After a while it turned into a joke, and they started to laugh at the absurdity of it all. They all gathered at the window for one moment when they saw one of their least liked teachers trip and fall with a zombie right behind him. The teacher, in a brilliant stroke of self defense luck, kicked the leg of the zombie out while he was flailing for his life, and he escaped at the last second. Secretly some of them wished the zombie had gotten him, but they were mostly happy to see someone survive. Stress does funny things to people.

At about seven pm they started to hear gunshots. One here, one there. Sometimes a short burst of three or four. That cheered them up. Guns meant cops to them, and cops meant rescue. The girls all had a sizeable boost to their morale. They sat in the dark, mostly quiet for another hour before there was another burst of gunfire. Many shots this time. From their window vantage point they couldn't see anyone shooting, or see flashes from the barrels anywhere. They just knew guns meant people were here to help.

Another hour later they stopped counting the dead people walking by. There was no sense counting living people anymore either, because there weren't any to count. One of the new girls was on watch at about ten when she spoke out.

"Hey! A living dude!" She pointed out the window as she exclaimed to the group. It had been a long time since they'd seen a real person. Several of the girls jumped up and went to the window. They watched for a minute or two before they walked away, dejected.

"Sorry. He looked alive for a bit there." No one responded. "Does anyone have any anti-itch cream? My boob is driving me nuts." She scratched at her boob, near the armpit.

The captain sat up on the edge of the top bunk she had been laying on, "What's wrong with your boob?"

"That fucking kid bit me through my shirt earlier," she said dismissively.

You could feel the tension increase in the room. Each girl's posture stiffened and they all retracted from the girl at the window.

"What?" she looked up at the others, finally half noticing the leprous gazes she was getting in the dark.

The captain hopped down off the bunk, and motioned for the shirt to come off, "Let's see it. How bad is it?" Several of the other girls got up and walked over to support their teammate.

"Not bad at all, he didn't even get me bad, it just itches."
She pulled off her shirt and revealed a white bra that was
stained dark red on one side. When she saw the blood, she
went still. A tiny keychain flashlight flared to life and
illuminated the wound. It was dark, ugly. Streaks of dark red
and blue blossomed away from the clear teeth marks in her
soft skin. Yellowish pus streaked out of the dozen
pockmarks like a thick, diabolical mucus.

"Fuck." The captain killed her flashlight.

*****

The arguments began almost immediately. The girl's two
friends wanted to save her. The teammates were divided
down the middle. Deb and Kim were silent, watching the
drama unfold. Voices eventually were raised, followed by
fists. The scuffles didn't last long though, they got too loud
too fast, and the ladies in the room who had maintained
more level heads managed to break it up. Unfortunately they
were unable to prevent several large scratches, a couple
broken noses, and several knocked out teeth.

In the end, once order was restored to the cramped, dark,
hot room they decided that they couldn't kick her out, and
they would not, under any circumstances, kill her. An
uneasy truce was reached. She would be put in a bed and
observed. If she started to act dangerous, they would knock
her out, or kick her out the window. It wasn't ideal in any
situation, but it preserved the peace somewhat. The bitten
girl's two friends sat on the bed with her, and the rest of the
group tried to sit as far away as possible.

It was an hour before anyone else spoke. It was one of the
underclass girls on the soccer team. She spoke one sentence
that spoke volumes about the strangeness of their situation,
"I have to poop."

Her statement into the hot void of the cramped room was
met with silence. Then an uncontrollable fit of hysterical
giggles erupted. All of the girls wound up rolling around on

the floor, sides splitting from trying to laugh silently. After far too long laughing the tears flowed, tears shed in the moment of a joke that's forcing the laughs out of every body part. It was shaking, crying, giggling, rolling laughter.

After too long the girls decided they shouldn't leave the room. Kim came up with the best idea for their potty issues, "Okay, we have little trash buckets. We pee and poop in one, and when it's pretty full, we toss it out the window. Hopefully they don't smell it and come here."

Plenty of girls argued that there was no danger in opening the bedroom door to use the bathroom, but in the end, paranoia won. Once they'd committed, they starting using one of the trash buckets as a toilet one by one. The stench became almost unbearable, but they cracked a window, and started spraying their designer perfumes wholesale to cut the smell. In the end, it wasn't that bad when weighed against being eaten alive.

Sleep came to them. Maybe it was the heat, maybe it was exhaustion, just as likely it was the fact that it was late, and they were naturally tired. One by one, two by two they all collapsed into various beds and chairs. Heads were nodding off, lolling back and forth. Bursts of quiet snoring here and there were frequent. Even Jenny, the captain who had volunteered for window watch duty nodded off.

Deb, in her top bunk was the first to come awake sometime in the middle of the night. She came to only half aware of her memories from the day. She hovered at the blissful moment when you are waking, yet still half asleep, aware that you are resting, happy and comfortable. Then a flash of the scene at the car accident jumped in front of her mind's eye, and her utopian dream was dashed. Her heart raced for a minute as she realized she actually was where she was, and what happened was reality, and not just a bad dream.

"Good God it smelled like someone died in here," she mumbled under her breath as she rolled over to look down into the room. She always loved having the top bunk in her dorm. She felt like a cat perched on a rooftop, all knowing, and all seeing. Deb's eyes adjusted quickly to the darkness of the room and she looked around. Most of the room was still, gently breathing in deep sleep. Those not still were moving around quietly, trying to get as comfortable as their arrangements would allow. Deb was thankful for the bed she was in. She yawned, and the stench of the room hit her again. This time though, she detected a new smell, something metallic and earthy. Coppery.

Blood.

She froze instantly. Without moving her head she panned her eyes over and down to the bottom bunk several beds over in the room. It was the bunk where the bitten girl and her two friends had laid down. Her eyes betrayed her though, and she couldn't get a good, square view. She squirreled her face in frustration and slowly moved her head sideways until she could see clearly.

The three girls were a knotted mass on the bed. They had fallen asleep on top of one another in the bed, and in the darkness their bodies were indistinguishable from each other. Deb watched the formless mound of teenager for minutes until she finally started to make heads and tails out of it. She watched what she thought was the bitten girl's head move rhythmically back and forth, up and down on the neck of the girl beside her. At first she thought they were kissing in some perverse, morbid sexual tryst, but she heard a popping noise that sounded far too much like chewing on gristle. She lost herself for a moment, and made a small noise.

"Oh my guh..." It was only slightly louder than a whisper, but the bitten girl heard her. So did the third girl. When they both moved Deb realized that the first girl bitten was eating the neck and throat of her friend. The other girl, the third girl, was helping devour her as well, eating from the stomach. Deb could see the dark circle of blood covering the sheets of the bunk now. Now that it was too late. The two dead cannibals turned and started to rise off their bed, reaching up for Deb.

Deb screamed as long, and as loudly as she could. The room became hysterical in the blink of an eye. The only light coming into the room was through the window, and that light was the orange haze of the streetlight down at the corner. The dim amber glow didn't illuminate the room enough for the women to figure out who Deb was screaming at until the two zombies had done more damage. Some of the girls rushed over to help Deb, thinking she was hurt, and inadvertently stepped into the path of the two undead. They were tackled to the floor from behind and savaged like a predator's prey. Their screams joined Deb's, throwing the room even further into chaos.

Jenny, the captain, was finally up and screaming for silence, "SHUT UP! SHUT UP! SHUT UP!" Finally her roars quieted the room. All that was left was the whimpering of the two freshly murdered girls, and the sickening chewing in the dark. The heavy wet sound of human flesh being torn from a body was there as well. One of the girls reflexively vomited, knowing even in the dark what that sound was.

By then enough of the girl's eyes had adjusted to the dark. Kim was pressed against the door her bunk was blocking, knees folded into her chest in a bizarre fetal position. She struggled to draw in every breath, hitching, gasping, trying to stay still, trying to stay silent. Right at her feet, not inches away she watched as the two girls slowly tore away strips of flesh from the girls she'd been talking to just hours before.

Jenny searched around her for a weapon. There was nothing. The only thing she was the television set on the bureau, so she decided to make that work. With a grunt, she ripped it off the top of the bureau and brought it down heavily on the back of one of the attacking girls. The plastic casing of the TV cracked with the heavy impact against the skull of the zombie. The TV rolled away and propped itself up against the frame of the bed next to them. Jenny skirted the zombie she'd just hit and went for the screen again, to smash with it once more.

The other girls in the room watched her making her assault, and suddenly built up the courage to join her. They started raining down debris on the heads of the two undead teens, trying to knock them down, trying to kill them. Minutes went on as they repeatedly tried to kill the zombies to no avail. In several cases their makeshift weapons went awry and hit their living allies instead, causing unneeded injuries.

Finally one of the undead girls went limp, flopping her bloody carcass down on the body of the teenager she'd freshly killed. Once she stopped moving the rest of the girls focused their rage on the remaining zombie. Jenny brought the television down over and over on her head, until all that was left was the heavy glass screen itself. Finally even that shattered, giving the zombie enough time to lunge at one of the girls.

The monster grabbed a random ankle, sinking her teeth deep into the flesh above the foot. The bite scissored through tendons and ligaments like rubber bands. The unfortunate victim screamed out and collapsed backwards, clutching her ruined foot. All the girls stopped, paralyzed for a second. Just long enough for the zombie to lunge once more at a different target.

The girl right beside Jenny had turned and knelt to help her fallen teammate. A final, fatal gesture of friendship. The zombie had coiled its legs just enough to propel itself forward, smashing into her target, sending her sprawling headfirst into the corner of a desk. Her head hit harder than her neck could take and with a sickening snap, her skull kicked sideways, finally resting at an impossible angle. Despite dying instantly the zombie bit her several times anyway, tearing into the soft meaty flesh of her hips. There was a sickening sucking sound as a chunk of flesh broke free into the dead girl's mouth.

Suddenly there was a flash of something metallic coming down in a wide arc, finishing almost level with the floor.

Kim's fist clutched a nail file, and with a giant haymaker swing she sank four inches of the etched steel deep in the ear of the zombie. The dead girl went limp immediately, and the mouthful of soccer player fell to the floor from her slack mouth, rolling a few feet before coming to a rest against the wall.

The room was silent again except for the sounds of gasping and wheezing. The surviving girls were trying to catch their breath, shed some of their panic, and gain some sense of safety. Some of them collapsed to the floor, others rushed to the aid of the girl with the bitten ankle. Kim and Deb grabbed each other in a desperate hug and started to sob, trying to make sense of the world and the horror suddenly thrust into their laps. Minutes later everyone was mostly calm again.

"What the fuck just happened?" One of them asked quietly into the darkness.

Deb answered meekly from her top bunk, "The girl who was bitten died after we all passed out. She killed one of her friends. I think they killed the third girl. When we all woke up, they got more of us." She left out the part about her rousing the undead women. There was a pause as everyone considered their situation.

"We're dead. We're all gonna die tonight," one of the younger girls blurted out suddenly. There was no fear in her voice, just the knowledge of the most likely ending to their story. The girls looked around the room at each other in the dim orange light, feeling sober about their possible fate.

Jenny tried to motivate her friends as she tried to bandage the destroyed ankle of her moaning teammate, "Look, we need to have a plan here. We have four more dead bodies in here that are gonna sit up shortly, plus one more of us has been bitten, and we all know now how that story ends." She looked sadly down at her friend as she finished with the tape. "We don't have much time."

Her words could not have been more prophetic. The two girls who had just been murdered began twitching, starting to rouse again to their deathless, murderous state. The third girl, the one who had been killed while the rest were sleeping, slowly sat up on the edge of her bunk blood running thickly from her tattered neck. The girls in the room started to back away, pushing things in front of themselves to put something, put anything in between the new monsters and their bodies. Some of the girls, Kim and Deb included, sprang to the top bunks to get some elevation from the new threats.

Jenny stood up confidently and looked around her space to find a weapon. The only thing she could see was a heavy wooden chair that was too heavy for her to lift. She grabbed it anyway and put her everything into getting into some form of striking position, but the effort was for naught. Just before she could get the chair to a destructive zenith, her two ravaged undead friends collapsed into her. In a twisted mercy, the heavy chair came down on her head, sending her instantly into unconsciousness. Her two friends ripped her open, and spread her innards without her knowledge.

Having lost their leader the room became complete anarchy. None of the remaining survivors mounted any form of a sensible defense. Kicking, scratching, screaming, one by one each was beaten, and eaten until they stopped moving. Deb and Kim sat shaking, clutching one another watching on Deb's top bunk, watching it all happen in slow motion. Even in the faint light coming from the streetlamps they could see the blood stains spreading on the carpet. Soon there was no carpet visible, just a pool of blood running from wall to wall.

The two friends sat there for what seemed like forever. After their piece of forever the room fell silent. The only sounds the two girls could hear were the crunching, chewing noises coming from the teammates that were slowly resurrecting, one by one. They were outnumbered by the undead in the room in short order. So long as they remained perfectly still, and perfectly silent in the dark, it seemed as if they were safe on the bunk. Both girls felt like divers trapped in shark infested waters.

They watched in horror as eventually the center of the room filled with the twisted, mauled shapes of their prior fellow survivors. They stood statue like, waiting for prey to present itself. They cast dark shadows onto the floor from the light of the window. Each shuffled their feet, occasionally bumping into one another, sending a flurry of uncontrolled rage at one another, an almost instinctive violence. These bursts ended quickly though, their true malice was only for the living.

Deb and Kim kept their hands pressed together tightly all night. Eventually the sun began to rise, illuminating the horror in the room that was obscured by the night. Nearly a score of previously young and vibrant women had been murdered in the room hours prior. Their flesh hung off their bodies in tatters, their throats ripped out, their entrails tossed aside. Some couldn't even stand on their ruined legs. Some of the girls had broken their own feet kicking at the unstoppable zombies. Those unable to stand crawled in circles, licking the blood smears on the walls and furniture absently. Even the indignity of the trash bin they had been using as a toilet had been knocked over, leaving the raw stench of human waste powerful and thick in the air, partially obscuring the smell of dead bodies.

Deb and Kim finally saw everything as it was in the dawn light. They saw the end of sanity. Deb started crying. As if controlled by some sadistic, evil puppeteer the zombie women turned on their strings, looking up at the two remaining survivors. They rushed to the bunk, reaching up, clawing, and scratching at their legs and feet. Deb and Kim pressed their bodies as hard as they could against the door the bunk was against, trying to stay as far from the edge and the undead as they could. Their efforts bought them some time, but not their lives.

One of the zombie women, a girl really, had been wearing a large ring. As she reached up to claw at her prey the ring caught on the sheet, ripping a hole in it. When she reached up again her hand slipped through the hole, catching there. In a confused rage, like a wild animal caught in a trap, the little monster pulled away savagely, tugging the sheets slowly off the bed, one inch at a time. Deb and Kim saw the sheets start to move, and shortly after felt themselves being tugged towards the edge of the bed. They started to scramble, to get off the top of the sheet, but Deb wasn't fast enough.

"NOOOOOOooooooo!" Kim screamed like an animal as her best friend stared at her in horror. As the hands got closer to her friend, Deb looked blankly at Kim. Her eyes went wide in fear.

The captain, Jenny, or what was left of her, was right at the edge of the bed, her long, strong arms reaching further onto the top bunk. Her powerful grip latched onto the ankle of the blonde, and tugged strong. And just like that, Deb's leg was snared, and she was dragged off the bed like a slab of screaming meat. Her body hit the floor hard face first and her breath was knocked from her. Unable to scream, she kicked and punched until she couldn't anymore.

Kim looked over the edge of the bed for a moment after she saw Deb's struggles cease. They feasted on her. Even as Deb's body was ripped apart slowly, she had a spasm, and kicked over one of the undead chewing at her calf. The undead girl scrambled back onto her body and bit her savagely in return, almost out of spite, tearing another chunk of skin and muscle clean off.

This infuriated Kim. She looked around the top of the bunk for a weapon, finding only her tightly balled fists. It would have to do. No one fucked with her best friend like that.

Kim let loose one bloodcurdling scream in the glowing light of the dawn coming in the window, and leapt from the top bunk. She would kill every one of these monsters, or die trying.

In the end, she died like her friends did.

Scared, and screaming.

December 2010

Continued

December 3rd

I have managed to survive to today despite my earlier attempts to jinx myself. Sometimes, I am stupid. I have been lucky lately though, and have dodged putting the kibosh on myself. I really need to watch what I say. Eventually I WILL say something and regret it.

Where to start? Let's talk about the weather Mr. Journal. It's fucking cold out. I've had to turn the heat up a little at night to stay warm. Currently I've got the heat on 60 at night, and it seems to be running almost all night. I'm still pretty chilly, but with Otis and pile of blankets, I'll survive. At this rate, I'll burn through my fuel supply much faster than I anticipated. I need to keep a good watch on how long my generator's tank lasts me. I suspect I'll need to get up to fill it during the night if I keep at the rate I'm going. I don't know, but I'll figure it out. I thought I was good at figuring this shit out too. I've been wrong on so many things.

As you might imagine it has also been cold during the day. Not quite as cold as at night, but still pretty cold. Solid 35 to 40 degrees during the day, dipping down to 20 to 25 degrees at night. It's only early December too, and if this trend keeps up, February is going to be a motherfucker.

My thumb is much better, but it's terribly stiff. I take a couple Ibuprofen for it every 6 hours or so, and that makes it more or less fine. I hate sprains, they take so long to heal and generally just gum up the works while they're taking their sweet ass time. Whatever I guess! It is what it is and it's almost all better. At least I didn't get bitten. Sprains are much less fatal.

My venison obsession has come to an abrupt halt. I've eaten far too much of it already. I set up my makeshift fridge for the meats upstairs in a room that I'm not heating. It stays about 40 degrees all the time, which is just good enough seeing as how it's all smoked. The meat has kept great for me, but I just over indulged and now I need a break. I have half a mind here one of these early mornings to try and bag some of the turkey I used to see roaming the fields before the shit hit the fan. I actually wonder if the zombies have eaten them? Turkeys can move though, so maybe they're safe.

The lake has started to freeze. There's a fine crust at the edges that's millimeters thick. In another couple weeks if these temperatures hold there will be a really good freeze going on. Kinda makes the whole island aspect of this place seem pointless eh? I guess it'll keep vehicles out, but any shambling zombies can just march across the ice once it's cold enough.

Speaking of cold enough, I wonder if the zombies will freeze? Is there any body heat being generated inside them? I haven't seen that many since the temperatures really dropped, so it stands to some reason that they're all freezing solid out there somewhere. Although it's strange, because when I shoot them now, they still kinda… ooze blood, which makes no sense at all. All their blood should be fully gelled up inside them.

This really makes me wonder what the hell is causing all this. A virus? Biological weapons? Is it supernatural? Fucked if I know. I wonder if anyone has found out what's going on. I'm sure somewhere on some huge military base they've got a good idea of the story. Out here in the sticks on campus I don't know shit beyond my doorstep. Hell I haven't even been into town in… a very long time.

I should talk more about my early times here. Before I do that though, I'll tell you about yesterday and today. Yesterday I finished clearing Auburn Lake Road. There were two houses left on the street, and I got them searched and emptied with no danger involved. Both houses looked to be left exactly as they had if someone was supposed to be coming back. My bet is the residents never made it home "that day." They're either holed up and stuck somewhere, or they died. Either way, their shit is now mine.

Two items came up at the second house that I was unable to retrieve. The people living there were snowmobile enthusiasts. This is a good thing. Sort of. For some reason there was no snowmobile trailer in their yard, so I had no way to get the machines back to campus. I'll have to wait for snow, and then just drive them back. They had two of them, incidentally. That little find will go a long way towards making winter safer, and more tolerable. The four wheeler is a nice toy, but in really deep snow it'll struggle. Once I get a trail packed for the snow machines, I'll be all set to get around in a pretty wide area regardless of the weather.

As I said, I didn't get a whole lot more of use. Blah blah. Today I started to work on the houses on Jones Road. If you'll recall Mr. Journal I mentioned before that there were nine houses on Jones Road, and the last one is a rather large farmhouse. I'm really hoping that farmhouse has cool shit. I'm saving it for last on this road. Earlier I did three houses on Jones Road. Lather, rinse, repeat. Apparently no one in this neighborhood made it home that day. Most of the houses coming up here have been abandoned. As in, the owners never came home, or they came home and left all their shit. Whatever I guess.

All three houses were stocked reasonably well. I found a few dead animals in them though, which smelled bad and put me on red alert. I'm always sad when it comes to animals getting hurt or dying. I always make myself feel like there was something I could've done. Shitty thing is there WAS something I could've done. I could've easily checked these houses long ago and rescued these animals. All I had to do was open the doors and let them out. Of course if I had done that, I would be exposed because of dumbass barking dogs. I guess it's a mixed bag. Dogs scare me. Not like, Adrian is afraid of dogs in that sense. More of a… dogs bark, barks are loud, noise is bad, noise brings zombies, therefore dogs are bad. Plus it's hard enough to feed myself ongoing. If I had done something about these animals I'd be the Dr. Doolittle of the post zombie apocalypse, and I'd likely be starving myself to save them.

At any rate, the houses were cleared out of bodies and

remaining decent supplies, and that's the end of the Jones Road story for today Mr. Journal.

I can rewind a bit here and talk about the early days here on campus. I went back and re-read the entry I put up awhile back talking about my trip back down the grocery store and realized I skipped the most informative part of that time period.

So the first few days were the last few days that there were television and radio broadcasts. I sat around plugged into the television while it lasted. It made me feel safe to not move around much, plus I was desperate for information. I think the television reports were up and running for about 3 days. However long it took me to build up the nerve to go downtown, that's how long the TV worked. The television abruptly cut out when I was watching it around dinnertime, so I'm wondering if there was some kind of severing of the service, rather than a "we're going off the air now," kinda thing. It was working, then there was static. Don't know. Maybe there was a fire at the cable company.

I didn't get shit for information off the TV at first. It was more of the same from the reports from "that day." I can say the spread of whatever it was that caused this was pretty thorough. Mr. Journal if you'll recall from earlier entries there was a widespread outbreak of attacks on people. All across the world these attacks occurred more or less at the same time. I now know that these attacks were perpetrated by what I'm calling zombies. At the time the media flat out refused to really jump on the bandwagon. It wasn't until the TV died and the radio became my source of info that they actually fessed up and said that the dead were returning to life.

So early on as I recall the TV and radio said the attacks were small business. One or two zombies, here and there. Most of the time I think the zombies were beaten back to death with little or no incident. The problem with it getting out of hand seems to have stemmed with corpse storage, and widespread media panic. I know, what the fuck? Right?

The media reported it was a virus, or perhaps a widespread terrorist launched biological weapon, or whatever. The media had no idea, and they were speculating. Humans, herd animals that we are, all panicked. Well not all, but the panic was widespread and severe. The bites infected the living, that much we knew then, and I know now. What was a bigger deal was that the dead were rising all on their own, all over the world. The outbreaks kept cropping up in different places that seemingly had no connection to previous outbreaks. One of the first and strongest theories was that a latent virus had been spread at the World Cup in South Africa earlier that month. Lots of disparate people from all over the world in one place... Then they go home, there's an incubation period, and WHAM. Global pandemic. I knew those vuvuzelas were bad news. Fucking horns.

What that meant (I think) is that people around dead bodies didn't take proper precautions. This explains why hospitals became such hot zones so fast. Many hospitals have morgues. Morgues are filled with dead bodies. These bodies, already inside the hospital, were sitting up, getting freed, and sending the hospitals into total havoc. Imagine a coroner who is tagging a toe, and his body sits up. He screams for assistance for the person who was almost dead, and proceeds to get bitten while he renders aid. People were rushing to the hospitals at the same time, thinking they were infected, and essentially ran right into their own doom. Now as best as I've been able to figure out, the bites seem to take hours to kill. However, someone who just dies... Gets right the fuck back up in minutes.

What they concluded, and I've basically confirmed, is that if you are bitten, it's like being poisoned, not so much being infected. The bites give you a terminal illness which kills you. However, everyone that dies comes back. Everyone. Bitten or not. That tells me if this is a virus, or a biological weapon, we are all already infected. That makes no sense to me though the more I've thought about it.

How did all these zombie outbreaks occur so quickly, so far apart from each other? How did the second wave of outbreaks occur? I mean we're talking about outbreaks from Indonesia to Russia to Qatar to Seattle, to Anchorage, to Nairobi to Krakow. It would've taken thousands of terrorists to pull it off simultaneously. Also, if this was some kind of naturally occurring virus, how the fuck did it spread so far, so fast? And how did the virus wait, essentially intelligently, to strike at the same moment all across the world? It's like a biological doomsday clock, counting down to "that day."

Now I'm speculating here Mr. Journal. Sheer guesswork. I think this isn't of this Earth. I am not saying aliens did this. I'm wondering if this is supernatural. It makes a lot more sense when you remove science from the equation.

If everyone across the world suddenly started rising from the dead, it makes a lot more sense to me if it were "God's will." Or if the Devil finally won some argument with God and got to use Earth as a playground for a bit. Oddly enough I am completely okay with those scenarios. I can wrap my head around it.

It explains why the geographical distance didn't matter. It also explains why regardless of cause of death, you get the hell back up as a zombie. Perhaps this isn't an infection, or a virus, or a weapon at all.

Maybe this is a curse. Surely humanity has earned some payback from up on high. We treat each other like shit, we wage war constantly, we fight over beliefs, we destroy our environment. We seem to do everything wrong en masse, and perhaps some greater power has decided that it's time we were put in our place.

I am okay with this. I don't know why, but whenever I think about it this way, I am not bothered by it. I feel like maybe, just maybe if this is why this happened, I can earn my place on this Earth again. I can deserve to survive. I can get back in the good graces of whatever all mighty beings are doing this to us. I can make penance for my "sins."

That's my current favorite theory. I just can't wrap my

51

head around an infection in the normal sense. Just can't do it.

Anyway, those first few days were a wreck. So many people were just ignorant of the dangers the dead posed. First responders paid the price I guess. They'd show up to a dying person, provide assistance, they'd live or die, and then the dice would get rolled. If the person died, they'd sit up, bite the medic, or fireman, cop or whatever and then they were down for the count. In the waning days of the TV broadcasts they said there were so few medically qualified trained responders 911 calls went unanswered. Doctors and nurses were right at the epicenters at the hospitals, and the EMTs, cops and firemen were the people most likely to get bitten.

I'm sure you can see what happened after that Mr. Journal. House fires and accidents went unanswered. Car wrecks received no attention, and the sick and ill that needed medical assistance got none. People who would've survived an injury suddenly weren't. Those trying to care for those people were in the wrong place to survive themselves. They often got killed or bitten trying to help, which caused it all to spiral further out of control. I remember hearing reports about the number of people bitten, and the numbers were mind numbing. Tens of thousands all over the place just that first night and day. Every bite victim became a zombie within a few hours, and quite likely, bit someone else.

Some areas of the world were flat out written off. Haiti was still recovering from their earthquake earlier in the year, and the sudden lack of foreign aid sent the country tumbling into a cholera outbreak. The entire island was written off in days. There were multiple plane crashes that caused entire regions to be turned into forbidden zones. Lots of planes crashed that day. Many went to Greenland after the US and Canada turned them away. I guess no one heard from them after a few days. Israel was a fucking wreck. The riots there caused things to get out of control in hours. Too much end of the world news caused the Palestinians and the Jews to decide to end their millennia long pissing contest with a stream of lead. The Greek economy had collapsed I think in May this year, and when this shit started, the youth revolted again there, causing more riots, causing more death and destruction. Mainland Europe was a disaster fairly quickly as I recall hearing. There were even sketchy reports that North Korea had a civil war break out right at the last moment. Fucked up shit. Some areas fared better than others, but it was all bad before the radio died.

This thing that's happening turned on every possible panic button you can imagine. The news had stories of people killing in the grocery stores, trying to get food and such. The government lost control quickly here, and it all fell down to might makes right. If you could take it and protect it, it was yours. The military was trying to secure their own bases and government centers, and with so many police hurt or killed, law and order became just an old TV show, as opposed to reality.

Man I'm tired. Talking about this depresses me. I have more to say to though. Maybe I'll put an entry in tomorrow too. There's more to say about the first week that shit went down.

-Adrian

Putting a Name to a Face

The morning shift was always Sabrina's favorite. There were many reasons why. She was typically able to get in a few minute early to talk with the night shift nurses on her floor, and get the skinny on everything that'd happened during their shift. No doctor orders ever really came in from the overnight either, so other than the hassle of checking all the logs, and doing an initial med pass, the mornings always seemed pretty great. Of course, things picked up as the day went on, but she also liked driving into the city to the hospital as the sun rose. Even if the dang thing was straight in her eyes half the drive. It was like waking up with the Earth.

Getting to where the hospital was in the city could sometimes be a hassle. There were large businesses all about, and after getting off the highway and onto the city streets just meant she had to fight through the five intersections to get to the multi floored parking garage the hospital had. Sabrina went directly to the fourth floor of the hospital when she left the concrete parking structure. She always parked on the uppermost levels, so the people visiting their family members could park low, near the lobby floor. If anything, she was courteous to the families, most of whom were already emotionally frayed just thinking about coming to the place where she worked.

The fourth floor of the hospital was the short stay floor, as well as the NICU. Hers wasn't the largest hospital, so each department wasn't always afforded all the space they would've liked. Patients who had just experienced surgery more robust than outpatient procedures and needed to stay a single overnight, or perhaps just a few hours went to her floor. She frequently spent very little time with patients before they moved along back to home, or to a different unit if they experienced some kind of setback. It was better that way, she felt. Less chance to get attached, and then let down if they fell more ill or died. She worked in the medical equivalent of fast food. Nothing too involved, and nothing long term. It was for the best though. Despite being forty years old, she'd only been a nurse for a year. With the economy shitting the bed she'd lost her longtime factory job, so she reinvented herself as a nurse. A few years of school later, she knew she loved it.

As Sabrina sat at the nurse's station, going over the overnight information, Catherine, the nurse she was replacing was talking absently about the night.

"Sabrina you could be up for a really bad day hun. I was watching the news almost all night long, and there are a lot of really crazy people out there. Europe is all in a tizzy, and I'd bet my mother's secret casserole recipe before lunchtime the ER is swimming in folks who are having panic attacks."

Sabrina looked up, her blue eyes picking out Catherine's through her brown bangs. "You are a paranoid lady Cathy. I think this will all blow over. I only caught a few bits of it on the morning show, and it's all the same. Bird flu all over again." Africa, Asia and Europe were all experiencing riots due to a strange series of infections that were causing people to become violent. It was almost like a strange form of human rabies, but Sabrina thought it was probably more like human paranoia. Things like these were always blown out of proportion by the media anyway.

"There weren't riots in London over bird flu Sabrina."

"And there won't be riots here in the city either. We'll

probably have our string of ten little old ladies who think they've contracted hyperthyroidism, or sudden onset diabetes, five suspected cases of rabies via cat bite, and that one guy who gets something lodged in his asshole because he's a closet gay man and is too ashamed to tell anyone about it. Happens every time something weird is on the news."

Catherine snickered quietly, afraid she'd wake some of the sleeping patients in the bays across from the station. "Oh Sabrina, you're so funny. I can see why your husband and kid love you so much."

Sabrina smiled. "Well if you keep them laughing, they have a much harder time being disobedient."

"Now that's wisdom. You have a good shift no matter what. I'll see you tomorrow morning," Catherine said as she gathered her purse from under the counter.

"Of course. Safe drive home," Sabrina said, returning to her charts.

Her goodbye to Catherine was the second goodbye she'd said that day, and just like the first goodbye, it was the last time she'd ever see that person again.

*****

Late in the morning, Sabrina was proven wrong. The emergency room had been busy the entire day. As the two nurses had jested about in the dawn of the day, there were the usual suspects. Elderly people who didn't know quite where to go with the strange events on the television, as well as the normal amount of sick and injured. Nothing too serious had happened all morning, right up until the major accident and shooting down the street.

At an intersection several blocks away an out of control truck had hit a handful of pedestrians. Something bad had happened in the aftermath of the accident, and there had been a police involved shooting. The ER had been notified by the police that multiple seriously injured patients would be inbound, but something went horribly wrong. As the hospital scrambled to get more staff to the ER to prepare for the glut of major injuries, word came in that the accident had escalated to more than just a shooting.

Apparently some of the injured people had attacked Samaritans as well as police officers that had arrived to help. The details were sketchy. Instead of four victims as initially advertised, the ambulances were transporting in nearly twelve, most in some fashion of critical condition. Sabrina was pulled from her quiet fourth floor to assist the ER crews when the number of victims on their way swelled from four, to fourteen.

She was pulled in person, under duress by the hospital's Nurse Manager, Phyllis. Phyllis was nearly out of breath, and looked frazzled. "Sabrina head down and find Doctor Barry. He's going to be working in room one oh four right near the lobby, and he'll be doing triage on the people arriving. Assist him as best you can."

Phyllis was a nice woman, but she was ruthless when it came to her job. Sabrina was only barely qualified to help in the ER under the best circumstances, so for her to ask for Sabrina to head down there must've meant the situation was dire. Sabrina thought of her son, and hoped he was safe at home with her husband, playing on the swing set in the backyard. It was a warm June day, and that seemed like a perfect vision to her.

She hoped their small town was far quieter than the city.

*****

By the time Sabrina reached the hospital's emergency room, the department was in heavy disarray. She saw four of the six security guards the hospital employed all attempting to maintain a semblance of peace in the entranceway and waiting room, but the men looked strained. Cabot, the largest and most imposing of all the guards was kneeling down low in a hallway to explain something to a frustrated woman in a wheelchair who had her leg elevated. She wore a splint and judging by the grimace on her pretty face she was in some pain. You could never tell how much pain someone was in just by looking at them though. Some people were predisposed to complain and feel pain more acutely than others. Sabrina's son David was impervious to pain. Just last summer he broke a bone in his arm and didn't say anything to her or her husband for a few days because as he said, "it wasn't so bad."

The look on the young girl's face said anything but, "this wasn't so bad."

Doctor Barry was a young doctor. She thought he was maybe thirty five. His hair was pitch black and trimmed neatly right down to his skin giving him a very military look. It made sense too as Barry came to the hospital after a career in the military. He had served as some kind of high profile medic in the army, and after getting out he'd completed med school as quickly as could be. Barry was a trauma specialist. If anyone came into their ER with a gunshot or stab wound, there was no better man to see. Barry was lean, and handsome, and was the subject of more nurse gossip at the facility than any other eligible man. She was scared to be in the ER with so much going on, but she was pretty damned thankful to spend some time with him. Her husband didn't need to know anything…

"Thanks Sabrina. I appreciate you coming down to help." Barry moved quickly and confidently. He arranged all manner of supplies on a series of trays and table in a waiting room near the ambulance entrance that was typically reserved for a single patient's intake assessment. He'd already prepared it to sit three, and had a series of beds in the hallway opposite ready to take those that didn't need urgent care immediately.

"Yeah Doctor, you're welcome," she said, failing to hide her apprehension about it all.

"Nervous aren't you?" Barry asked with a smile, his hands never stopping, prepping more and more supplies for the ambulances that were only a minute or two away.

Sabrina swallowed, "Yeah. I'm not really the kind of person who deals well with this kind of thing."

"This kind of thing? You did go to school to be a nurse? They did tell you that at some point in time you might need to step up and help save lives right?" The Doctor replied, still smiling. He was almost flirting with her.

Sabrina laughed at his jest, "Yes Doctor, I'm aware of all that. I guess my preference is to work with people who aren't in critical conditions. I like helping folks with an existing problem, on the upswing, not necessarily the ones who are coming in with who knows what going on. I think I'm also scared I'll make a mistake and get someone hurt."

Barry nodded, handing her several medical instruments. "Look at how I have my things arranged and put those on your scrubs the same way. Nice flower pattern shirt by the way. Aren't those worn by pediatric nurses? Brings out the green in your eyes."

Sabrina blushed, "Well we've got several young kids on my floor right today, so I'm borrowing this from Deanna. Thought the little ones would like it." She slid all the tools into the small pockets and folds of her scrubs as he continued to talk.

"Let me give you very simple advice Sabrina, and if you can remember some of it, we'll get through this okay today, and we might even help some folks out in the process. First off, stay calm. Panic kills. Panic makes you do things too fast, and even though time is a factor here in the ER, you need to do things at a controlled speed. As long as you're under control, you'll be able to do the right things, right?" Barry asked her, his voice instilling her with a measure of confidence.

Sabrina felt encouraged. "Yeah, right."

"And remember, ABCDE and compression Sabrina. Just go down the check list, and if they are meant to be saved, then it will happen. I'll try to direct you as best I can, and you stay calm okay?"

"Deal."

"You can do this Sabrina," Barry said as the wail of an ambulance's approach could be heard through the heavy ER sliding doors. The first of the victims was here.

Sabrina said a short prayer, and hoped that she could indeed do this.

*****

Very quickly indeed her confidence was thrown out the window.

One after another a series of ambulances pulled in and vomited out a crew of EMTs and blood soaked people that needed incredible levels of skilled medical treatment. She felt like a tornado had descended on her and the hospital, complete with death and destruction in every direction. She focused cleanly on the good young Doctor, and did her level best to follow his every instruction. There were many, many instructions.

The first four injured were whisked directly into the trauma rooms where they were put into direct emergency care. Immediately thereafter a man with massive chest trauma was wheeled directly into surgery. And from there, things went downhill.

"This is where we step up Sabrina. When the ER is full, we need to triage, okay? Decide who can be fixed and who can't, okay?" Doctor Barry was serious now, his voice flat. His tone authoritative.

All Sabrina could do was adjust her gear and nod. She hadn't even helped anyone yet and there were already large smears of blood on her scrubs. It seemed like blood was everywhere. She heard the voices of the next batch of EMTs, and it overwhelmed her.

"Large human bite wound at the neck, appears that the carotid is perforated, blood loss is severe-" and that voice trailed off, loudly and quickly giving Doctor Barry a litany of medical facts that frightened her.

"Blood pressure is dropping-"

"IVs are in and running. But he's lost a lot of blood-"

"Need plasma-"

"Intubate immediately, the airway can be made clear-"

"Gunshot is a flesh wound, send him to the lobby. He waits."

And more. It all sounded like death to her.

Seconds later another patient came in on foot, likely from the same ambulance. He was wrapped in a neutral gray blanket that was stained purple, brown and red from wet and drying blood. He had a lost and vacant look on his face as he stumbled past other people sitting in the ER waiting room. They looked at him with forlorn expressions. He was the nearest thing to normal to walk into the department since the scream of the first ambulance.

It was the closest thing Sabrina had seen to a typical patient in her world, and her mind leapt at the opportunity to help a slice of her mundane. She moved across the room with purpose, and slid an arm around the blanket covering the man like a shawl. "Follow me sir. I'm Sabrina, I'm a nurse here at the hospital. If it's alright with you I'm gonna take you into this room here so I can check out your wounds and injuries. What's your name?"

The man blinked a few times, his feet blindly putting one in front of the other as Sabrina steered him towards the room she was sharing with Doctor Barry. Finally, as they were about to sit in one of the smooth plastic chairs in the triage room, his mind put everything together. "Oh hey, I uh, my name is Matt. Someone bit me." The man named Matt dropped the edge of the blanket that was draped over his shoulder, revealing a massive bite wound on the outside of his arm near the tricep. It was a strange place to be bitten.

Sabrina gasped at the wound, but started to treat it automatically. She didn't even realize that she was treating the man. "Well that's a strange wound sir. Someone bit you then?"

The man was delayed, and his answer took a few extra

moments to come out. He almost seemed in a strange kind of shock. "Yeah. Some guy hurt in a car accident over in the finance area of town. Someone hit some pedestrians in a crosswalk. I don't know if he was the driver, or someone in the street. I just saw him hurt, and went to help. I thought he was passed out, or dead, and he sat up and attacked me. I turned away, and he bit into my arm. The police shot him, they had to, but he didn't die. He kept trying to bite people. He hurt a bunch of us. I think he was on drugs. Other people were shot in the crossfire too. It was insane."

"Crazy story Matt. I'm glad this was all that happened to you. Lift your arm for me," Sabrina said. She watched as the torn muscles below the skin flexed painfully for the man.

"Ahh, dammit, that hurts. It burns," Matt said, yanking his arm away.

Sabrina made a face to console him. "I'm sorry Matt. But we need to flush this out real quick and make sure there are no teeth broken off in the wound. Once we check it real quick, I'll get you wrapped up and the pain should start to subside really quickly, okay?"

Matt nodded through gritted teeth.

"Alright then," Sabrina said. She grabbed a bottle of saline solution and after pulling a pair of purple gloves on, she flushed the wound into a metal tray. Water and blood cascaded down Matt's arm, revealing even more damage. He would almost certainly get an infection. Human mouths were dirty beyond belief.

"Sabrina, can I borrow you for a second?" Doctor Barry said from the hallway. He had his sleeves rolled up and was covered in blood. He looked calm, but definitely tense.

"I'm dealing with this man's bite wound Doctor Barry, can it wait a minute?" She asked, her hands never stopping their care.

"Not really Sabrina, I need you now."

Sabrina saw the intensity appear on the young Doctor's face suddenly. He was displeased for some reason, and she felt it was her, "Okay, give me a second."

"Thank you," the Doctor said briskly before disappearing down the hall.

"I'm sorry Matt, but the Doctor needs me. The good news is, you will survive. All you've got is this single bite wound, and it's clearly not damaging anything serious. Just hold this bandage on, and I'll be back soon to help more, okay?"

Matt pressed the large square bandage onto his wound and nodded. He wasn't happy about being left, but he understood. There were cries of pain coming from every direction.

Sabrina tossed her purple gloves into the waste bin and left the small room saying yet another final goodbye to the man. The hallway was considerably louder than the little room she'd worked on Matt in. Doctor Barry was leaning over a gurney in the hall checking a young girl's chest and abdomen with his hands. She cried out in pain when he put pressure on her stomach.

"What can I do for you Doctor?" Sabrina asked once she reached his side.

The young doctor rattled off a quick assessment of the girl to another nurse, then turned to Sabrina. He started to talk but checked himself instead, and gently took Sabrina by the arm away from the young girl. Once out of earshot, he continued what he started. "How is that man?" Are his wounds life threatening?"

Sabrina shook her head happily, "No, he has a nasty bite wound on his outer arm, but nothing major. I don't think he'll need anything more serious than a skin graft or stitches."

"Excellent. How long did it take you to assess his condition?" The Doctor was going somewhere with this line of questioning, and she didn't like it.

"A minute maybe."

The Doctor nodded. "And after you realized he'd survive his wound, you continued to treat him anyway?"

Sabrina nodded, "Well yeah. He was in pain, and I knew I could help him."

The Doctor nodded, clearly a little frustrated. "Sabrina we're doing triage right now okay? We quickly assess survivability and seriousness of injury, then move on. We aren't trying to treat anyone, least of all someone with a fairly minor bite wound. I know it's our instinct to help, but right now everyone is in pain, and we need to focus on helping those that have serious life threatening injuries. I'm not trying to be an asshole here, but I could've used your help with that little girl with internal injuries."

Sabrina felt very defeated. "Okay, I'm sorry. I won't do it again."

The Doctor rubbed her shoulders reassuringly, "Sabrina don't apologize for caring about your patients. I get it. This is a rough spot to be in. Just try to focus on looking for the worst case in the room, and assess them fast. If they're minor, steer them to a seat. If it's major, funnel them deeper into the ER, or perform trauma medicine with me as I direct you. You're doing okay."

He was gifted with presence she thought. He had that calming way, and his choice of words was immaculate. She felt like she could take on the world again. "Alright. I got this."

"You got this."

As the two of them shared their reasonably quiet moment amidst the cacophony of the emergency room, more injured and sick were coming in. The hospital was already flooded, and this situation was getting so much worse.

Exactly how much worse neither really knew.

*****

The accident and subsequent violence a mile or so away had nearly ruined the small city hospital. Combined with the incredible number of other accidents and injuries experienced that morning, the wait to be seen was hours upon hours unless you were bleeding out, facing the loss of a limb, or clearly in need of surgery.

Sabrina and Doctor Barry worked together for another hour, checking the incoming patients for their level of medical need, and making quick decisions as to whether or not the person could wait for additional help, or if they needed immediate attention. Over the course of the hour, Sabrina watched six more nurses come in from their day off to help, as well as three doctors. She was very proud. The dedication of the medical community was unquestionable in moments of crisis.

Everyone's stress seemed manageable. With the extra ER nurses, and the number of doctors now on hand, Sabrina was gifted with a moment of respite. She had no patients flooding in, and with Doctor Barry's blessing, she decided to sit in the lobby and sip on a cup of coffee. She'd selected a little hazelnut flavored K-Cup, and even now that she drank her coffee black, it was still pretty yummy.

She'd picked a spot in the lobby far away from the television screen. There were a surprising number of available seats due to the fact that the entire lobby had crowded over to the flat screen mounted on the wall. She watched as she sipped the hot drink as the faces of the sick and injured were plainly in rapture from the news streaming across the network feed. Normally at this time of the day they'd be watching the last of the morning talk shows, or perhaps the noon news. She had no idea what time it was. The face of her watch had been covered in a smear of dried red blood for a very long time.

Curiosity got the better of her, and she walked over to take a spot at the back of the nearly silent crowd. She sat on one of the end tables next to a row of seats. The news anchor looked desperate. She was reading over notes that were being handed to her nearly every second. The poor person running the teleprompter clearly couldn't keep up with the flood of information, and the anchor was in very awkward ground. She was pretty; dark hair and eyes, though she had faint blue rings of fatigue around those eyes, showing how long a morning it had been.

The anchor and a small host of experts talked about how whatever it was that was overtaking Europe and Africa had somehow jumped to Asia, and was now spreading across North America. They even showed a disparaging graphic of a world map that had red dots for every death linked to the strange plague, and subsequent riots and madness that were linked to it. The map was still primarily not red, but when they showed a time lapse comparison of the past twelve hours, the red was spreading at a dramatic rate. Things got strange when one of the experts got into a very brief argument with the anchor.

"Sir I can't condone in the least your odd suggestions here," the anchor said with a frustrated and dismissive tone.

"I don't think the suggestions I've made are odd at all Natalie. If you read the police reports, and the eyewitness reports, and watch some of the public videos, they are staggeringly similar, and until we have the science to back it up, we need to keep our minds open to new and strange possibilities. This is the real world and not a horror movie, this much we all know, but like any intelligent person knows, sometimes life imitates art. The facts are supporting a lot of what I hope to be false. People who are simply bitten are dying. Human bite wounds are rarely fatal if treated with even basic first aid."

"Sir, the idea that the dead are returning to life as murderous, poisonous maniacs is sheer nonsense."

The expert looked sad. "Natalie, I certainly hope so. I don't think our world can handle that kind of situation."

A guttural scream came from the back of the emergency room that ripped the crowd's trance apart like tissue paper caught in a gale force wind. Sabrina paused her sip of coffee, mouth full of the drink. She listened again as she heard a new series of noises; those of commotion, and of confrontation. She stood and sat her paper cup down on the nondescript, fake wooden magazine table and hurried around to the hallway that led from the lobby to the ER, swallowing her coffee as she went. She walked past the makeshift triage room she had helped set up with Doctor Barry, and headed straight into the heart of the ER core; six trauma rooms around a central nursing hub.

In the middle of the large space were the security guards, clearly wrestling with a pair of patients, or family members. One man was completely naked. Everyone was covered in blood, and she couldn't tell exactly what was going on. The large security officer she'd seen talking quietly with the young woman in a splint, Cabot, had a man wearing some clothes pinned against the edge of the nursing station, the man's arms wrapped around and held firm at his back. The two other security officers were grappling a man completely covered in blood to the floor, and as Sabrina ran around as fast as she could, she was multiple other people writhing around on the floor, either in pain, or trying to escape on the slick, blood soaked floor. In the back of her mind she laughed at the claim that the hospital executives had made that the floor was slip resistant. She wondered if the manufacturer had prepared for situations like this.

Even without an eye for trauma medicine she caught glimpses of several people bitten. She immediately thought of her first patient Matt. He had been bitten too.

"Knock that prick out. Cuff him!" Cabot yelled over his shoulder at his two fellow officers struggled with the person. Sabrina watched as one officer swept a leg backwards powerfully, clearing the subject's leg out from under him, and sending them all crashing to the floor in a strangely well executed martial arts maneuver. The two uniformed men crashed down atop the bloody man, all struggling, and on any other day, with any other person, the weight of the two large men breaking ribs and collar bones alone would've stopped the fight altogether, but not this day. The rules had changed.

The now floored man, IVs still dangling from his arms twisted his head just enough to sink his teeth into the black uniformed shoulder of one of the guards. Sabrina didn't know his name. She saw instantly that there was something profoundly wrong with the man trying to bite everyone. Something had turned his eyes a deathly, pus shade of white, and all reason and soul had left him. The bite caused immediate pain in the guard, and elicited a powerful punch from the wounded man. Sabrina watched as the biter's head rocked back from the powerful punch, and saw several of his teeth fall out onto the blood red floor. The other guard slipped a cuff over a blood slickened wrist, and deftly got the other wrist restrained. The bitten guard rolled away, darkening his already black clothes. The cuffed maniac rolled around wildly until an officer sat down firmly on his back, straddling him to hold him still.

The noise of someone flat lining in a trauma suite sent a flurry of bodies through the room as some semblance of control returned. Cabot and the bitten officer were handcuffing the standing aggressor, and Sabrina, struck nearly dumb watched as that man's large white eyes rolled around. He was biting at the air madly, trying to snap at anything living that he sensed or saw. A nurse with more smarts about her than Sabrina slipped a mesh spitting hood over his face, hopefully mitigating the biting threat.

"What-, what happened?" She asked as Cabot walked over near her. She wasn't asking him directly, but he answered.

"They had two die in surgery or something. They wheeled the bodies out, and moved on, and not long after they died, they both sat the fuck up again. Angry. I guess they weren't quite dead. You see their fucking eyes? White as hell. Pure motherloving evil if I ever saw it. They bit a handful people on the arms and back before we got over. Your good Doctor Barry was one of them. He got bitten on the arm."

"Whoa. How many people got bitten before you got them cuffed?"

Cabot did a quick count. "Eight. Ten maybe? They seem okay." Cabot looked at his hands, stained red from someone's blood. Sabrina thought they looked like bear

69

paws.

"You know Cabot, some guy on the news said that bite wounds were fatal. And that the dead folks were coming back to life and attacking people," Sabrina said, turning her gaze upwards from the man's large hands to his big eyes.

"Are there any patients with bite wounds that aren't being directly supervised right now? Because if there are, we need to put them together and observe them away from the other patients. There's no sense risking anymore injuries."

Sabrina thought of Matt just as she heard more screaming from the lobby she just left.

*****

Matt had gone on a gory rampage. The room he had died in was right near the lobby, just a scant fifteen feet from the flat screen television the crowd had all watched intently. Matt must have been able to leave the makeshift triage room and approach the crowd from behind.

As Cabot and Sabrina rounded the hall and came into the lobby there were several people wounded already. One person had been killed; their neck ripped open by yet another human bite wound. The burgundy colored rug of the waiting room was sickeningly blackened by the spread of blood from his still pumping neck. Three or four people were backing away from Matt as he stumbled into the ring of fleeing patients and family members. They were bitten, some badly, others not.

"Matt, stop!" Sabrina yelled, but he didn't respond.

Cabot pulled out his extending baton and with a whip of the wrist extended it to full length. He pursued Matt as the dead man stalked towards a pair of women that were pinned against a couch in the center of the room.

"Hey you!" Cabot barked, and somehow that got Matt's attention.

The dead white eyes that were starting to be all too common fixed angrily on Cabot. A silent snarl of rage crossed Matt's bloodied face and Cabot shattered it with a stroke of the metal baton. Sabrina's mind and eyes collected enough of the event to realize Matt's jaw caved in, broken apart like a tooth filled piñata. Matt simply staggered backward for a moment, and pushed forward at an incredulous Cabot.

"What the fuck?!" Cabot exclaimed as the man came at him, fury unabated. The large guard took a step back and hammered the baton down again, this time into the forehead of the man lunging at him. The blow would've knocked a horse senseless, but Matt pushed forward, the only affect appearing to be a dent in the brow where his skull had shattered. Cabot took another step back and whipped the baton across Matt's face, hitting him hard enough to spin him around and cross his feet up, causing him to lose balance and crash to the floor on his destroyed face. Cabot tucked the baton into his armpit and in an incredible display of quickness, agility and precision, produced a pair of cuffs and put the metal bracelets on the prone assailant in one deft maneuver.

"He should be fucking dead. Or unconscious. There's no fucking way a normal person could take those hits. No way." Cabot was out of breath from adrenaline and exertion. The five second encounter had been exhausting.

"Check his pulse Cabot," Sabrina said, taking stock of the situation in the lobby around her. More of the nurses and at least one Doctor were rushing into the room to help stabilize the situation.

Cabot looked over at her with dread on his face. He kneeled, reached down carefully and slid a pair of fingers around a slickened neck, and pressed them where the drumbeat of a pulse should have been. He left his fingers there, pressed hard against the struggling man's throat, and then moved them a bit, searching.

He looked up. "Nothing. This man is dead," Cabot said quietly. Only Sabrina and a doctor walking past heard her. The doctor froze and looked down at Cabot, clearly angered by the guard's assessment.

"Nonsense," the Doctor said. "Roll him over please."

Cabot looked at the doctor and shook his head. "You're fucking crazy if you think that's happening Doctor. You're welcome to check his pulse exactly like this if you don't believe me."

The Doctor looked furious that the 'lowly' guard had disobeyed his medical command, but Cabot's stature, even kneeling as it were was too intimidating for the Doctor to say anything. The Doctor dropped down to the writhing figure on the ground, and carefully slid a finger to the spot Cabot had tested for a pulse. After nearly a minute of searching, the Doctor moved his hand near Matt's mouth to feel for breathing. Matt's broken jaw snapped shut quickly at the Doctor's fingers, narrowly missing severing a finger. Cabot put a knee into Matt's skull to hold it still against the floor, and the Doctor returned his hand, suddenly appreciative of the massive security officer.

"No pulse, and as best I can tell, the only breathing he's doing is entirely based on how much pressure you're putting into his back. Hold still," The Doctor said, and Cabot obliged as best he could. After a few moments, the Doctor nodded. "He is dead. That… doesn't make any sense."

"Sure as shit doesn't Doc, now does it? I'm thinking we are in a very bizarre world all of a sudden," Cabot said.

Sabrina started to think out loud, "What do we do? How do we treat the dead? I bandaged him up perfectly, and he still died. All of these people are bitten, and if the news was right, they are all going to die, and they are all going to do exactly what Ma- AHH!" She stopped suddenly as she felt a stabbing pain in her hand.

Looking down, she saw the man with the severed neck artery biting her hand at the base of the pinky finger. His teeth were sunk in deep enough to be locked into the bone, and her training kicked in. She grabbed the man's head and pressed it against her hand, all the while pushing the blade of her hand deeper into the man's mouth, trying to feed the bite, and trigger the gag reflex to get him to stop. It was textbook self defense when bitten, and it would've worked, if he was alive. At her expense they had just learned that dead men don't have a gag reflex.

Instead it gave the white eyed dead man more flesh to bite, and he eager chomped his teeth up and down over and over, rendering much of her hand pulpy and ruined. She screamed over and over until Cabot's massive black boot came down on the back of his head, rescuing her and shattering the skull of the man, smearing brain tissue across the wine colored carpet. Sabrina's stomach heaved, and a jet of vomit, still mostly coffee came out across the dead man's body. She pried the man's mouth open, and backed away, holding her damaged hand up, and staring wild eyed at the corpse of the man who just bit her.

Cabot watched her scurry backwards until she hit a chair. Sabrina gasped for air and wiped the thin vomit from her chin with her good hand, her mind obviously not functioning in the shock of the moment. Cabot called out to her, "Sabrina. Sabrina!"

She snapped to at the baritone of the large man. "What? What? I'll be okay."

Cabot knew she probably wouldn't be. "How long do you think that guy lasted between being bitten, and dying and doing this?" Cabot gestured at Matt's dead, and still quite active body.

Sabrina thought about it carefully, and took a wild stab, "I don't know. An hour. Maybe an hour and a half? Why do you ask?"

Cabot's face became dark, and sad, "You have a kid at home right?"

Sabrina put the two elements together, and her emotions welled up, causing wetness to flow down her face. "Yeah. I should probably go to them shouldn't I? Just in case the bite really is fatal."

Cabot simply nodded.

"Okay then. I'll get my purse."

73

"Angela, remember. The bitten are violent when they die, or so it seems right? If you die, you might harm them. Make sure you don't do anything horrible, trying to do something nice."

Sabrina simply nodded, holding her ruined hand high.

*****

Her exit from the city was disastrous. Everyone else in the mid sized metropolis had the same idea as her, and the traffic, coupled with the idiotic driving, cost her extra minutes, and blood from her wounded hand. She'd bandaged it up in the car on the way out, and while stuck trying to get around a vehicle roll over just off an exit, but she'd still lost a lot of blood. The ragged wound had refused to knit enough to stop the blood flow. She felt lightheaded, and the wound itself burned like unnatural fire. She tried to call the home landline to get in touch with her husband, but that rang busy. She also clumsily dialed his cell number, but the cell networks were overloaded. She might as well have tried smoke signals.

She and her family lived in a condo complex near the center of a small town about forty five minutes from the city. It was a forgettable town, off a forgettable highway. A few businesses were there, keeping the town afloat, as well as a large private school nestled in the hills that employed a good number of people. It was a nice place to raise her kids, and she figured it would be a good enough as any place to die.

By the time she pulled off the small highway and onto the town's surface streets, she knew she was a goner. Her temperature had soared, and her vision was complete shit. Her skin was a pasty shade of pink, like the skin of a chicken in the butcher's plastic wrap in the grocery store. The bite had drained her of life, literally and figuratively.

She pulled off of the street and into the back section of the condo complex. The neighborhood of townhouse style condos was almost terraced, with her row of homes being the rear, and higher buildings. Hers was right near the street, and she only had to drive in a few doors before she aligned her car between the white lines noting where her familiar parking spot was. Her husband's pickup was still there.

She put her car shifter laboriously into park, and eased her head back onto the headrest of the driver's seat. One hand pulled the door release of the car, then freed up her seatbelt, setting her free. Sabrina's eyes closed, knowing she was home, and that she would see her kid and husband soon, she let herself take a short nap.

One from which she would never wake up from.

*****

"David, go ahead and get into the car. I'm sure you're Mother will be home soon son," Sabrina's husband Dominic said to their son David. David was that child that looked just like both parent's. Enough shared features that anyone could see both his mother and father in his face. Right now Dominic could see the worry in his wife's eyes on his son's face, and he wanted to get his son in the car quickly. His wife would have to catch up at their friend's house later. He'd tried to call her already to no avail. She'd know where to look.

"Dad we need to wait for Mom!" David pleaded from the doorway, screen banging against his back. The warm sun of the early afternoon was beating in from the open door frame, and Dominic worried how many of these days they'd be able to enjoy. The world definitely seemed like it was on the precipice of long and dangerous times.

Dominic lowered his voice, and tried to appeal to his son, "David. We need to leave right now. Your mom is a smart woman, and she knows we will be going to Uncle Jake's house near the lake. Remember the note we made for the door? See? It's posted right on the door there. She'll meet us there. I need you to go get in the car, and make sure that if you see anyone acting weird, you get in and lock the door, okay?"

David's facial expression was defiant, and as he stormed outside to get in the car, Dominic knew his son would be angry at him until they reunited with Sabrina. Dominic picked up the last box of stuff after slinging his hunting shotgun over his shoulder, and headed for the door. He backed out of the door, pulling it shut and seeing the note he and his son made. Before he turned, he heard his son's faint voice from the car a few feet away.

"Dad. Mom's home, but something's wrong."

Dominic turned, his mind filled with dread and diminishing hope for a happy outcome. When he finished his slow spin, he saw his wife's car parked in her regular spot. Inside the vehicle, he saw her sitting, looking around the inside of the car sluggishly, as if she were drugged. Dominic caught a flash of her eyes, and saw that all the color was gone just like the maniacs that were infected with whatever was causing this epidemic.

"David, please walk around to the driver's side of daddy's truck, and get in. Mommy might be sick and we don't want to startle her, okay?" Dominic slowly lowered the box he was carrying to the pavement as the son blindly obeyed his father. Dominic remained rock steady still as his son walked around the truck, and climbed in. When the door shut loudly, his wife snapped to attention.

Sabrina was feral. She whipped her head to the side where the noise of the car door closing had come from. Dominic saw her hand was bandaged, and judging that she'd died by so small a wound, she was either fully infected, or had been bitten. Either way according to the news, she was dangerous. Dangerous to Dominic, and certainly dangerous to their beloved son. As Sabrina climbed out of the car like some predator on the hunt, Dom got his shotgun ready, and racked up a shell in the chamber. The noise of the weapon's action twisted Sabrina's stare from the truck and their son, back to the father.

"Sabrina, please follow me. Talk to me if you can baby.

Don't look at David."

She gnashed her teeth in response. No words came from her, or even the recognition that the words meant anything. Dominic backpedaled slowly, making sure he didn't trip over anything, or run the risk of backing up into an object that might cost him his life. All he had to do was get her away from David, and then pray for the strength do what he knew he would hate himself forever for.

"Baby, I love you."

The grinding of her teeth answered him. Dom had her twenty feet from the house, and the kid.

"David loves you."

A lunge. Awkward.

"I'll tell everyone you came to say goodbye."

A swipe from Sabrina's well manicured fingers. A stream of a husband's tears.

"I'll tell them you loved us." Dominic looked over Sabrina's shoulder and saw that David was watching out of the rear window of the truck. He motioned for David to turn around, and his eyes full of fear and tears, he did what his father asked him to do. Dom made sure he wasn't aiming anywhere near his son, and he raised his hunting gun towards his wife's head. The news said you had to shoot them in the head. Dom said his prayer.

"I love you Sabrina. I hope I see you on the other side."

When the shotgun went off the birds in the sky flew away, and Sabrina's headless body fell to the ground, streaming her red blood across the pavement. Dominic, overcome with emotion ran off to his truck, and got inside to hold his son tight. They drove quickly away before anything got any worse.

When the shotgun went off, a man awoke in a nearby home. He'd been sleeping all day, but the blast stirred him from his slumber. Unknowingly, Sabrina's death, her final death, was the first event that would start a long series of events that would determine the true fate of the world.

Upstairs, just a few dozen feet away, Adrian Ring

decided to investigate the source of the noise that woke him up.

December 4th

It occurs to me tonight that almost every plan I make hinges on something I know fuck-all about.

How many people are left?

I don't know. I haven't the goddamn foggiest idea, and wouldn't even be able to hazard an educated guess. When the television died it seemed like there were still a lot of people around. Billions served so to speak. After the radio stations faded a week or so later, the reports made it sound much more grim. As in perhaps only a billion of us left. Math isn't my strongest subject, but that means about 6 out of every 7 people died, give or take.

Some areas of the world seemed to be faring much worse. Africa for example was wiped out almost immediately. They've always been on the razor's edge for health anyway, and when this hit, they went downhill in a hurry. No infrastructure, shitty transportation resources, a general lack of secure locations, etc. I don't know the exact details, but I recall the radio people saying Africa was bad, from what they could glean.

America and Europe, and most of Asia though… I just don't know. All I can worry about is here though. America has a shitload of guns, tons of securable locations, solid infrastructure, decent healthcare, good media for communication, and plenty of food in the pipeline to maintain a large surviving population for some time. We also have huge tracts of arable land to grow food on after society has stabilized.

This is all assuming there are enough survivors to even establish some form of society though. It's really hard to gauge what's going on because I am so secluded. In a small town that's off the beaten path at a private school that's even further off the beaten path my intelligence on survivors is somewhere between slim and none. So how many people have survived? Where are they? Are they hungry? Starving?

Have they reformed some kind of shitty government right down the street?

No idea. These are the things that keep me up at night. That's not entirely true.

I think about Cassie a lot too. Some nights when it's cold and I'm feeling more lonely than usual my mind gets to wandering and I inevitably go full circle and come back to her. Recently it's been worse than normal too.

Remember that black fancy car I saw drive by me the other day? The one with a couple of people in it? The one with the redhead in it?

Cassie was a redhead.

You have any idea how much that tears my ass up inside? Is it her? It could be. The color of red was about the right shade. Of course this could be my memory fucking with me. Being very selective about the details it wants to recall. It's entirely possible the girl in the car had brown hair with red highlights, and my brain thinks of Cassie, then equates that with red hair, then I see the girl, then I think red hair, then I think; holy shit, that was a redheaded girl; it was probably Cassie.

Sigh Mr. Journal.

This is going to bother me. As I was thinking in bed last night with Otis sitting on my chest keeping me warm I was debating doing a stake-out. I mean literally sitting in one of the houses on the side of the road down there waiting to see if they drove by again so I could get a good look at them. You realize how stupid an idea that is Mr. Journal? It would be an enormous waste of time and energy likely for nothing.

The rational thinker that I am tells my idiot self that if Cassie were in fact alive, and had made the trip all the way out here, she would've come to the school looking for me. I took a lot of stuff from the house, which she would notice, and I always told that if the world ended, I would hole up here. So if that is her, it means she doesn't care about finding me anymore.

Ouch. Just fucking ouch.

I don't want to think about that. It's bad enough that the undead are roaming the streets, let alone having to think about my girlfriend abandoning me up here.

Ouch.

I wonder if that IS her and she's pissed at me because she thinks that I abandoned her.

Ouch.

Sitting here typing this entry is just causing me emotional pain and distress. I need a new frigging hobby. One that involves me not wishing I were dead. This sucks.

It isn't her. It can't be her. She would've come here first if she was in town. Even if she was furious at me, she'd come up here at the very least to beat the shit out of me and let me know she was furious at me. She'd kick both of my balls up high enough to pass for earrings. I know that much.

That makes me feel a little better. Curious that the idea that getting my balls kicked up to my neck is a comforting thing nowadays. What a world Mr. Journal, what a world.

Cassie, if you're still out there, I love you. Always will.

I am feeling a little under the weather tonight. I think something I ate for dinner isn't agreeing with me. I got that... Squishy feeling downstairs like I'm going to be spending some time on the shitter in a bit. Getting a little warm, and there's a light film of sweat on my brow. All signs point to diarrhea. I'll cross that bridge when I get there. More likely, I'll shit all over that bridge when I get there.

Having discussed my digestive issues, I'll recap you up on what happened earlier today. I cleared three more houses on Jones Road today. Took me forever, which usually means good things. As I said before I've already cleared three houses on Jones, and today I did three more, which leaves three left, one of which is that huge ass farmhouse which I've got a great feeling about. Old houses are usually great places to find useful stuff from an older era. We'll see what it brings in a day or so I guess.

The three homes I cleared today were all relatively small by this neighborhood's standards. Maybe 2,000 square feet.

Still out of my price range, but much more reasonable homes. There were several great finds in these houses too, which is pretty awesome. None of the homes had any zombies in them, which was great. Found another dead pet though, a cat, which sucks. Makes me think of Otis.

One house had two items of note worth mentioning. Beer. Lots and lots of beer. Now after my single experience turning myself into an emotional wreck since the end of the world, I am not going to drink any of the beer. I'll save it for barter should I ever find other living people. Not sure how long it'll keep for though. The other item that house had in it was a shotgun. Another Mossberg pump action 12 gauge. It's a hunting model, only holds 6 shells, but it is in very good condition. They also had 8 birdshot shells, and 18 buckshot, which is a nice shot in the arm for my dwindling shotgun ammo supply. (How many times can I fit the word "shot" in a sentence you think Mr. Journal?) Hopefully one of these houses will have some 9mm ammo, because that's starting to get into the red zone. The same house also had some extra gun cleaning supplies, which is always useful. There's got to be more houses up here with weapons in them. Got to be. The new shotgun is going on the shelf for now. My current shotgun holds 8 shells, which is sort of a big difference if the shit hits the fan, plus it has a little shell holder on the stock which allows for less fumbling for ammo if I'm in a hurry. Devil's in the details as they say.

One house had a single awesome item, but it was a pretty awesome item. They had a small gas powered electric generator. Well, it's not that small. It's a 16HP generator, which is enough to power one of the small dorms. It looks more or less brand new too, which is another big bonus. They had it set up in their garage likely in the event of a power outage in the winter. It would just need to be plugged in to the electrical system at the school and bam, juice to a new building. Add this generator to the wood stove that I want to get up there and we are seriously looking like a success story in the making.

The third house had the dead cat. The third house also had a few bags of cat food. Guess that's how that works right? Otis lives another day at the expense of another kitty's life. Sorry bub. Same house also looked like the home of a hoarder. Useless bullshit piled ceiling high in every corner. It was clean thankfully, but amazingly cluttered. They had a lot of really great books that I took. I always took the internet for granted. The last few months it has occurred to me that "Googling" how to do something isn't a fucking option anymore. If I don't know how to do something, then I fucking don't know how. There are no more easy solutions Mr. Journal. These people had an old school encyclopedia, which will be useful.

Great haul earlier. Really pleased. The generator and the shotgun make it a total victory. Add to that I got a bunch of good consumables as well and we're looking like champions. Really happy.

So yeah, just had the shits. Of course you can't understand the passage of time because in your world Mr. Journal this is just the next sentence. No time has passed for you! But for me I just nearly soiled myself. Jesus that was terrible. Smelled like someone set a corpse on fire after they took a shit on it. Fucking terrible. It was like evil cement sausages.

Colorful, aren't I?

My guts are killing me. I hope I'm not getting sick. That really worries me. I think I'm going to get some water and lay down Mr. Journal. See if I can't lazy this thing out of my guts.

-Adrian

December 5th

Mr. Journal.
I am hurt badly.
I don't know what to do.

-Adrian

December 6th

I finally out of pain enough to make some sense. I tried to write yesterday, but it was all a goddamn jumble. Right-click delete. As it stands, the Percocet I'm on right now has me a little loopy, and it's taking me forever to write this out. I'm at that happy period of time with Percocet where I'm not feeling much pain, but I'm largely still coherent. Really stoked the old couple above the gas station had some in a pill bottle. Hooray for the little things.

I am hurt. I was hurt yesterday afternoon during my house clearing on Jones Road. I'll get to that in a few minutes. First, I'll explain how I got to my injury. Hopefully I can finish before the pills knock me the fuck out.

As you might recall, the night of the 4th I came down with a case of the Turkish trots. Mr. Journal if you are unfamiliar with that expression, it means powerful diarrhea, typically in a vibrant green color. I think it was food poisoning. I was up late that night off and on the toilet, so sleep was basically nonexistent. However, by dawn I had shit myself empty, and after rehydrating myself I was much better.

I should've stayed in the dorm yesterday.

I left early this morning with a full belly of food and high hopes for a quiet day. I feel like I'm falling behind on my stated goal of having these houses cleared by the 14th. The sooner I get these houses cleared, the sooner I can start trying to find people. I am definitely not going to make my Dec. 14th date now. Not happening.

There were three houses remaining on Jones Road. Two pretty normal houses, both good sized, and the final huge ass farmhouse at the end of the road. I've been itching to get into that farmhouse for days now to see what could be inside it. Frigging place was huge and I just knew there'd be a lot of good stuff inside. I was right about that at least. Of course that wasn't the only thing I found at the farmhouse.

ALONE NO MORE

The first two houses I did were great hauls. Nothing equipment wise that's new, but there was a really good amount of food and stuff, which I was more than happy to remove. I finished clearing those places by about 1 in the afternoon, and both houses were totally empty of anything sketchy or dangerous. I guess that's the calm before the storm. I loaded the truck up with the food, and ran it back here before I tackled the farmhouse. Turns out that was a really fortunate choice on my part. I got it all inside here to sort out last night, but it's still sitting there untouched. I'm having a hard time getting around right now, and it's not going anywhere anyway.

God I feel so vulnerable.

The farmhouse is on a slight raise at the edge of a field. There's a typical farm style post fence running around the majority of the property. Maybe 4 or 5 acres of clear land I think. They had 3 or 4 cows, and it looks like 2 horses. I can't be sure because the animals were pretty much devoured. Their smelly ass carcasses were in the far edge of the field away from the house. I only saw them when I went into the barn when I started to clear the area.

For some reason I forgot to honk my horn. I've only skipped honking the horn once, and that was when I was clearing the cape the other day that I was pretty sure was empty, or filled with zombies. I can't be sure either way, but I'm thinking if I honk my horn earlier today, I'm walking around fine tonight. Fuck me. This is what cutting corners gets you I guess.

So I parked the truck next to the house where the previous owner's cars would've been parked. There was a gravel driveway right there, plus it was next to the gate for the fence. I was so goddamn giddy to check the place out I didn't clear it quite as thoroughly as I should have. I gave the outside of the house a quick walk around, then headed straight to the barn to see what was out there. I saw the animal bodies on the grass and double checked them to make sure they weren't sheltering any zombies. All clear.

CHRIS PHILBROOK

The barn was pretty good for stuff. Biggest thing was a small tractor. I left it there because right now I have no use for it. Come spring though it will be awesome when I start to plant crops. Assuming I make it to spring. Assuming I make it to Christmas. There was also a bigger gas powered chainsaw in the barn, which I did grab.

I let myself into the house via a back porch. They screens were all still open from the summer months, and it was really cold. The back door to the house was wide open as well, which told me no one was here. If there were people living here, they wouldn't have left the back door open in 25 degree weather.

I cleared the bottom floor of the giant ass farm, then for some reason decided to clear the basement. I can't say why. Just decided to do that next. Easily the creepiest basement yet. 10 out of 10 for sure. The house had to be 200 years old and the damp, dark, cold cellar was straight out of a horror movie. There were no windows either, and once I got down stairs I switched to the Sig and my new Maglite instead of the shotgun. I couldn't safely clear the cellar holding the shotgun and the flashlight. Despite giving myself a complete mind-fuck in the scary ass basement, it was empty. I perused down there for a few minutes and found a pretty decent supply of canned food. Gotta love farmers and their need to stockpile food. Salt of the Earth, those people.

I came back to the first floor and made my way up the wide stairs to the second floor. It was bitterly cold going up the stairs. I realized there was a, um. A big window open in the stairwell letting the cold in. I shut it when I walked past it. The upstairs was a single long hallway with a handful of rooms off of it. All of the doors were shut, and the hallways smelled like death.

This house had really nice hardwood floors. They were stained a dark cherry color, and for all I know, they might've actually been cherry. They were old, worn, and they've been scuffed up by years of dragging feet, but the color was still rich. Almost like a patina on silver.

ALONE NO MORE

The hallway was covered in giant piles of dog shit. Huge piles of dried up brown nuggets. Big nuggets. Looked like fucking kielbasa. Everywhere. Wall to wall poop. I actually had to laugh that a dog had shit that much in the same place when the doors were wide open the whole time. Getting through the hallway was actually a pain in the ass. Only way to make it anywhere was to tip-toe in between the landmines of poop. I knocked on all the doors, one by one, and the only door that had a response was the one with the biggest piles of shit in front of it. The floor and door looked like someone had attacked it with a garden rake. Scratches on the door all the way up past the knob.

When I gave the door a rap or two there was that insistent rattling again. The tell tale bumping of something trying to get through the door at me. I could hear a few quiet scrapes as nails were drawn down the wood of the door, attempting to scratch at me from the other side. That sound makes my bladder weak. I sighed, leveled the shotgun off at what I guessed was neck height, and blasted a hole in the door. I was actually hit in the face by a few shards of flying wood which stung like a bitch. I think I got a sliver in my cheek of all places.

I leaned over and looked inside the room through my new fist sized peephole. Getting up off the floor was an elderly woman. She was clearly dead, though not in the permanent sense that would make me feel good about it. My shotgun blast had hit her in the chest and cleanly took her arm off. She was shakily pulling herself to her feet and I decided to get in the room and kill her with the sword. The door was locked, so I drew the sword and booted the fucking thing in.

The old lady zombie had just steadied herself using the bed to make a lunge at me when I gave the sword a good swing and embedded it in her eyebrow. She went down in a heap. It took me a few seconds of see-sawing to get the blade out of the lady's head. It stank in that room. There was a huge pile of crusty shit in the center of the bed, and right next to that was another dead body. This one was dead-dead though. The body was an old man's. Very frail and thin. What was left of him looked at least 80 years old. He was holding a handgun, a small snub nosed .38. The old guy's melon was busted out the top and he had a finger sized hole in his chin. It was surrounded by a grey halo from the gun powder. Pretty clear suicide. He had been bitten multiple times all over his arms and legs, but the bites were pretty superficial. Most of them had barely broken the skin.

False teeth.

I grabbed up the pistol, slipped it into the cargo pocket of my pants, and searched through the small bed stand drawers. I found a box of ammo for the pistol. It had 12 bullets in it. The pistol itself held 6, and had 5 left in it. I was pretty excited. That's when I heard this weird clicking noise coming from the hall. Tick-tack-tick-tack-tick-tack. It was getting closer faster.

I got the shotgun ready and went to the hall. Just as I got to the doorway I froze. Not five feet away was the biggest motherfucking dog I have ever seen. I don't know what breed it was, but it was a beast. I think it was part Dane, part Rottweiler, part pony, because it looked huge, and it looked mean. You know when a dog curls its lip when it growls? And you know that primal growl they can let loose when they're feeling scared, or territorial? It was doing both.

It was then I put two and two together. All this dog shit in the hallway. The open doors. The dead cattle and horses. The scratches going up the bedroom door.

The dog had gone feral when its masters died. It lunged at me. I don't know why but I didn't try and shoot it. I half assed and missed a butt stroke with the shotgun which was completely useless of me. Fucking dog hit me like an all-pro linebacker and took me out at the hips. The inside of my left thigh exploded in pain as it sank its teeth into the meat just below my balls. The dog landed on top of me, fully engaged with the meat of my leg and started shaking on me. I can't even begin to tell you the agony I was in.

When I hit the floor I lost the shotgun. I was half twisted up when the dog hit me and I had to drop the gun to prevent my head from smashing into the floor. At least I did that right. Once I got some semblance of balance back I started punching the dog in the nose but all that did was cause him to bite me again, punching a whole new set of teeth marks into the meat of my leg. He had his front legs pinning my lower half to the floor and I could barely move.

Big fucking dog Mr. Journal. I got my right leg free and kicked him in the gut. He let go for a second. That bought me enough time to draw the Sig from the holster, but it also caused him to bite the shit out of my right foot. When he latched on he turned sideways and I emptied the Sig into his side, right at the spot where I thought the heart was. It wasn't until the pistol's magazine was half dry that I felt his jaws loosen some, and he didn't flop to the floor until the gun clicked empty with the slide locked back. He still had my foot his jaws when he went down, and my ankle twisted almost 90 degrees from his weight falling awkwardly. I remember screaming out and kicking my foot free.

I reloaded and just sat there, breathing hard, pistol aimed at the empty hall. I had a feeling there would be a second dog, but none came. Once I cleared my head I cut my pants open with my hunting knife, the one my uncle made.

My leg is messed up bad Mr. Journal. Bad. There are at least 8 puncture wounds half an inch deep or more. When the fucking dog shook me his canines tore the flesh of my inner thigh pretty good, and there are rips in the leg an inch long leading from the bite holes he was holding me at when he did it. The bleeding wasn't too bad surprisingly. I mean it was bad, don't get me wrong, but I wasn't bleeding out. My CLS training kicked in and I realized I was about 3 inches at most from having my femoral artery severed.

Three inches higher and the last thing the world hears from me is that I had diarrhea.

The fucking indignity. I am now out my favorite pair of pants. Had to cut the leg all the way down to the cuff to get at the wound. Insult and injury. Having a rough go of things Mr. Journal.

I had my small first aid kit in the hunting vest I wear, which a good decision. I had enough Bacitracin, bandages and tape to get a reasonably good field dressing on there. I couldn't bend my right leg up to get a good look at my foot right then though. It hurt far too much to try and balance myself at the moment. In a terribly ironic moment I had to pull myself to my feet using only one leg whilst damn near face planting in the corpse of the old lady. Unreal. I am really starting to feel like the punch line to some cosmic fucking joke.

I emptied the shotgun of shells and started using it as a makeshift crutch. Every time I had to move any muscles in my left leg it was like putting a blowtorch to it. Oh my God it hurt. My right foot was painful as well, but not that all that bad. Turns out there were a couple of really bitching bruises where the teeth had hit bone in my boot. No punctures though.

I steadied myself against the wall every step or two. I think it took me almost 5 minutes to make it back to the stairs. I was all kinds of excited that I hadn't fallen, so as you can probably see coming Mr. Journal, I ate shit going down the stairs. I think I had 3 or 4 steps left to get to the first floor when I had a sharp stabbing pain hit my left thigh and I stiffened up. My foot missed a step, and in complete slow motion, I teetered forward, arms swinging wildly to and fro like that coyote from the cartoons, and I smashed face first into those nice cherry stained floors. I blacked out for a few seconds from the pain. It wasn't another concussion thankfully, just the swooning stars of having to choke down the throbbing from my foot and leg.

I got myself up and hobbled all the way out the back door. It was then I had a fit with myself over leaving the fucking back door open. First time ever. Shows you what even a simple mistake can do nowadays. The margin for error now is razor thin.

ALONE NO MORE

What the fuck ever man.

I almost went teapot over kettle again when I was going down the back porch steps. Luckily they had handrails on both sides. I had to toss the shotgun on the ground to catch myself, but that's better than putting my face into the freezing cold gravel of the driveway. I already split my chin open in June and I don't want an instant replay of that bullshit.

I wound up nudging the shotgun along with my bad foot until I got it back to the truck. I nearly went down for the count when I bent over to pick it up, but I used the truck as a leaning post and got upright just as the stars filled my vision. The drive back here was a fucking joke. I couldn't get my left leg bent and into the cab so I had to drive with the door open. My foot was sticking out into the road, but I didn't fucking care. I don't even remember the drive back to be honest. Today when I looked out the window the Tundra was practically rammed into the side of Hall E. Must've really wanted to avoid walking. Don't know how I got the door open to get in it was parked so close.

I'm exhausted right now. All I've done today is clean my wound, go in the basement, eat, and type this. I can't get over this Mr. Journal. Sigh.

I don't remember much about last night when I got home. I vaguely remember getting into the shower and cleaning myself off. The warm running water hitting the holes in my leg was not soothing, that I recall with distinct clarity. Felt like someone was driving nails into me every time the water hit the wounds, but it had to be done. I washed the wounds out with antibacterial soap, and when I got out of the shower, I must've doused it with hydrogen peroxide. I found an empty bottle on the bathroom floor today. That's about where Adrian's big old head checked out for the night.

When I woke up this morning I was laying in the recliner. Otis wasn't on me either, which is unusual. He was sitting on the shitty dorm couch watching me intently. It was kind

93

of creepy.

The wounds on my thigh were very red when I woke up. Angry, puffy welts that is still very sore to the touch. It was freezing in here when I got up too. I hadn't refilled the gas tank on the generator in some time and I'd run out. Took me forever to refill the tank in the basement, but I got it done.

I showered after that. Wasn't thrilled for that, let me tell you. I found something a little disturbing when I cleaned the wound again. A tooth. Lodged pretty frigging deep one of the holes. I felt it as a hard lump just under the skin. Used a pair of tweezers to dig it out. That nearly sent me to the black hole of pain right in the shower. I will say the pain lessened immediately, and that was a relief. Gross to think I left a giant dog tooth in my thigh overnight though.

Washed the wounds again, slathered around the wound with Bacitracin, and got something to eat. I'm kinda pissed I used hydrogen peroxide when I got in the shower right after it happened. I am pretty sure that's not the best idea for a wound like that. Hope it doesn't fuck me up. I don't have much of an appetite, but I know I have to eat. I forced down some canned shit and now here I sit, typing this, letting the air get to it. I think that's the right thing to do. Bandaging it seems wrong, but the Percocet I took earlier has got me a little wobbly upstairs.

The pain is bearable at the moment, but I only have three more of the pills. I figure that'll get me through tonight, and maybe tomorrow, but then I'm on ibuprofen by the handful. I hope that's enough.

I hope this doesn't get infected. Even just a regular infection is fucking game-over for me. Wave buh bye to Mr. Ring Mr. Journal. C'est la fucking vie. I took a ballpoint pen and gently drew a circle around the edge of the redness earlier. If the redness spreads out beyond that mark, I need to do something in a hurry. I'll need to go downtown.

I don't know what to do right now. I need rest, I need food, and I need water. All the shit at the farmhouse can wait til hell freezes over for all I care. I need to get well.

If these wounds get infected though…..
Well that's a problem I just can't think about.

-Adrian

December 7th

Very, very, tired Mr. Journal. My leg has swollen up a fair amount since last night. I drew ink boundaries around the redness surrounding the wounds before I went to sleep, and over the course of today the redness has crept about a quarter inch past the ink markings.

I think it's getting infected. No, no I know it's getting infected. I'm not running a fever yet though.

I need antibiotics. Something powerful that will stave off an infection like this. I don't even know what ones to take.

I have to go downtown.

Fuck.

-Adrian

December 8th

I'm out of Percocet. As it turns out fistfuls of Ibuprofen don't even begin to put a dent in the pain I'm in. Looking at the bright side, my nausea from the Percs has subsided. I'm sitting in the recliner right now with my leg elevated as high as I can get it. That isn't very high though, as my wounds are all near my cock. Right in that slab of meat next to your groin Mr. Journal. Feels… Awesome.

The redness is a little further out today than it was

yesterday. There's a clear fluid building up around the deepest wounds, and the fluid is just slightly off from clear. A vague yellowish color to it. I'm starting to feel flush, and my temperature has begun to creep upwards. My handy dandy electronic thermometer tells me I started today at about 99.1 degrees F, and as I write this shortly after dark, I am sitting pretty at 99.7. I'm going through fluids like a fish.

It's infected. But we knew that didn't we Mr. Journal? Could I have expected anything else? Remember that punch line to the cosmic joke bullshit I was talking about? It's not funny anymore.

I don't want to die like this. Let someone shoot me, let me get eaten alive, let me get hit by a goddamn falling airplane. I don't want to slowly die from an infection. This could take weeks to kill me, and I don't think I have the balls to kill myself.

Sigh.

There are four places to get antibiotics in town that I can think of. There are two chain store pharmacies. One is on this side of town, the other is on the opposite side of town near my condo. The closest pharmacy is right near the grocery store. The further pharmacy near my house is in a small cluster of businesses, but more importantly, it is right near a residential area. There could be a lot of people, or undead over there.

The third place to get drugs is the town clinic. I'm sure they have ample supplies of various medications for samples and in case of emergencies. The clinic is a two story building right near the closer pharmacy and the grocery store.

The fourth and last place I can think of is the veterinarian's office. Granted probably not ideal, but antibiotics are probably antibiotics, and in this situation it might be the only place that hasn't been raided yet. If there are survivors in town, there is a very good chance that the clinic and both pharmacies have already been picked clean.

I can't get around for shit Mr. Journal. I can hobble, but if I spend too long on my feet the thigh starts to pulsate right along with my heartbeat, and the pain becomes unbearable. I start seeing all those pretty fucking stars, and then whether or not I want to, I go down in a heap. What that means is that I am not very mobile, and I need to sit down or lay down after being upright for a short amount of time. I can't afford to be out in the open at all. I really need a drive through here.

Literally and figuratively, a drive through. The pharmacy closest to me is the one nearest to the clinic. It also has a drive through window. I can literally drive the truck up the window, smash the window, get right into the pharmacy area, throw what I need through the window into the truck, and then climb back out. In theory, unless there are undead in the pharmacy, I will never even encounter undead at all.

I can shoot the undead inside through the window before I go in as well, or draw them out with the truck. If the pharmacy is untenable, I can cross the street and try the clinic. That's really, really not a good idea though. Anyone sick around here during the fiasco days will likely have gone there, and if they died, the place could be crawling with zombies. As in balls deep.

If plan A and plan B fail, I can hit the vet's office, which is about a mile away from there. If that fails, then I can cross town and hit the pharmacy near my old condo. And won't that be a piece of cake.

So that's the plan. Try and hit the pharmacy via the drive through window. If all goes well, I'll be in and out in no time flat.

What's that Mr. Journal? You want to hear the bad news? Oh there's plenty of that still left to share sir.

I can't shoot the shotgun. I can't balance enough to brace for the recoil. If I let loose a single shell I fucking know I'll tip over in slow motion and crack the back of my skull open on something. Shotgun is just not going to happen. This sucks too because I just double upped on my shotgun shells with the stash I found the other day.

Which means... I need to use my pistols, or the rifles. The

rifles would be decent, especially the .22, but I don't feel comfortable moving around holding a rifle right now. I can't balance like I said, and having to stop all the time and rest means I'd have to sling it, or set it down. Rifles get in the way, and I need to move fast as I possibly can, which means this is a pistol only mission.

Yes Mr. Journal, I did say the other day my 9mm ammo was almost in the red zone. Oh what's that? How many 9mm rounds did I use to kill Cujo the pony? Sigh, the shame. I emptied a full magazine of 15 rounds into it. Are you suggesting that was overkill? Well Mr. Journal despite our close and otherwise amicable relationship, I'm offended at the suggestion of overkill in this instance.

That fucking dog was huge, and had nearly bitten my balls clean off. Not that I should let that of all things get to me. I haven't really used my balls in forever. Well, besides for beating off, and I'm not really "using" my balls per se. They're just sort of in the neighborhood of the process. Men wouldn't beat off at all if we had to do to our balls what we do to our cocks. Well, some really fucking weird men might.

I am down to 32 9mm rounds. I have 17 .38 caliber rounds, and 18 .45 cal rounds. I hate revolvers. I mean mechanically they're superior. They're easier to clean, easier to maintain, less prone to jams, etc. But reloading a revolver in a hurry without speed loaders is a fucking death sentence. The .38 is a last ditch thing.

So I'm rocking the 9mm and the .45. I am pretty fucking glad I found that thing now. Plus the sheer knockdown power of those slugs can't hurt. I can easily take the recoil of the pistol without going down in a jumble.

Um, what else for bad news? I can't walk for shit. I need to go downtown. I'm low on 9mm ammo, I can't shoot my shotgun, I have a festering leg wound, I think I've got a few bones broken in my right foot too, which is just about right all things considered.

Fucking A, right? I mean seriously. What else can go wrong?

Ah DAMMIT! Why do I say that shit? Definitely gonna pay for that jinx. I've half a mind to hit backspace and hold it down until it's gone. But you know Mr. Journal just as well as I do that what's said is said, and I'm fucked even if I delete it. Whatever. Gonna throw my hands up at myself. Stupid Adrian.

Back to the topic at hand. The Pharmacy. It makes some sense to go down at night to avoid anyone seeing me, but as I've said, I'm scared of moving around at night. I can't see well, and it's not like I have NVGs. I'll go in the morning, as soon as I can get up, get showered, get bandaged, get dressed, get fed, and get motivated. I'm guessing that puts me at noon.

Pharmacy drive through, that failing I'll try the clinic. If that falls through I hit the vet. If the vet is a failure, I go to the pharmacy near my place. If that fails, I might be a dead man. Once I get the meds I need I get out and get back here. I lock the damn door, wash off, put my leg up, take some pills, and heal up.

No problem, right?

-Adrian

December 10th

I made it.

Paid a high price Mr. Journal, but I am here, and I am still alive. Let it never be said that I was not a little lucky here and there. Even if it was my own mind numbingly powerful ignorance that imbues me with said luck. Both good luck and bad I guess.

Yesterday I went downtown to the pharmacy. What a trip Mr. Journal. Just like I suspected it took me almost until noon yesterday to get my shit together for the trip down. I had to gear myself up after wrapping the leg tightly in bandages. Speaking of my leg, it was ugly yesterday morning. The redness was a solid inch and a half out from the edges of the wounds on all sides. There was a faint red line starting to form near the deepest and most angry looking hole in my thigh. That's not good at all, right?

I already know the answer Mr. Journal. It's bad news. So I cleaned it, bandaged it, got my shit together, and worked my way out the front door despite having the Tundra parked about 8 inches in front of it. I have no idea how I got inside the dorm the other day. I must've thought very thin thoughts and squeezed my way in. I think I scraped a frigging rib off on the way out yesterday. Gotta cut back on the desserts I think.

Geared up, ready to rock and roll. When I left campus I realized I hadn't done a patrol in some time, and vowed to do one when I got back, but I forgot. I also had forgotten to move the two school vans into the normal V formation on the bridge, which was a huge lapse in security. Anyone could've driven across and onto campus while I was laid up. Bad, badness Mr. Journal. I hopped out and got the vans moved so they were set up while I was gone. Did I mention it fucking freezing out? What a miserable time to get my leg mauled. As if there were better times for that to happen.

The drive downtown was clear. I saw nothing out of the ordinary on Route 18, which is normal I suppose. No shambling undead, no people walking around, nothing. I drove really slowly as well so I could look around and see if there was anything of value I could come back for after I was healed up enough. Every trip out is a recon op.

I saw some cool shit, but nothing really outrageous. I made my way down to the Main Street area near the grocery store. Remember when I went down there before and I said I saw a couple of houses on fire? Or burnt down or something? There were quite a few more burnt down this trip. I'm guessing here, but if there were people holed up in them, they probably started fires in their houses to stay

100

warm, and I'm betting they set their own damn houses on fire. That or idiots using gas generators and electric heaters. Might as well throw a match on your fucking couch. Dangerous shit right there.

Just as before the more urban-ish, retail-ish areas were loosely populated with shamblers. I think I ran over about 10 of them heading down to the pharmacy. I was most definitely a little less careful about the Tundra, I'll admit that. The windshield is all fucked now, one of the headlights is busted, and the grill is cracked. Don't even get me started on the paintjob. Good thing insurance isn't really an issue anymore. So I carefully lined up my zombie speed bumps and made sure to hit them with the tires. I wasn't worried about killing them I just wanted to make sure all they could do was crawl, instead of walk. That'd buy me the time to get in, and get out.

I noticed a few things that were eyebrow rising. The small metal caps that go on the tops of gas station storage tanks were removed at the gas station I stopped at when I was heading up to the school back in June. Someone has been getting gas out of there manually. I guess that makes sense. It means there are, or were survivors in the area. That's scary and encouraging at the same time.

There were also several new car wrecks along the main drag. I remember seeing a few small ones, but there were a LOT now. So many in fact that at one point I had to slalom the wrecks in the truck to get through. A couple of the cars were flipped over on their sides, complete with zombies still seat-belted in. It was almost funny when I drove by the wrecks and the zombies reached out, trying to grab me as I drove by. Creepy more than anything.

The good news right off the bat was that the pharmacy parking lot was pretty clear. There were maybe 5 or 6 undead wandering about, and as soon as they saw me they started heading my way. The cars in the lot were spaced out nicely, and when I did a loop around the building, the drive through was unobstructed. The bad news was the front door of the pharmacy was destroyed. Someone had obviously driven some kind of vehicle through the sliding doors to get inside. I was hoping they'd left something for me.

I swung back around again and checked the surrounding areas. The only thing I could see for threats were about eight undead wandering in a small plaza across the street. They were heading over my way, but I figured I had enough time to get inside. On my third trip around the building I swung into the drive through so the passenger side window was nearest the building, and climbed over to smash out the drive through window.

I think I sat there staring at the steel shutter in the window for about thirty seconds. I had totally forgotten about the steel shutters. I think I've seen them a hundred times in the past few years. When they close up shop, down they come. Matte steel, just like a garage door, only reinforced. I think I cried a little. I'm man enough to admit that. I mean by that point my leg was in excruciating pain contorted in the cab of the truck, and I felt totally fucked. I mean serious anal pillaging fucked.

I was bending myself to get back behind the wheel when I saw into the bed of the truck and gave myself a mental high five. The chainsaw. I had left the chainsaw I found at the barn the day I was bitten in the bed of the truck. Fucking A! I slid the back glass window open, reached out and grabbed it. My leg protested in pain hardcore, but it had to be done. The saw was heavy, but I got it in the cab and shut the back slider. Now it can't be a particularly bright idea to start a chainsaw in a car Mr. Journal, so I really don't recommend it, but I was in improv mode. The saw started on the first pull. I gave it some gas, and like a fucking champ the chain moved perfectly. I leaned out the window of the truck and brought the chainsaw down into the glass. It shattered and went everywhere. Luckily it was safety glass, so it wasn't too sharp or anything.

One I got the glass removed I started to lean on the saw as best I could, pressing it against the joint where the shutter and the frame met. It took about thirty seconds, but eventually the whizzing teeth ate their way into the locking mechanism, and with a giant shudder everything broke loose. I grabbed the metal shutter and lifted it, and smooth as silk it slid upwards into its hiding spot. I'm a fortunate motherfucker Mr. Journal.

I left the saw in the truck, double checked that I still had my handguns, and threw the big black gym bag through the window into the pitch black pharmacy. I could see inside enough to tell the gate to the rest of the store was still closed, so unless there were zombies inside, I was good to go. The darkness was a worry, but I was pretty confidant

I worked my way up and out of the truck, onto the drive through window's edge, and I toppled over onto the counter, then somersaulted onto the floor with a painful thud. My back was killing me from the fall, but to be frank, getting my leg straightened out was such a relief I hardly noticed it. I laughed for a second, then opened my eyes. And you know it, there was a form coming down on top me in the dark.

I couldn't tell at the time if it was a person, or a zombie, so I just reacted on gut instinct. I punched the motherfucker in the side of the head. The female body went sideways like a mule kicked it and I crawled backwards, further into the pharmacy. It was then that I noticed the smell. That God awful smell. So here I was, crawling backwards to get away from the zombie that had just tried diving on top of me, and I come to sudden halt against an object at my shoulders. I had backed into the shins of another one. I looked up just as the zombie of the pharmacist, white lab coat and all was leaning over to rip into my guts. I got lucky and punched kinda upwards at his right knee just as he started his plunge and it threw off his aim. He went from savage plunge to face plant right between my frigging legs. I actually heard his nose and teeth break on the tile, and could hear the scraping sound of his jagged teeth scratching the floor as his body stretched out on top of me.

Worst.
Sound.
Ever.

I was so horrified by the sound of his teeth scratching and breaking on the tile I hardly noticed one of his hands had smashed into the bandage on my wound. Holy shit the burning agony. Using my good leg (the one with the bad foot) I kicked the shit out of him mostly to get him off of me. In the background the female pharmacist zombie was already up and coming back at me. Once I got my hip free I pulled the Sig and double tapped at the chick. First shot must've sailed high, but the second hit home. She went down backwards and I used my hips to escape from under the guy on top of me. I went with his motion as he tried to turn into me to bite me, and wound up bringing the barrel of the Sig right into his shattered face. I bucked the pistol twice and he fell back on top of me, really dead this time.

I think it was about then I realized I had shit myself. I forgot to mention that Mr. Journal. The uh, stomach issues I had the other day have been making cameo appearances in my underwear. Sort of a wet fart problem I'm trying to shake. It's embarrassing, yes, but I've no dignity left anyway. This diarrhea has been so sneaky I've taken to calling my ninja shits. I never know when they're coming, and they always kill me when they show up. It's a good thing there aren't any women around me. Even if I was the dead last guy on Earth I'm pretty sure I'd never get my dick wet at the rate I'm going. I am so fucking unsavory lately. I was letting out a stream of curses when I realized the zombies from outside had reached the window, and were reaching in to get me. I was a good six feet away though, and I've never seen them get past an obstacle that high, so I felt safe.

That was an incorrect assumption. I think there was something on the ground they could step on. A tall curb maybe? Plus their clustering action in between the truck and the building apparently was enough to get a few of them lifted up high enough to start falling into the building. I crawled backwards some more, leaving a nice fat brown streak on the floor and started firing at the silhouettes in the window. It felt like I was at the bottom of a fucking barrel with the fish being thrown in on top of me. I shot and shot and shot but the zombies kept falling through the little hole into the dark and on top of me. Figuratively of course. Although their pile inside the crowded pharmacy eventually was at my feet when they stopped coming through.

I fired the Sig until the first magazine was empty. I dropped it and slapped in the second, and aimed as carefully as I could. When that went empty I put my final magazine in, and fired the last two rounds in that. That was all she wrote. I'm out of 9mm. Dry as a nana's vagina. I holstered it and grabbed the .45 that I'd stuck in my waistband. In the small of my back. Right where the poop was. I only had to use it twice before the stream of zombies finally dried up, but let me give you this public service message Mr. Journal:

Guns covered in poop smell terrible when they're fired. You're welcome.

My ears are still ringing loud as can be from all the gunfire. Guns are so fucking loud inside enclosed spaces. You've no idea what the hammering does to your eardrums. I guarantee in a few days when the ringing finally stops, I'll have permanent hearing loss. I'd put money on it.

I shook the poop off the pistol and reloaded the magazine from the spare shells in my vest. When I finally got to my feet I think I did a one legged dance for joy. Then I shut the window shutter to make sure nothing else got in with me. Everything was still there. I mean everything inside the drug section of the pharmacy. Everything. All shelves stocked as full as normal. Apparently these two dropped the gate to hold up and no one since had gotten in. Unfortunately they'd died in here. Made me wonder right then why whoever had driven in the front didn't just drive into the shutters inside the store? I found out, I'll get there Mr. Journal. Patience. Incidentally with the window closed it may have been much warmer, but all those fucking zombie bodies were capital R RIPE. Btw I'm about to be all fucked up on vicodin Mr. Journal. Might get a little wiggy up in here shortly.

I had no idea what to grab, so I grabbed everything. Just in pill bottles alone I filled the entire duffel bag. I knew I couldn't leave after having gotten this far with just the one bag, so I knew I needed to transport more shit somehow. I had to get into the store to get more bags or something. I slid the shutter open, checked to make sure it was clear, and then tossed the gym bag into the truck. I couldn't reach the chainsaw, so I wasn't sure how the hell I was going to open the inside gate to get out.

Then, like the epic jelly dong I am, I realized the pharmacist probably had the key in his pocket. Once I yanked his corpse out from under the pile of zombie and searched him, I found the keys. God what a bitch that was. Bodies are frigging heavy Mr. Journal. The lock was right at floor level, so I got the .45 ready, and got down on my belly. I tried to be as silent as I could turning the key, and was largely successful. My fear was that I'd slide the shutter up, and see nothing but feet. Bloody undead feet pressing against the shutter, trying to get inside to me.

I said a little prayer, and hefted the shutter upwards slightly. It went up much easier than I thought it would. So easy in fact the thing flew wide open. I watched it sink into the ceiling from my stomach, neck bent all the way back to get a good angle.

Then I looked into the store and saw the handful of zombies standing right there looking up like retards at the shutter going up, just like me. As fast as I could I dropped them. I break-danced myself into a better shooting position on my back and got three of them dead as a doornail before the other three realized what was going on. Fascinating fucking door for zombies. If it were portable I'd consider it a potential replacement for Lady Gaga.

I managed to squeeze off accurate shots and dropped the last three before they got to me. It took me a few minutes to get back to my feet, but once I did I realized why the driver of the vehicle hadn't rammed the shutter. Inside the store were row after row of shelves, just like any other store. The idiot driving the SUV who rammed his way into the store flipped a few of them over and managed to drive up on top of a few of them. The SUV's wheels were totally off the floor, and it was smack dab against a support column in the middle of the store. No way around it, and no way to push it out of the way without taking down the column. The driver was history, so maybe he or she escaped.

I scoured the store as fast as I could on my bad leg. By that point I was in near agony just taking steps. I kept an eye on the smashed out front doors, but nothing came inside. I found a handful of backpacks which would do well for transporting stuff out. I also found a few of those Sterilite plastic bins, which were pretty clutch too. Exhausting walking around with my leg all fucked up. My back is now sore as hell from favoring the one side so much.

Most of the rest of the store was completely ransacked though. I mean to the floor empty. A few things here and there that were at best fringe useful. However, there were plenty of goodies left inside the pharmacy. For some reason condoms were in there, which was cool, as were the diabetic supplies. I'm not diabetic, but someone somewhere might be. I took everything. Any by everything, I mean fucking everything. I was tossing armloads of shit I couldn't fit into the bags into the bed of the truck when I was wrapping up. In amazingly awesome news, there was a desktop reference for drug uses and drug interactions on the shelf. That'll be REALLY good to have kicking around.

By then my leg was bleeding badly, and I could barely walk. It took everything I had left in me to get back through the window and into my truck. Spinning my body around to get behind the wheel was like pulling teeth. However, once I was situated, I peeled the hell out and blew that pop stand.

Drive home was… quiet. I drove in an aggressive fashion I should add. I veered to and fro to hit the zombies on the ground I'd merely disabled on the way in. I figured why leave them half or three quarters dead when it was just a few seconds of driving to get rid of them.

I made it home fine. I stopped like a good doobie and reset both vans into their V formation to prevent anyone from just driving onto the campus. The Tundra got parked near Hall E as normal, and I got everything inside and tossed into the kitchen with the rest of the shit from the farmhouse I still hadn't sorted through. The pain was worth it.

I took a breather for a few, then got into the shower to clean my leg and ass off. I was covered in blood, gore and shit. My leg looked like absolute hell too. I'd managed to tear off the scabs that had formed already, and I am pretty sure I ripped the tears in my thigh a little bigger too. When I do things Mr. Journal I do not half ass them. If I'm gonna be fucked, I want to be totally fucked.

Cleaned it, got some Bacitracin on it, and got sitting in the kitchen to go through the book I got about medications. I found the names of a couple antibiotics recommended for wound infections and dug them out of the pile. I have several bottles of the stuff, and the book said I need to take 2 a day for 7 days and I should be good to go. I started the first pill immediately

Then I found the VICODIN! Oh sweet blessed relief. I spent the entirety of last night in a narcotic induced coma, and it was wonderful.

I woke up fairly early today when the pills wore off though. I popped one more, stumbled my wounded ass to the basement and filled the gas tank on the generator, and then came back up here.

The vike is finally kicking in here and there's no pain at all anymore. I can feel the wooziness coming on though, which means that's fucking all for fucking today Mr. Journal.

I am out of 9mm. That's pretty shitty news. I'm also down to 10 .45 rounds. I've got over a thousand rounds of . 22 left, which is cool. I've also got the .30-06 and the shotgun, but those are less than ideal to use as clearing devices. If I weren't hurt as fuck I could use the sword more, but I can't risk melee combat. Lol. Says the guy who punched and kicked two zombies today. One might successfully argue that I am intellectually challenged Mr. Journal.

You know what has me thinking right now Mr. Journal? Like, seriously thinking? What the fuck is the middle of town like? I blasted through how many rounds going to the fucking pharmacy? What's Main Street near the center of town like? What about the residential areas where Steve and I used to live? I mean... shit... What're the big cities like?

What a life. I'm gonna go lay down in my recliner with a big fat glass of orange juice made from concentrate and hope the antibiotics start to work. Today is a do nothing day, and I think I deserve it.

I might just pull through this. Cross your fingers Mr. Journal.

-Adrian

Exodus

People underestimate the value of being warm. Abigail lay on her mattress on the living room floor with the covers pulled up over her face. It had gotten so cold the last two weeks that she and her family had dragged their beds into the living room near the fireplace to stay warm at night. Her father had shut all the doors and put black trash bags on the windows to try and seal in the heat. It only marginally worked. They were also almost out of wood to burn. Soon they'd be breaking furniture apart to put in the fireplace.

Things were bad now, but they had been much worse over the fall. The Fall. It had been the fall of mankind, not just the season of autumn. Abigail Williams was one of the few people that survived until cold weather, and for that she was somewhat happy. She'd almost go so far as to say she was thankful. The world, as she and her family knew it, ended on June 23rd, 2010. Abigail herself didn't see much of the news the first few days of the end. She was away at her private high school an hour away from home when it happened. When "it" happened.

No one had agreed on what to call the end of the world. There was no catchy moniker like Y2K, The Apocalypse, or Z-Day attached to it. Most likely because the world ate itself alive that day. Or at least it started to. At her school Abigail's first experience with the end of the world was a car accident in the afternoon. Two of the parents had come to the expensive private school to get their son and somehow had crashed their car into the side of one of the school buildings. Abigail had rushed in to help the mother, getting dirty and

111

covered in blood in the process. The driver, the father, had died very quickly. His arm had been severed in the accident and he bled out rapidly. Right after he passed on he got to his feet and attacked one of the school's athletic coaches. The driver was unmistakably dead, and yet he stood up and bit the coach.

Abigail knew right there and right then everything she had ever known was going to change. She saw him sit up. She saw his pasty white skin, the ragged stump of his destroyed arm. His milky white eyes already empty of the soul. He was the undead, the nosferatu, a demon, a zombie, and he was the beginning of the end. The father bit the coach on the shoulder and pounced on his own son. Abigail ran then, she didn't want to see what was going happen next. She'd seen enough horror movies to know what the undead do the living.

It was a long time before the 17 year old girl realized that her decisions that day saved her life. It took her weeks to forgive herself over not helping the people being attacked. She'd seen far too many people since then helping and paying the ultimate price. You can't help the undead. They're beyond the reach of mortal hands she knew now. Even helping the living now was dangerous.

After the father's initial attacks Abigail had run to the nearest building, one of her school's administration buildings. She found a cluster of the staff standing in windows, watching the father kill his own son just a few dozen feet away. She couldn't believe that they were just standing there, doing nothing. Looking back on it, she understood panic now.

The staff inside frantically dialed 911 over and over to no avail. No one answered, or the calls got cut off. Too many phone calls can flood the network she knew. It had to be bad everywhere else. It was bad there.

That afternoon was a blur. She can remember seeing the undead father return at some point and bite more people. A few of the staff rushed out to help the victim, but they got bitten or killed too. Eventually someone took him down by beating him to death for a second time. The son and the mother were still undead and dangerous though. It was a cycle that had only just begun. The evening was a matching blur as well. All she could remember to tell her parents about it later was being abandoned by the remaining school staff. Once they had left two more girl students came in to the nurse's office. Abigail hid upstairs from them because she wasn't sure if they were bitten or not. They came in, ransacked the nurse's office for a few minutes, and then left in a hurry. Apparently there were some survivors left. She just didn't want to see any more of them right now. After an hour of building up the nerve she decided to turn off all the lights and barricade the downstairs doors.

Abby was motivated by the sound of gunshots outside. Normally she would be scared of guns, but that night it was the sound of safety. Every loud crack of gunpowder was something dangerous being shot. It was the sound of the living fighting back. She pushed every bit of furniture she could in front of the main door. A desk, a bookcase, a file cabinet, some chairs, even a potted plant or two. The back door had a kitchen table and some chairs pushed in front of it. It wasn't Fort Knox, but Abigail worked with what she had.

When she finally got the kitchen table and chairs propped up in front of the door she was scared out of her mind as one of her fellow students banged on the very door she was standing in front of. The door was a sturdy industrial door, but the small glass window in it seemed bare and fragile with his face on the other side of it. She screamed at him. He wasn't alive anymore. His face had been bitten open, and lips and cheek hung off him in bloody tatters. He hit the window with slow mechanical repetition, staring at her with those lifeless white eyes. She killed the lights and ran upstairs, locking herself in an office.

There were more gunshots too. Many more before the night was out. She huddled in the office as quietly as she could all night. The students who were dead yet still moving stayed at the kitchen door downstairs all night long. She sat alone in the dark for hours that night, hiding underneath a desk. She waited for the banging on the door to stop downstairs. She expected to hear the creak of the steps as her dead classmates came up the stairs to eat her, to feast on her. But the banging never stopped. The horror never beat down the door, and she made it through the night.

She starved for hours. Her stomach growled hours on end as she searched the room for something, anything to eat. She found nothing. The windows in the office showed her little of what was happening on the campus. All she could see was a dorm down the street, the river that circled much of the campus, and part of the school's cafeteria. Early in the morning as the sun started to rise she saw the coach that had been bitten stagger out of the cafeteria, his grey hooded sweatshirt stained burgundy from his blood. He was dead. He was still walking.

It wasn't long after that she started to hear music coming from outside. Something upbeat and trendy. It came from the other side of the building, but it was muffled. It wasn't long after the music started the streams of the dead started to form. Dozens of the undead came out from their previously hidden resting spots. They all moved with stiff legs, jaws reflexively going up and down, trying to eat the sound that was drawing them in. Abigail still shudders when she thinks of their looks of blank hunger. The memories almost make her feel as cold as the late December air in her living room now. The memories made her feel cold even back then, back in the warmth of June.

Laying on her bed now in the living room, letting the warmth of her breath fill the blankets she still hated to think about the state of the world. She was angry, bitter even, but still thankful for being alive. She could thank one of the good staff at the school for that. Mr. Ring. She started to hear a lot of gunshots after the sunrise. A little while after the music started. Sharp cracks. Dozens, maybe over a hundred before it finally stopped. She didn't know much about guns, but she knew the sound of precision. One shot, then silence for a second. A second shot, then a moment of silence. She got the predatory rhythm of his shooting down enough that she could tell when he was about to fire again. The shots were coming from close by, maybe the school building across the street, but she never found out.

After a few more gunshots in a different area, she heard the front door open downstairs. Her heart stopped cold, waiting for the undead to smash through her makeshift barrier. Instead she heard yelling. There was quite a pause while she figured out what to yell back. She never did figure anything clever out, she just started yelling; "hey, up here," as loud as she could. She let herself out of the office and came down the stairs. She saw her debris had been moved, and she was both excited and scared to meet the person who had rescued her. When she turned the corner at the bottom of the stairs she nearly met his ammunition. Luckily he didn't shoot her, and she didn't die of fright, so all's well that ends well she thought.

He gave her the most delicious energy bar she had ever eaten, and they exchanged information in a hurry right there on the steps. He was the shooter from earlier, and his plan was to secure the campus, to make it safe and call it home until whatever was happening ended. She thought it was laughable now, months after the fact that they still thought there would be an ending to this. She just needed to get home to see her parents and her brother that day.

They left the building together. Mr. Ring stopped her in the door and handed her his small rifle. This she remembers vividly. He drew a small sword he had on his belt and he walked across the small yard towards one of the undead classmates that had survived his shooting rampage earlier. The zombie was moving awkwardly towards them. She'd never seen anyone move quite like Adrian before. He approached the zombie with no fear, just deliberate violence and determination. At the last second he sidestepped it to the left, dodging its lunge, and brought the sword in low and fast, taking the kid's right leg off at the knee. The dead student toppled forward as his foot and calf tumbled out into the road behind him.

Adrian circled him like a predator, all the time watching her reaction. It was like a lion teaching a cub. This is life now. Kill or be killed. This is the cost of survival. He brought the sword down once, sinking it the width of her hand into the head of the student. His body twitched a few times then went limp, and his eyelids closed over his pasty white corneas. She dropped Mr. Ring's rifle and threw up while he wrenched the blade out of the kid's head. To this day she can remember hearing his skull crack when the blade came free. It sounded like a coconut cracking, or a stalk of celery being broken. More shivers from her memories.

After he cleaned the sword off she remembers him walking straight up to his rifle and picking it up off the grass where she'd dropped it. He looked around slowly, assessing the campus around them for danger, and then he turned to her and said his final words of advice.

"Abby, if you want to leave, I won't stop you. It's not safe though. These things are going to be everywhere, and they're not even the most dangerous thing you'll find. Plenty of people are going to be panicking, doing things they normally wouldn't." She remembers him looking down at her torn shirt, at her exposed bra. "Things they might not do to a 17 year old girl otherwise."

The thought of what he meant still makes her swallow some rising bile, even now months later.

"To kill them you need to destroy the brain. I don't know why, I just know it works. Shoot them, crack their skulls, whatever. Kill the brain, kill the threat, ok?" She remembered nodding at him, wiping the puke from her lip.

"You will need fuel, food, and water. Most grocery stores are already empty, and most gas stations will be dangerous, or out of fuel already. Go straight home. Do not pass go, do not collect $200. If your parents need to, if you have to, come

116

back here. I think I can make this place safe. Be smart. You made it through last night like a champ and you can survive if you're smart." He looked around again, checking for danger.

"Remember, if you have to, run. Run to a safe place and hide. Now let's get you a car."

They found a small station wagon with the keys still in it fairly quickly. He shut the door for her, wished her good luck, and that was the last time she saw Adrian Ring. Underneath her blankets, still chilly from the cold air in the living room outside them, she silently wished she'd never left school that day. It was probably warmer there right now.

*****

Abby and her mother were making dinner together later that evening. The older Williams woman was wearing an expensive black wool ankle length coat in the kitchen. It was something you'd expect to see a powerful businesswoman wear to her corporate job, not something a pale and emaciated woman would wear in her kitchen. The two women silently did their chores, their breath faintly visible in the cold air. Her whole family didn't talk much to begin with, and since they'd locked themselves into their house, they didn't talk much at all anymore. Her mother stood over a trash bin and opened a can of green beans, draining some of the juice out. Abby noted they were the infinitely more expensive "French cut" green beans. It must be a special day she thought dryly. Abby herself was portioning out a can of peaches onto plates as her mother came over to do the same to the green beans. They arranged each plate until the portions were all roughly equal. The two women stood and looked down at the meager meal.

"Mom how much is left?" Abby asked her mother quietly.

Her mother didn't answer her, instead she took a deep breath and exhaled, watching the steam drift away absently.

She shook her head and quickly wiped a tear away from her cheek.

"Maybe a couple more days. Four at the most." She looked over at her young, vibrant teenage daughter and wiped another tear away. Even her daughter's hunger couldn't put the fire out in her eyes.

"Randy and I can go looking for food tomorrow. Dad can stay here and protect you again, like last time." Abby tried to reassure her mother with a smile and a gentle rub on her back.

"No honey. It's too cold, and there are too many of those things out there again. That truck that crashed the other day on the corner brought too many of them near here." She leaned over and lifted the black trash bag covering the window above the sink. It was dark out, and little could be seen in the pitch black outside. "Besides, we've checked all the houses around here and with those assholes at the high school running around town, there isn't going to be anything left anyway."

The two women, one young, the other older, looked at their delectable meal of cold green beans and peach slices for a minute. They shared a silent chuckle at their misfortune.

"We can always go back to ALPA. Mr. Ring had the place pretty safe Mom. I'm telling you we should do it." Abby pleaded in a whisper. She knew her father heard her he would object strongly to any trip anywhere. In his mind the only safe place was locked in here, together.

Abigail's mother stood contemplating the idea for a few seconds, then responded back in her own whisper, "Tomorrow. Tomorrow when we show him how much food is left, maybe he'll decide we have to leave. Maybe I can persuade him to see the writing on the wall. It's not safe here in town, even locked in here. There's too many of those things, and there are far too many people who think they're the law now."

Abby nodded, and the two women picked up their pauper's dinner plates.

*****

Bringing up the idea of leaving their home did not go well the next day. After eating their little lunch meal Abby's mom Patty brought it up. The four of them were huddled close to each other in their living room, next to the fireplace. They were finishing off the last can of peaches and a can of cold peas.

"Charles, we're almost out of food." Patty made eye contact with her husband, trying to show the seriousness of their situation.

"I know. Randy and I will go out looking for more food tonight, after dark. Those assholes can't see us then and we can outrun and lose the dead people." Abby thought he looked strange as he said it. He seemed excited about the prospect of finding more food, but he looked afraid or scared at the same time. Abby had never seen that expression before.

"Charles, there isn't any more food out there. We've scoured every house in this neighborhood twice and taken everything. The people who took over at the high school have taken everything else in town. Tomorrow we start starving if we don't go somewhere we can find food. I know it's dangerous but-"

Charles cut her off. "No. Leaving is too dangerous. You've seen how many of those things there are just outside the house. Can you imagine what we'll find if we drive somewhere? Where would we go anyway? Your sister's place?" He asked in an accusatorial whisper.

"Abby and I were thinking the school. Her school," Patty replied quietly.

"Are you two crazy?" He said almost laughing. Abby's 12 year old brother Randy sat on his sleeping bag stiff as a board, watching the argument unfold. Normally he couldn't be shut up to save his life and now he was paralyzed from the argument. If only one good thing came out of this discussion Abby thought, it was shutting him up for five minutes.

"That's over an hour away. It's over halfway through December, those roads are probably covered in foot deep snow or ice by now. We would never make it." He stuffed his last peach slice into his mouth angrily, chewed it twice and swallowed it.

"Well, you should've savored that Charles. It was our last peach." Patty gathered up the empty plates and walked out of the living room.

Charles licked his lips sorrowfully and looked over at their bleak, unlit Christmas tree.

*****

Two days later on another cold late December morning the parents found themselves all alone in the kitchen. Abby and Randy were in the darkened living room with the slowly burning fireplace. Charles was gently washing dishes with water made from melted snow as Patty dried them and put them away.

"Charles..." Patty whispered.

"I know." The dad chewed his lower lip as he watched his two beloved children play Yahtzee on the living room floor. Both kids were covered in blankets and only exposed one hand and their faces. Even from the kitchen he could see the faint white vapor from their breath. Their faces were starting to look gaunt, stretched. Too little food and too much stress in their short lives. He had a knot form in his stomach when he thought about what they'd look like next week, after they'd completely run out of food.

"Maybe we can go to the people at the high school. Maybe they'll take us in. We can work, gather things. You still have the shotgun and a few shells, maybe they'll trade for that or something?" Patty was talking absently, thinking out loud.

"No." Charles looked back her. "The people in the high

school have no need for us. You're an accountant, and I'm a civil engineer. Abby has no usable skills and Randy will irritate them almost immediately. We'd be excess baggage to them. We would be extra mouths to feed. I'd hate to think what they might do to you girls too." Charles face tightened in a grimace when he said that. He'd been having bad dreams for weeks now, waiting for the people in the high school to come knocking, looking to take his daughter and wife away. It was inevitable. He knew they ruled this town now, with their guns and their trucks. They knew where his family lived too; there was no hiding the smoke coming out of the chimney.

Patty stopped drying the dish and hugged her husband tightly.

*****

Charles rolled over onto his back. He couldn't get any sleep on the damn floor, same as every other night. He'd lay there until he was exhausted, then pass out and get maybe 4 or 5 hours of sleep at best. His 50 year old back had no interest in hardwood floors, but his 50 year old body didn't want to freeze to death either. Tonight there might not be any sleep.

It'd been two whole days since he and Patty had their private moment. It'd been over a day since they'd eaten. Earlier that day he and Abby had gone slinking house to house further out from home looking for food. It was a dangerous waste of time. Charles only had eight shotgun shells left and that was hardly enough if things got bad. There were far too many of the dead walking around and if they were cornered, he and his daughter would be fresh meat. If they were dead at least they wouldn't worry about being cold any more. He wondered if all the dead people walking around were hungry, maybe that's why they kept trying to eat everyone. Another couple days of not having food and the idea of eating someone would start to seem less outlandish.

He and Abby counted 30 of the dead people walking around that day. Moving slowly, bush to bush, house to house they'd avoided being seen. Charles was just as worried about the living lately as the dead. Even if he did fall asleep that night he'd still dread it. The nightmares kept getting worse and worse. Visions of rape, torture and worse would fill what little sleep he would get. At least exhaustion was tolerable. His dreams of late were not.

He looked at his lovely young daughter with only her face poking out of the blankets. She'd always be seven years old in his eyes. Even asleep she was scowling at the cold, and at the gnawing emptiness in her flat belly. He still envied her, despite the bleak future she seemed to have in front of her. Still young, still fit, still funny. She was still in the awkward, lanky portion of her life too, and in a few years he knew she'd blossom, and be just as beautiful as the wife sleeping next to him. He'd die for them if he had to. He was fully expecting to, possibly before Christmas.

Christmas. What a joke he thought. The season of giving has arrived, and there's nothing left to give his family. They had even run out of wood to burn this week. Tomorrow night they'd be breaking apart furniture to stay warm, and after that, they'd have to sit in the car with it running to stay warm. Of course the noise of the engine would bring them in. The dead people.

Charles wiped away the tear at the corner of his eye and steeled himself. He wouldn't sob in the dark. Despair would not tear him or his family apart. He distracted himself and thought about their options instead. The high school was not an option. He knew some of the people who were pretending to be in charge down there, and he knew how it would play out. The town selectman, a few asshole cops, city council members, and car dealership tycoons. All they were now was petty tyrants abusing their power. His family wouldn't last down there and he knew it. He could take his family to the homes of his extended relatives, but that was a stretch. The only family that was close was Patty's sister, and she had an apartment a few towns over that just didn't make sense to move to. She was in a more heavily populated area, and just getting there might kill them all.

It made a lot of sense to go to Abby's school. His daughter said the man that rescued her had killed a lot of the dead people that day, and that meant it might be a lot safer. Charles was trying to remember what the campus looked like, thinking of how safe it'd be. He knew it was rural, miles off any real road. He knew there was a large cafeteria, likely left alone when the shit hit the fan. He remembered you had to cross a bridge to get there, and that seemed excellent. And from what Abby said, this man had several guns, and was really quite good at using them. Charles wasn't sure if that was good news or not.

He looked over at the face of his son Randy. Little Randall was a hellion, every bit the precocious 12 year old he could be. Randy struggled to make friends, and was very awkward socially. He'd talk at length about silly childish things for hours, and then get angry if you didn't engage him. Frequently they spent all day trying to keep him occupied so he didn't go off wandering, trying to elude the dead people for fun. Even in his sleep the haircut he prized dropped down low, covering one eye. Trendy kid that one. Charles got a quiet laugh out of that. His wife Patty stirred against him, and he pressed himself against her warmth. She felt like the only warm thing in the world.

The roads to Auburn Lake Preparatory Academy might be terrible Charles thought. It was hilly, and mostly in a valley that turned into a collection bowl for bad weather. It could be awful driving to get there. But if Abby was right, safety was there, and possibly some food. At this point, staying here wasn't an option Charles could consider for his family. Their home would not become their tomb. Tomorrow he would break the news that they were leaving.

In a world empty of gifts to give, he would give his wife and children the gift of hope. He would try and give them one more chance for survival.

*****

"We leave tomorrow. On Christmas kids." Charles finished his speech with a grin on his face a foot wide. All night he'd gone over the details of his plan, and all these hours later, he was sure of it. For the first time in three weeks his daughter danced for joy. She leapt off the couch and strut her stuff around the living room silently. They didn't dare make much noise today. For some reason a few of the dead people had wandered down to the end of their cul de sac and were just outside. Abby tore her little brother off the couch and got him dancing with her. It was the first time he'd seen them get along since everything changed.

He looked over at his wife Patty and saw the quiet satisfaction in her face. She agreed with him earlier when he told her his idea for the trip to the school. Together they tweaked the details and the plan was set. Tonight they would pack everything they wanted to take with them. Only the things they could carry would go. Everything else stayed behind. At dawn they would load the station wagon Abby got from the school the day the world went to shit. It was all wheel drive and would give them the best chance of making the trip. It was also inside the garage, which meant it could be loaded safer.

Charles would drive. They'd leave as soon as they could in the morning and head straight to the school, taking the route all the way around town to avoid driving anywhere near the high school. The last thing Charles wanted was to drag those bastards behind him. Fucking lampreys were all they were in his mind now.

They would drive the same route back to her school that Abby had taken to get to the house that day. She had already given them detailed information on where she had seen clusters of the dead people, and where she had seen some car accidents. There had been a lot of car accidents since the

124

world ended Charles thought. People driving scared are dangerous animals.

He savored the celebration of his children for a minute, and then headed upstairs to begin packing his things. Patty waited a minute longer, then followed suit.

*****

In the garage the next day the engine of the station wagon turned over immediately. Charles was intensely thankful for the engineering prowess of the man who designed the car. He, his son Randall, his wife Patricia, and his daughter Abigail all sat in the car, excited and scared that they were finally leaving the home they'd taken to calling a prison. Charles waited a minute for the engine to warm up, and then he hit the switch for the garage door opener.

Nothing happened.

Patricia reached up and hit the switch again as Charles looked out the back window, perplexed. He'd put the garage door opener in this car just last night. He'd even put new batteries in it just in case.

"Dad," Randall said in an irritated tone as he brushed the hair out of his eye. "There's no electricity, duh." He exchanged ludicrous looks with his sister. Parents. So stupid.

Charles kept the sternest face he could muster and gave his son the evil eye. Inside he was laughing at himself. His wife covered her mouth to stifle the smile on her face.

"Well then kids. Seatbelts on?" They nodded in response.

"Merry Christmas!" Charles put the car in reverse and punched it. The beige garage door blew off the tracks with a loud, cold shriek. It flew up and over the car as the wagon hurtled out into the middle of the cul de sac. A handful of the dead people were milling about around the car as he spun the wheels to straighten it out into the road. Two of them got close enough to grab at the window as they sped off.

"WOOOOOO!!!!!" Randall yelled as he gave one of the

dead people the middle finger. His older sister Abby stabbed two powerful middle fingers up as a sign of solidarity with her brother. They high fived each other as Charles weaved around the other dead people in the road. He didn't want to risk running over one and blowing a tire now. There wouldn't be a second chance right here.

At the end of the cul de sac was the wrecked truck from a few days ago. The assholes who thought they were the new militia had crashed one of their lifted up Chevy trucks during a chase for the dead folks. Something had gone wrong, as was so often the case and one of the trucks had flipped over against a street lamp. Charles gave the truck a wide berth. Several of the dead that had flocked to the scene of the accident were already headed their way as they sped past.

The roads were a mess. Snow and ice were covering the streets in moderate amounts, but it was just enough to make driving the car feel loose to Charles. Every time he turned the wheel to go around a corner he felt the ass of the car sway a little further out then it should have. To avoid a spinout he kept the wagon at a steady and manageable 20 miles an hour.

Getting out of town turned out to be a piece of cake for them. They only encountered maybe 30 or 40 of the dead people walking around, dragging furrows in the snow as they went. Most of them were so bogged down by the few inches of snow they posed no threat to the family in the car. Charles actually thought to himself several times that if he had a good bat or an axe, he could clear most of the town out all by himself. That wasn't the priority though, and he got the car and his family out of town and onto Route 18, the most direct route to Auburn Lake Preparatory Academy.

*****

It wasn't anywhere near as bad as he'd expected. The roads were bad, but as long as he stayed slow, it was fine. It helped tremendously that there was no traffic. In fact, they never saw another moving car, or a human being the whole car ride. For that, Charles felt like he was given an invaluable gift that Christmas day.

The car ride was initially nerve wracking for the whole family. They hadn't been this far outside of the house in months. In fact, most of the trip they spent squinting from the harsh glare of the sunlight. They'd avoided going out during the day almost entirely, and they'd put those trash bags on their windows to block the dead people from seeing them, and to try and keep in the heat. Their seclusion made their eyes weak to the bright daylight. After they'd left the house once they realized the dead people were spaced out enough that they could drive around them, and that the assholes from the high school weren't following them, everyone's demeanor dramatically improved. It almost turned into a driving version of 'catch me if you can.'

What should have been an hour's drive turned into a multi hour marathon. The slow speed Charles had to drive at combined with the constant need to go around crashed cars, downed power lines, broken tree branches, entire fallen trees, and the occasional walking zombie made things move at a snail's pace. About three and a half hours into the drive Patty noticed that Charles had gone very quiet. She noticed he was gripping the steering wheel tighter than he had been, making his knuckles go white, and he kept looking down at the dashboard every few seconds. Patty waited until the two kids in the back were half asleep before she said anything to him.

"Chuck hun, something wrong?" She put her hand on his thigh, the typical comforting measure she took when he was driving stressed. Mostly it happened in heavy city traffic.

Chuck smiled and laughed at her, "Well I'm fine. It's just this little light here has been on for about ten miles now. It's right next to the big fat E on the gas gauge."

Patty's stomach dropped. They were easily 5 miles from the school still. And right on cue, the car coughed a few times, and the engine went belly up. Charles wrestled with the wheel and they drifted slowly to the edge of the road where the car died. They were out of gas.

The two kids in the back asleep slowly roused after the vehicle came to a full stop on the shoulder of the road. Abby wiped the sleep from her eyes and leaned forward between her parents.

She asked in a half asleep whisper, "What's up?"

"Looks like we are walking the last few miles to Auburn Lake babe," her mother replied soberly.

"Are you shitting me?" Abby rolled her eyes.

"Watch your language Abigail. Of all days it's Christmas," her father scolded her mockingly.

Randy sat forward and set his head on his sister's shoulder. "Are we screwed here?"

The mom and dad contemplated their response before Charles finally snickered, and responded to his son, "Well Randy, that really is a subjective question. Are we screwed because dead people are staying kind of alive and trying to kill us? Then yeah, we're screwed. But in reality, things are decent. We just need to go for a little walk to get where we need to be."

Randy scratched his head and sighed. "You suck dad."

"Thanks son. Let's get our stuff and get moving. If we hustle we might be able to get to the school by dark."

*****

The snow wasn't deep in the road mercifully. They had the good fortune of traveling from home, so they all had their winter boots and jackets. Randy of course being the typical 12 year old boy decided long ago that boots were "for pussies." All he wore on his feet was an extra pair of socks, and his sneakers. Charles walked first, using his bigger feet to drag paths through the snow so his family didn't have to wade into the full five inch deep snow.

When the sun was as its peak they saw the first dead

128

person walking in the road since the car died. They came up behind him and got to within 20 feet before Charles motioned for them to stop. He turned around and got the golf club from Randy, handing him the shotgun in return. The family all readied themselves for the worst, and Charlie took off at a run at the zombie.

Even at his age Charlie was in good athletic condition. It helped dramatically that he hadn't eaten a normal meal in a month as well. All that was left on him was skin, bone, and muscle. He trudged at a good jog behind the zombie and it wasn't until he was ten feet away that it heard his muffled footsteps in the snow. It was a large man, very tall with broad shoulders. He had a full reddish bread that was clumped and matted with frozen blood and gore. All down the front of his tee shirt was the remnants of who knows how many human meals. Streaks of person covered him head to toe.

Charlie swung the 4 Iron as hard as he could like a baseball bat, aiming for the forehead of the dead man. The timing was off though. The huge bearded zombie raised his arm just enough to deflect the blow slightly, causing it to glance sharply off his head. The blade of the golf club took a divot right off the side of the zombie's head, leaving a brownish patch of skull exposed. The patch of flesh flew twenty feet off into the snow, landing with a faint, wet thump. Charles wouldn't be replacing that divot.

Charlie lost his balance and stumbled forward, losing the golf club and hitting the zombie in the chest. The two of them tangled immediately and fell together onto the snow. The wife, daughter and son screamed and bolted towards the melee.

The father and zombie rolled around multiple times in the snow before the huge body of the dead man had Charles pinned in the freezing white fluff. The desperate father shoved both of his forearms into the neck and chest of the hulking dead man, pressing his desperate advances away. His beard, fetid and rancid hung directly into Charles' face, leaving him gagging on the smell. The mouth of the bearded monster snapped shut over and over, trying to sever chunks of Charles' flesh to no avail.

Randy, shotgun in hand, made it to the struggle first. He aimed the double barrel shotgun right at the side of the zombie's head and squeezed one of the triggers. With an ear splitting roar the bearded man's head disintegrated, sending a shower of gore all over the father's face. A cone shaped swath of human destruction went out on the snow from where the blast happened. Randy was sent backwards a few feet from the tremendous kick of the shotgun. Charles gasped up breathlessly under the zombie at his family, and they got the headless body off of him.

Lying in the snow they clutched each other, desperate to survive. Charles labored hard for a long time, but when he finally caught his breath, they started moving again. No one said a thing to each other.

*****

They made the turn up the hill onto Auburn Lake Road about an hour before the sun set. The family was shivering in the cold air and they knew they had to move fast to get to shelter, or to get to the school. It was already cold, after it got dark, it would be frigid. Shuffling through snow is exhausting. Trudging through snow on an empty stomach is nearly impossible. Doing the same while heading uphill is nearly insurmountable.

Patty was the first to suggest they find shelter. "Charles, we need to stop. I can't go on. Next house, we need to stop." She was out of breath and her face was nearly blue from the frigid winter air.

The family of four stopped, all panting. Secretly they were all thankful that someone had finally spoken up. Charles bent over, putting his hands on his knees. His chest heaved repeatedly until he caught his breath. "Yeah okay. Next house."

And they started again. Much slower this time, but they knew their trip would be over soon. Abigail envisioned finding a home with a fireplace like theirs. They could eat some snow, curl up in front of a fire, and spend one last night together as a family before they got to the campus. She smiled as much as her face would allow. It felt to her as if it was nearly frozen solid. Her teeth hurt it was so cold.

"Isn't it weird how we haven't seen any dead people?" Randy said in between deep breaths.

"A little yeah. But who knows. Maybe these people never made it home that day," Charles replied as he grunted each step out, clearing the snow out of the way for his family.

Abigail saw the truck first, and pointed it out, "Hey, that's one of the school's maintenance trucks on the side of the road there." The family all saw the Ford truck parked on the side of the road. It took them a few minutes to reach it, but after Charles approached it with his double barrel shotgun, it was found to be free of danger. He peered through the driver's side window and saw the keys hanging in the ignition.

"It's got keys!" He yelled back to his family.

"Try and start it!" Patricia yelled back to him as they moved to the truck to rejoin Charles. The dad opened the door and maneuvered his way into the driver's seat. The seat was cold on his ass, but he was thankful to be off his feet. Pulling his glove off Charles flexed his fingers, trying to force warm blood into the tip so he could even feel the key to turn it. After rubbing his hands together fast and blowing on them, he closed his eyes, crossed the fingers on his left hand, and turned the key with his right.

The huge truck coughed a few times, and roared to life. Everyone started yelling in celebration. The truck hiccupped a few times as the moisture in the fuel line worked its way out. They all piled into the single bench seat and sat there for a few minutes, waiting for the truck to warm up, and the heat to come to life. Charles noticed the fuel was very low, but he knew the school as only maybe 2 or 3 miles away.

"Let's do this kids." And they were off.

Charles pulled an ugly nine point turn in the road and started the truck off up the hill to the campus. Eventually the road leveled out and he slowed when Abigail warned him the bridge onto the campus was ahead. They all leaned forward on the seat as they rounded the final curve, exposing the giant 800 acre island that was Auburn Lake Preparatory Academy.

Dozens of buildings were spread out over hundreds of yards beyond the bridge. The bridge itself was obstructed by two large passenger vans, parked end to end in a V formation, blocking any vehicles from crossing.

"Smart." Charles pointed at the vans. His family nodded their approval with him. "Well Abby, what now?"

Abby leaned even further over the dashboard and looked around at the expanse of the campus center. She saw the staff building she hid in that night so long ago, as well as the admissions building across the street. Beyond those buildings were half a dozen brick maintenance buildings as well as the school building and the cafeteria. The first car crash that started it all was still leaning against the school right where it happened in June. She shuddered at the flash of memory seeing the wreck gave her.

She peered further, searching the campus for more details. She saw the tops of the dorms, some far in the rear of the campus, visible only by their snow capped roofs. She looked to her left, down the campus street that started the big loop. Hall A was the closest dorm, and next to that was Hall E.

Abby's eyes widened in amazement when she saw Hall E. Wordlessly she raised her finger and pointed at it. Her family leaned forward and looked at the building, failing to notice what had caught her interest.

"I don't see anything moron," Randy said.

With a smile, she replied, "merry Christmas shit for brains. There's smoke coming out of the heating vents."

And smoke meant a furnace, and a furnace meant heat,

and heat meant warmth.

Abby would never again underestimate the value of being warm.

December 12ᵗʰ

Have you ever heard of the expression "bone cracking cold" Mr. Journal? The thermometer tells me it's a pleasant 12 degrees Fahrenheit outside, and I can see the wind blowing the trees back and forth in the faint moonlight. I would hate to not have heat right now. When it gets this cold, people die even with heat.

How am I you ask? I am pretty Fucking A Mr. Journal. Huzzah for painkillers. I'm trying hard as hell to moderate my vikes so I don't get dependant on them. I knew a few guys in the Army who got a little hooked on pain killers and it was hell for them to get clean. Last thing I need to do is take a few too many because I can't deal with the pain and wind up getting addicted. I already have enough fucking problems without that. More shit going on than a one armed wall paper hanger.

Speaking of problems! My infection seems to have halted its forward progress. The ink lines I drew a few days ago are mostly gone, but enough of them are still there that I can see the redness hasn't moved. The little red line is gone too. The pain has subsided dramatically as well, and that's not just the vicodin talking. It's really much better. Very fucking stiff, and it's still difficult to get around, but we are miles away from where we were a few days ago. My right foot is almost all better. Being off my feet all day yesterday and today has done a world of good. There are a few ugly little bruises that are dark purple where the teeth got me, but as long as I don't hit them on something it's fine.

As you can imagine, it's been a little slow around the homestead. I haven't been outside since I got in on the 9th after my pharmacy shenanigans. I moved the recliner closer to the windows of the common room here in Hall E so I can see the campus grounds a little better. I've got a decent vantage point where I'm sitting to the front door, and as long as I'm not blacked out from the painkillers I think I've got it under control. I can easily shoot the .22 while sitting here so it should be all good.

I've been carefully tending my potted plants. Sheer thrill for you there. I put away all the food I got from the two houses I cleared before the farmhouse the other day. I beat off twice. Pretty sweet.

Oh I sorted those sports cards. Lots of really cool stuff. Nothing super duper old but a lot of great cards. I could definitely open my own card shop if the world suddenly rights itself. Like that's happening.

So I am as bored as plywood Mr. Journal, and I have nothing but time on my hands. I think I've got an hour or two before the pain pill I'm about to take shitcans my ability to form crappy sentences, so I think I'll tell you a little bit about myself. I haven't talked much about myself lately, well actually I haven't talked at all about myself. Lots of little mentions of things here and there, but no real stories, or information. It's long overdue that you learn a little bit about me the person.

I shall remedy that! Slowly but surely. I also wanted to fill in the story about my second trip to Moore's and the few weird things that happened between late June and mid September when I started the journal. Not a ton to talk about there, but enough to get a good entry in or two. With no new info coming in while I heal, I might as well tell you about older shit.

I grew up in a small town in the middle of nowhere near the east coast. Millions of people grow up in towns just like it all over the world. As a kid I hiked, fished, played a lot of sports with my brothers, and read profusely. I was the rare jock-nerd. I played football, specifically Tight End and Linebacker. I also played some baseball. I was a catcher. I got scouted for football but nothing ever came of it. My brother Caleb was offered basketball scholarships to several places but declined to go in the Marines instead. Always thought he was moron for that.

I had a little trouble with the ladies until I was a senior in high school. My mother was quite frankly a bitch to us kids, and I think I was scared of girls until I realized it. I'm still not sure what my mom's issues were, but my brothers and I always thought that she was angry about marrying our dad because she was pregnant. I think she always felt like she missed out on something because of us kids. Whatever. She was snarky with us our whole childhoods and we resented her for it. We knew she loved us, but she took shit out on us a lot. Spiteful bitch, I think is the phrase. I think I was scared any girlfriend I fell in love with would either be just like her, or get scared off by her, so I avoided any kind of real relationship with girls.

Don't get me wrong, I had some fun, but I was unable to take it seriously. I really feel bad now, years later about it. I misled a lot of young girls for selfish reasons and I can't take it back or say sorry about it. I just hope they look back on their relationships with me as fondly as I look back on them myself. The ignorance of youth I suppose. I wish I was brave enough to be a more honest kid. Regret is a motherfucker.

My whole family revolved around the military. My grandfather served in the Army, my father did 8 years in the Air Force, my older brother Caleb did 4 years in the Marines, I wound up doing 5 years in the Army, my two younger brothers Tommy and William were both still active duty Navy when it all went down. I hope they're okay somewhere on a boat, or in a base.

Service was a thing in our household. My father didn't expect us to serve in the armed forces, but all us boys knew we would. It was the Ring measuring stick. How far could you go? Were we more bad-ass than dad? I think of all of us my brother Tommy was the most bad-ass. He was one of those freaks of nature that could run jump and swim forever. He went into the SEAL teams out in Coronado and thrived there. We didn't get to see him much. Those guys are always out fighting somewhere now. God I miss him. I think he and I were the closest.

I joined straight out of college in '99. I realized that after I finished my business degree I wouldn't use it. Oops, right? I really wanted to make my dad proud, and I really always wanted to follow in my grandfather's footsteps in the Army. During college I satisfied my hunger for action by working as a bouncer and bodyguard. Saw some impressive shit those years. I couldn't even tell you how many times I've laid hands in a rough manner on people. I moonlighted for a few security places around here after I got out of the military too. Free concerts, late nights with pretty girls. It's addicting, the thrill of confrontation. Good times.

All of my family called me an idiot ground pounder for going green, but I was happy. I enlisted as infantry, and I got my wish. Right after I finished all my infantry schools 9/11 happened. It was a good time to be a grunt I guess.

My units never deployed to Afghanistan, but we did eventually get sent in to Iraq when we invaded. I did one tour in Iraq from early '03 to a little over halfway through '04. Remember when Bush declared the end of combat operations? I was on a plane heading over there when he gave that speech and I assure you, there were plenty of combat operations.

My best friend in the Army was a guy that I met right after I went into my unit. Kevin Whitten. When we met he was Specialist Whitten, just like me, but when I left the Army he was Sergeant Whitten. He and I were acorns from the same oak tree. You want to talk about a hardcore motherfucker.

He and I were on the same fire team our whole tour in Baghdad. I would gladly have fed both of my balls to Cujo back at the farmhouse to have him here right now. He and I both re-enlisted when our stop-loss ended at the tail of '04. We were insane, not gonna lie. Kicking in doors, patrols through al-Mansour, firefights with the Mehdi Army, convoy protective details on Route Irish, shit it was hardcore. We did everything, we volunteered for every QRF detail we could. I think Whitten did it trying to get me to tap out so he could finally admit he was scared too, but neither of us did. Too proud to admit any fear. We were lucky idiots.

When we re-enlisted we did it under the condition we could go to Ranger School. We both wanted to be elite, and RIP, or the Ranger Indoctrination Program was one of the Army's first steps to get there. We sailed through the initial 61 day school like champs. We were near the top of the class coming out of the Florida phase of the school and we had inquiries coming at us to join the 75th Ranger Regiment. Those guys are fringe Special Operations Mr. Journal. Borderline black ops shit. Happy as could be, us two.

We returned to Fort Benning in Georgia and that's when my wheels came off. It was the ass end of '04 and we were killing time until the graduation ceremony. One of the DIs at the school invited us out for some drinks that night at his apartment off base to celebrate, and we went. Kevin and I got completely trashed. We were so proud of the fact that not only had we kicked Ranger School's ass, but we'd done it and bested almost everyone else. We wound up crashing at the drill instructor's place that night.

The next day we were brought up before our company commander and summarily ass invaded. We were told that we were essentially AWOL, and we were to be thrown under a bus, driven over, then backed over again for good measure. Our careers in the special operations community was over before it began. Kevin had no college education, his family had nothing. He was dirt poor South Boston Irish all the way and if he got rolled from this, his life was over. He'd work in a fish packing plant in Quincy if he was lucky. If just I got rolled, I would be fine.

I offered myself up. I told my platoon commander I'd accept the court martial and full responsibility if Kevin was allowed to skate. After some screaming at me he took it up the chain of command, and it was done. A few days later the paperwork was finished, and I got discharged the day before graduation. One day I'm riding on the clouds, the next day I'm booking a plane ticket home trying to figure out how I was going to tell my parents I was kicked out of the Army.

It's not all bad news. My platoon commander was an asshole, but he pulled some strings and had the discharge written up as a medical separation. Apparently I had a chronic ankle problem that precluded me from a military life. His "favor" saved me the dishonorable discharge. That would've been a death sentence on my record I think. The real treat was when Kevin dropped me off at the airport.

He and I bullshitted about everything, about some of our crazy times in Iraq, and all over the place. Soldiers find the craziest ways to entertain themselves. Makes for great stories. We laughed a lot as we waited for my plane. Anyway, Kevin hugs me, and puts something in my hand. It was about three inches long or so, and made of fabric. He shook my hand and told me the squad felt I had earned it, and he hugged me one last time and left me.

After he left I opened my hand and looked. It was my Ranger tab. I hadn't graduated, but the guys in my squad felt I'd earned it. I can't even tell you what that feels like. My men, my boys, my fellow brothers felt I'd EARNED the tab.

Fuck Uncle Sam.

I heard from Kevin quite a bit after that. He did three years in the 75th Rangers and wound up seeing some bad news bears shit. Those guys have a very high operational tempo, always deploying. Somewhere in northern Iraq he took some shrapnel from a VBIED and got discharged medically. A legitimate medical discharge that is. A few months later he had his DD214 all squared away and was working for private military contractors all over the world. He called me a few months before everything went south and told me he was on his way overseas working for the State Department doing executive protection for some high falootin diplomat. Hope he's ok. I tell you this with complete certainty, if there's anyone that is okay, it is him.

That's my military life. Lots of highs, lots of lows. I wouldn't do it again, but I'm glad I did it. I told my family the real story, and they understood. Actually my dad understood, my mom didn't care either way. Shit like that happens in the military more often than you know. Neither of my younger brothers have had any problems like mine though, and I'm happy for them. Maybe they learned from my mistake.

After getting out in '04 I wasn't sure what to do with myself. My old buddy Steve, the one I already told you about Mr. Journal, worked here at Auburn Lake PA. He asked if I was interested, and I interviewed, liked the idea of doing damn little and getting paid for it, and I took the job. I've been here ever since.

So that's a lot more about me. I think I might try and build up the testicular fortitude to talk about Cassie soon. Maybe tomorrow or the next day. It's still very sensitive for me. This week has been strangely good about my feelings, but I 'm gonna chalk that up to the power of the pain killers washing my memories away Mr. Journal.

Tomorrow I will try and tell the story of how we met. Tell you a little bit about her. I might even try and explain why I never married her. I should probably try and figure that out too. I'm still not sure why I didn't.

Talk to you tomorrow Mr. Journal. Thanks for listening. Sua Sponte.

-Adrian

Jerusalem

"This'll be a pretty standard in and out. Myself, the Senator, Kyle and the aide will be in the middle vehicle. Lead vehicle will be team A with Alan, John G, Mike, and Quan. Tail vehicle will be team B and will have John F, Corey, Nate and the other two aides. It'll be a little cramped, but it's a short trip to the ribbon cutting in Jerusalem." Kevin Whitten addressed his team of operators from a plush high backed leather office chair. They all sat around a ridiculously expensive long mahogany table deep in a subbasement of the U.S. Embassy in Tel Aviv Israel. The walls were a neutral beige color and the lighting was harsh and fluorescent.

Kevin shuffled the paperwork in front of him detailing the trip for later that morning and looked for any information he might've missed. He had aerial photography, CIA intelligence reports, FBI input forms, and the written statements of a half dozen locals that worked covertly for the embassy doing information gathering. Everything on the paperwork said easy in, easy out. Kevin was always suspicious of anything that had the word "easy" on it.

Kevin was dressed like the rest of his team in the room. He wore khaki cargo pants that were fitted close. No extra fabric or loops to catch as he moved. He wore a plain dark blue button up shirt over a $5,000 ballistics vest. Slung low on his right thigh was his handgun, a Glock. He had a plain white baseball cap and sitting in front of him on the expensive table were his Wiley X ballistic sunglasses. Even

143

sitting you could tell Kevin was a rugged man. Not a large man by any means, barely reaching five foot nine, but his body was corded, and his shoulders broad. His weathered skin showed years of rough living, but his eyes showed the life of someone who'd felt a lot of adrenaline. Kevin would eternally be the 13 year old boy adventuring wherever he went. Now, he carried real guns instead of BB guns.

Kevin's team was dressed nearly the same as him. Like him they all wore the same style pants, and had the same button up shirts and bulletproof vests, but none had his white cap. They either had no hats at all, or they wore dark colored baseball caps. Kevin was what they called a white cap, or a protective detail leader.

These men were all employees of Warden Protective Group, or WPG. WPG was a newly formed private military contracting company that had been picked up by the U.S. State Department to fill in the void with diplomatic security overseas. Each of the men and women that were operators for the company were decorated veterans of various militaries from across the world. Kevin was thankful to have his British, Australian and Vietnamese men with him. WPG hired the best to protect the best.

"We are rolling in 2 hours. Team leaders will have HK416's, and team A will be full gear as well. Team A is the counterassault force if needed." Kevin rifled through the paperwork again, noting the relative calm Jerusalem had experienced of late. Pleasant change of pace he thought to himself. "Extraction location is here at the Embassy. If that fails we'll extract to Ben Gurion airport in Lod. Drivers make sure you know the route in and out. It's all in your briefings."

"Kevin, how long are we going to be out for? I have a video conference call with my wife and kid at noon?" Alan, the leader of Team A and the detail's sole British representative asked. He was a tall ex SAS member and if you didn't know he was a trained killer, you'd of thought he belonged selling you your home insurance. Alan scratched his graying goatee as he waited for Kevin to answer.

"Shit Alan I would guess you're gonna miss it. Sorry mate." Kevin winced at his longtime compatriot. Kevin had put his years in, and he hated shooting down the older guys with families. In this profession, there were too many long trips, and far too much danger to miss phone calls home. Plus he knew Alan's wife and little daughter personally. He'd spent a few leaves with them at their flat in Manchester.

"It's alright man. I'll just call home later." Alan scratched his bald head trying to hide his frustration. Everyone hated it when they missed a chance to call home.

"Alright, two hours, make sure your gear is ready to roll and double check the three SUVs. I want a full comms check on the vehicles as well as our personal mics. All signs point to a calm day for us folks, and now that I've jinxed us all, dismissed." The team all stood up and left, heading off to take care of their last minute tasks. Waiting in the hallway was a cheap suit wearing junior aide to the Embassy staff. He looked Jewish to Kevin, dark skin, dark hair. The yarmulke was a dead giveaway he thought. In his hand he held a sheaf of papers.

"Come in." Kevin sipped his coffee as the young official strutted in urgently.

"Mr. Whitten this briefing just got released by the DOS. Senator Henke thought you should see it. He thought it might be of use to you." The aide held the paperwork out as it if were the Holy Grail itself. He had a serious look as if this single briefing was going to change the world. Kevin stifled a laugh at the seriousness the kid exhibited. No briefing was ever that important he thought.

Kevin recalled his name finally, "Thanks Aaron, you making the trip to the ribbon cutting with us?" Kevin sat the folder down on the huge mahogany desk in front of him and sipped his hot coffee again. Black, with a smidge of sugar.

"Oh no sir. I'm supposed to stay here and get some visa paperwork processed. Plus it's damn hot out there. I'd melt."

The kid adjusted his yarmulke and laughed. Kevin liked him again.

"Poor baby, make the trip all the way back to Zion just to wilt in the heat." Kevin grinned at him.

"Yes sir, to each their own." The aide smiled back, and excused himself from the briefing room.

The former Ranger sat his cup down and turned his attention to the quarter inch thick folder stamped "Department of State: Confidential Briefing 23rd June, 2010." He flipped the folder open and thumbed through the pages. It was ten minutes before he really grasped what the briefing was trying to say. He wasn't sure if it pertained to him and his mission here in Tel Aviv, but any intelligence is good intelligence. If it was right.

As best as Kevin could tell from the disorganized briefing, Africa had shit the bed. Africa always had a shitty bed in Kevin's opinion, so how far could they fall overnight anyway? Pretty far apparently. Multiple nations and regions on the Dark Continent were hot spots for terrorism, or instability. Somalia, The Democratic Republic of Congo, Sudan, Uganda and Rwanda had all been red flagged as trouble spots just this month in his meetings. It had even been a good month.

Sometime shortly after midnight in Somalia there had been a skirmish over something, which wasn't news by any means to Kevin. At about the same time there was a substantial engagement in the Congo, something about a few buses being robbed by rebels on a highway. Pretty standard fare for that part of the world Kevin thought. Also in Sudan, somewhere in the suburbs of Khartoum overnight, there had been an enormous loss of life connected to a cholera outbreak. The report guessed at perhaps 50 or more deaths in the Sudan. In the two engagements in the Congo and Somalia there were a large, unknown number of casualties. Again Kevin thought, not news.

The strange noteworthy aspect was the sudden reports of violence in the three different regions following the attacks, especially following the deaths in Sudan. Almost as if the populace itself had risen up in a fury, and taken their vengeance on their attackers, and released their mourning in fury. The odd bit is that the surge of violence occurred in all three places, more or less simultaneously. A very conspicuous coincidence Kevin thought.

Aid worker reports, embassy spies, and local media all reported that these attacks were vicious affairs, carried out in almost mindless fury. Almost as if the perpetrators were sick with some form of rabies. Just mindless violence. Kevin looked at the printouts of pictures taken in the area, and even though they were taken a few hours ago in the dark, you could see the complete loss of reason on the faces of the people. They were soaked in blood, and seemed vacant. The black and white pictures reminded him of that old horror movie Night of the Living Dead. Well, if Night of the Living Dead took place in the heart of Africa and had the cast of Friday he thought.

There were no reports of similar violence here in Israel yet, but as a precaution anyways, the Israeli national airline El Al, had already shut down flights in coming from Africa. Gotta hand it to those Israeli people Kevin smirked. They do not fuck around.

*****

The ride to the housing development in Jerusalem was about an hour long. They sped past several security checkpoints with their Israeli police escort, but certain chokepoints of traffic slowed them down. Kevin sat in the backseat of the glossy black armored Suburban next to Senator Henke. The ex soldier's HK416C carbine was cradled low in his lap with the barrel pointed toward the window. Kevin and his team paid close attention to their surroundings as they closed in on the ribbon cutting ceremony. Despite it being only eight in the morning, it was already almost 90 degrees outside. The Mediterranean sun was beating down with force.

"Kevin why the hell would all these people want to build more houses here? Don't they realize it's hot as hell here?" Henke wiped his brow of the sweat beaded on there as he took a break from rehearsing his speech. Even the truck's air conditioning was struggling against the sun.

"Sir why do so many people move to Vegas? It's hot as hell there and most people lose all their money to boot." Kevin's disdain for the heat showed through, causing his Boston accent to slip out.

"Ah! Gotcha!" Henke slapped the veteran on the thigh next to his weapon. "That hit a nerve didn't it?" Henke took a sip from a bottle of water.

"Sir I hate the heat. Spent far too many years of my life sweating in places people shouldn't live, let alone fight in." Kevin kept his eyes on the road as he corralled in his native Southie accent. His mind drifted back to some memories of hot places. Baghdad in the summer was his last stop on memory lane. 120 degrees more often than not. The heat reminded him of his old Army buddy Adrian. Now there was a hardcore motherfucker like him. He still wished Adrian had taken the offer to join the WPG team. He changed the subject before he got distracted any more than he already was. "Why are you even here sir, if you don't mind my asking?

Henke swirled the water in his bottle as he stared out the window at the ancient city passing by. "The Ambassador had to be at some meeting today, and I've got a few years in the diplomatic core. Plus I speak fluent Hebrew and Arabic." Henke shrugged. "You read that briefing that came through earlier this morning?" Henke took another sip, fixing his thinning hair in his reflection in the tinted windows.

"Yeah. Very odd." Kevin leaned forward and looked out the windshield in between Kyle, his team member driving, and Anna, the Senator's platinum blonde aide in the front seat. He hated moving around like this, he felt nervous, and exposed.

"Think we're in any trouble?" Henke asked seriously. He was picking up on Kevin's body language.

"Sir we're headed into the heart of the millennia old conflict between Muslims, Christians, and Jews. What could possibly cause us trouble in a place like that?" Kevin said dryly.

"Not funny Mr. Whitten. Not funny at all." The Senator brushed the lint off his pants as he sighed.

"Wasn't a joke sir. I hate this part of the world. Too many people with their hands in the cookie jar for my liking around here. Fact is many of them have one hand reaching for a cookie, and the other holding an AK. Now if you're asking me if the stuff from the morning emergency briefing will cause us trouble today? I'm going with no on that." Kevin sat back in his seat and adjusted the throat mic that connected him to the rest of the team. In his earpiece he could hear the drivers quietly calling out traffic movement to each other, organizing the small convoy to avoid slowdowns and cars acting suspiciously. These were good operators he thought to himself.

"That's reassuring Kevin. Hopefully we won't be there for more than half an hour or so." The Senator slid his glasses back on and lifted his speech to read it again.

"Sir with all due respect, I've been through a few of your half hours, and they're rarely ever actually a half an hour long." Kevin laughed. The Senator gave him a dirty look over the rim of his glasses and returned to reading his speech. The rest of the drive the only talking that happened was in the operator's earpieces.

*****

360 degree protection was the WPG rule for Senator Henke in Jerusalem. Kevin instructed his security personnel to form a loose triangle around him every time he moved, and when he was stationary, Kevin was no more than 3 feet away. When the Senator finally took the steps up to the

outdoor stage for the ribbon cutting ceremony, the WPG people were in position. One each at the corners of the stage with Kevin sitting mixed in with the local officials sitting behind the podium. His counter assault team was spread out at the edges of the crowd, ready to return heavy fire should something go wrong. The microphone podium was reinforced as requested, and Henke was trained to drop down and take cover behind it should he be attacked. Now if a bomb went off… Well everyone was fucked and it didn't matter. Kevin could only hope the Israeli bomb dogs had done their job. Besides, he didn't have a limitless reservoir of worry to waste on things out of his control.

The WPG drivers kept the big black Suburbans ready to go in the dirt parking lot behind the stage. The men stood just a few feet apart from their driver's doors with their eyes peeled for anything approaching them. It was a good system for what the government was willing to pay, and Kevin was satisfied. If anything did come at them, he and his team could handle it. The heat made everyone uncomfortable, but it was the fact of life here. Kevin did his best to tune out the different speeches, especially when they shifted to Hebrew and Arabic, but when the speaker finally called out the Senator's name, Kevin's guts dropped an inch as his adrenaline spiked. Showtime.

As was his typical MO, Henke greeted the people in Hebrew, then in Arabic, and then started his speech in English. You had to give it to him, he was good at the languages here. Kevin watched him go through his motions, reciting the speech perfectly he'd rehearsed in the car on the way. He could speak. No doubt about that.

Kevin's eyes wandered to the crowd of a few hundred gathered at the industrial site they were at. This whole shindig was about a new housing project that was supposed to represent a union between the different cultures of Jerusalem. This was to be a building where Jews, Christians and Muslims would share their lives in order to blend together, hopefully creating a unity that had thus far been like water in the desert here. Fictional.

Kevin looked at the faces of all the people, every single one of them as he scanned the crowd. Far in the back, on the other side of the chain link fence circling the site he could see protestors. Most of them were Palestinians that were opposed to the idea of yet another Israeli building project in Jerusalem. Those were his real worries. Everyone at the speech and ribbon cutting inside the fence was searched by the police, and vetted mostly. However, one of the protestors with just a few rocks could make for a bad day.

Far off in the distance, less than a kilometer away, a deafening boom came rolling. A blast wave tossed paper and debris down the street behind the protestors. Car alarms began screaming in all directions. Kevin stood to his feet with no hesitation and walked to the side of his ward, pushing his way past the local officials. Henke stopped talking for a few seconds as the crowd turned to face in the direction of the explosion. In those few seconds a column of pitch black smoke rose from behind a building down the street, and the wail of ambulance and police sirens could be heard starting. Half of the police assigned to the speech took off running towards the explosion. Henke swallowed and started his speech again, right where he left off. His voice trembled a little, but he soldiered on defiantly.

Kevin didn't like this one bit. As soon as the Senator finished his speech they were history. The ribbon could be cut in his absence. The white capped leader reached up and keyed his throat mic, communicating with his people, "Eyes open, that first blast might've been a distraction. Drivers get your vehicles ready to roll. We're out in three."

Kevin reached behind himself to his back right hip and slowly swung his carbine more to his side so he could shoulder it fast if needed. He had his Glock holstered on his thigh, but he wanted the firepower of the fully automatic weapon should things come to it. He rested his thumb on the safety switch, ready to go at the drop of a hat.

Henke's speech continued on for a few more tense

151

CHRIS PHILBROOK

minutes. The crowd had largely been distracted by all the
sirens from the rescue and police vehicles whizzing by in the
narrow Jerusalem streets on the other side of the chain link
fence. Kevin took it as a good sign that the protestors had
shut up and were turned, facing down the street out of his
field of vision at the site of the explosion. Judging from
where the smoke was rising, and the proximity of the
ambulance sirens, Kevin guessed the blast was right on the
street that they were on, just a block away perhaps.

Henke finished his rallying call for unity and peace then
thanked the crowd. Kevin could see he was a little shaken by
the explosion in the distance, and he moved to his side and
pressed him immediately, "Sir we are moving." Kevin's
voice was forceful, authoritative. Henke moved immediately
and without protest, allowing Kevin to usher him off the
side of the stage and into a waiting semi circle of WPG
security personnel. These were the Team B men, the core of
the protective detail. Team A was still spread out, more
heavily armed and able to counter assault should violence
erupt from the crowd.

Whitten addressed his team via the throat mic again, "To
the cars, back to the Embassy. Roll out the back entrance if
we can, heading away from the explosion." As he finished,
gunfire erupted from 40 feet away, behind the stage on the
dirt lot, right in the direction where they were headed.

The two youngest men on team B were Corey and Nate,
both ex Marines. Their job was to shield the Ambassador,
and that's what they did. Without hesitation the two men
dove on top of him, forming a human shield. In unison they
rolled into different firing positions, one kneeling covering
the Senator, the other laying across the Senator's body.

John F. drew his Glock and took aim at the back corner of
the stage, where the shooters would come from. Kevin fully
shouldered the HK416C and flicked the safety to semi-auto.
He tabbed the mic once more, "Team A respond, weapons
hot and clear the vehicles. Make a hole for us." He moved up
beside the older operator John and took up position near the

stage.

As he dropped to a knee he heard return fire. Clear and distinct the sound of Glock handgun fire rapped out in two round bursts. Pap-pap. Pap-pap. Pap-pap. The return fire was precise and controlled. It was his drivers returning fire, protecting the vehicles, their lifeline for escape. As the crowd ran screaming he could hear radio traffic in his ear. His Team A was making their way to the back of the ceremony, pushing through the panicked crowd, assaulting into the gunfire fearlessly.

Within seconds he heard the high pitched cracks that belonged to his people's carbines. Just like the pistol fire two shots at a time. Snap snap. Snap snap. He could hear the gunfire echoing in the open space where the new apartment building was going to be built. Kevin turned and looked down at the Senator, covering his head with his hands, pale white and scared shitless. He made eye contact with his two youngest men and they looked good. Sharp, scared of course, but they were on point.

Kevin lived for this.

"Sir, all clear. Shooters were police firing into the crowd." Clearly over the mic he heard his Brit team A leader, Alan call out.

Kevin responded with the throat microphone on, "Let's move. Get out of the box immediately." He motioned to the younger operators and they got the Senator to his feet. He was so out of it they had to hold him up with their arms and walk him forward. John and Kevin began to head around the back end of the stage guns up and searching as wounding, bleeding civilians stumbled past them. They screamed and begged for help in a mixture of languages Kevin could only barely understand.

His men were trained well; none of them shot the civilians. When they finally got around to the back area of the stage they saw dozens of scattered bodies. Most had been pretty clearly wounded or killed by small arms fire. Groans of pain in any language are unmistakable. It pained

Kevin to not render aid, but there were plenty of people already on their way who could, and he had to get his principal and his team out of here. This gunfire meant a lot more real danger than just a bomb going off in Jerusalem.

Kevin watched carefully as he moved the Senator and his detail across the open construction site to the rear where their Suburbans were parked. As he stepped over and around the fallen, he knew something wasn't right. Kevin had earned a reputation in the Special Forces community for his "sniff test." Everyone knew when Kevin got the creeps, it was bad juju.

He slowed his gait and took a few seconds to evaluate was happening around him a little closer. Nate, Corey and John continued moving past him with the Senator in tow. He watched the wounded as they struggled to staunch their bleeding, or put their mangled limbs back into place. Some would succeed, some would fail. Combat teaches you what a lethal wound is quickly. There's no time to help those who cannot survive, and Kevin could see several lethal wounds slowly bleeding their victim to death. That wasn't it though, that wasn't what was setting him off.

The Senator was about 20 feet from the middle of the three Suburbans when Kevin noticed some of the dead bodies were twitching. Kevin had seen dozens of bodies in his time in the military. Hundreds even. Many twitch, but not like this. They jerked in spasms, hands clenching over and over into fists, jaws tightening reflexively, sneering the faces of the dead into an expression of sinister evil. Kevin felt his stomach drop out on him again, but this time, there was no spike of adrenaline, just hollow fear.

As he watched on in horror, a dead Arabic man missing half his chest sat up and made vacant eye contact with him. The man's lung slipped down and out of the hole in his side and dangled there, like a morbid pendulum. Kevin stopped breathing as he watched the man turn his head and look at the wounded people lying around him. A man moaning a few feet away was oblivious to the situation with the rising dead man. The man was preoccupied holding his mangled thigh together. The dead Palestinian locked onto the rocking victim near him, and pounced with animalistic hunger. Soft moans of pain quickly turned into high pitched screams of agony as the dark skinned murderer bit into him, ripping fist sized pieces out of his chest and neck.

Kevin finally breathed. Operating on complete instinct he lifted the HK416C and placed the red dot of his Aimpoint sight on the torso of the dead man. He squeezed the trigger once, sending a high velocity round straight through the space the man's heart should've been in. The impact of the tiny bullet rocked the dead man forward, but didn't knock him down. He spun, and with a noiseless snarl, rose to his feet, and started approaching Kevin. Kevin held his ground and squeezed one more round off, hitting the blood drenched man in the chest, directly where the Kevin knew the heart should be. In his earpiece he could hear one of his men call out that other dead bodies were moving, and getting up. Kevin knew they were running out of time.

The man coming at the team leader started to pick up speed, closing the dozen or so feet between the two of them startlingly fast. Kevin snapped out of his disbelief and double tapped the rushing predator. One bullet hit him in the throat, and as the muzzle of his carbine lifted slightly, the second shot went straight into the nose, blowing the back of the skull clean out, sending brain matter a dozen feet away. The dead man died again, crashing face first at Kevin's feet.

He bolted for the Suburban as he saw more of the dead surrounding him rise. He keyed his throat mic as he went, "Shoot them in the head, shoot them again, they're coming back from the dead!" He was screaming. He never screamed. Had the Senator heard him, he would've mocked his thick Boston accent.

On all sides as he sprinted to the center Suburban he witnessed the dead coming back to a twisted mockery of life. They were sitting up and immediately ravaging the defenseless wounded all around them on the ground. Kevin snapped off a few hasty headshots and re-killed a few of the freshly risen corpses. He got a few, but even for an expert marksman like Kevin, head shots on the run were next to impossible. Eventually he saw they were hopelessly outnumbered by the violent, risen sea of the dead and he gave up trying to fight. The only safety here was inside the armored SUVs.

Kevin's team stood in the open doors firing into the mass of undead closing in on them. He couldn't believe what was happening. This wasn't real, this wasn't possible. Dead people are dead. Dead people do not sit up and bite other people. That shit happens in movies. Not in real life. As Kevin's mind struggled to wrap itself around the reality of the moment he watched as one of the lead car's team A members was overwhelmed by several of the walking dead. He wasn't shooting them in the head as Kevin instructed, and he paid the ultimate price. He thumbed his HK416 to full auto as he was pulled to the ground, spraying automatic fire everywhere. One of his errant bullets hit Alan, the senior Brit team leader square in the chest, sending him sprawling into the open SUV door as if he'd been struck by a sledgehammer.

"NOOOOOOooooo!!" Kevin screamed as he saw his buddy go down. Alan looked like he'd been hit by a truck. No blood was visible, and for a moment Kevin thought his vest had stopped the round. For Alan it turned out to be a moot point, because as he was pulling himself to his feet half of the dead turned their attentions to him, and they ripped him apart right there as he tried to get to his feet. He managed to empty his rifle into them, but most of his shots were ineffective. Kevin watched as Alan coughed up a thick gout of blood with his last breath. There would be no call home to England tonight.

Kevin screamed in primal rage and had to restrain himself from getting their bodies. There was no chance he'd survive. The Ranger creed of leave no man behind did not account for the living dead. By the time he got to the bodies there would be twenty of the near un-killable monstrosities on him. They'd have to get their bodies from the Israeli police later.

"Wheels up, we're out!" Kevin said as he slammed the heavy armored door. Not a second later there were Jewish and Arabic undead smashing their limbs and faces against the tinted windows. Kyle the driver floored the gas pedal and the heavy vehicle lurched forward behind the lead car. They spun in a large circle turning around to head out the back of the construction site. The SUVs jumped up as they ran over the bodies of the living and dead, smashing Kevin's head into the ceiling

"Head out go right," Kevin heard Kyle say into his mic, instructing the front driver which way to go to get out. Immediately the lead SUV picked up speed, hitting a few more of the undead, sending them flying. The giant black Suburban in the lead barreled through the closed chain link gate, blasting it violently to the side. Kevin checked the Senator's body next to him as his vehicle moved into the street.

"Are you wounded? Are you hurt?" Kevin ran his hands all over the old man's shirt and legs, looking for red wet spots. His hands came back clean as the Senator shook his head in shock. Kevin looked out the windows as Kyle got the truck pointed away from the ceremony site. He looked at the blonde aide Anna, clearly panic stricken in the front seat. She didn't even realize he was looking at her. She had a random smear of blood on her cheek that stood out starkly. He suddenly realized that she was very pretty, but he didn't like her much, and he couldn't figure out why.

Out the rear view mirror Kevin could see the intersection closest to the area the bomb had gone off. Emergency vehicles were parked or parking as far as they eye could see, and just as they turned off, he watched a body in the street begin to sit up.

Maybe that briefing he'd gotten this morning really was going to change the world.

*****

They were a few kilometers away before Kevin felt comfortable enough to start radioing in the situation. Kevin used an advanced communications suite built right into a special center console in the back seat of the Suburban. He started making the calls according to emergency protocol. First step was notifying the Embassy, and getting the other actual diplomats back inside the compound. An attack on one usually led to attacks on the others.

His second call was to the Department of State office of security back in Washington. The call went all the way back to D.C. via a satellite uplink. In a calm voice born from years of being shot at he relayed all the information he'd gotten to a faceless, nameless intelligence officer. He explained the bomb, then the shooting, and finally the worst part, the dead rising. An intelligence officer put him on hold, and after a few seconds a different voice picked up the line.

"This is Director Lancaster, is this Mr. Whitten?" The voice was older, rough. Not a diplomat's voice at all, it sounded more like a drill instructor's. From years of habit Kevin was instantly respectful to the man.

"Yessir."

"You say dead bodies got back up? How sure are you of them being dead? Dead as a doornail dead, or just mostly dead and they got themselves a second wind?" The voice sounded skeptical, but Kevin caught a hint of seriousness. He was instantly afraid of what to say back. Life in the military teaches you to always know enough, but also to never know too much.

Kevin swallowed and replied, "Sir they were dead. I watched a man missing most of his torso get up, lose a lung, bite another man's chest open, then come at me. I put four rounds into him before he went down for good. Last shot was a head shot."

Silence. Finally Kevin could hear the other man clucking

158

his tongue, mulling over what he'd said. Finally there was a long, tired sigh. "Son that Senator is a pretty important pencil pusher. You may think he's as useful as tits on a bull, but there are many who think otherwise. We need him extracted from that region immediately. Head to the airport per your exfil plan. We'll get the DOS bird ready and you are to head straight to London. Stop for no one. Anyone even fucking looks at that man funny you put two in their face, capiche?"

"Uh yes. Yes sir." Kevin unscrewed the cap on the Senator's old water bottle and drained it of the last swallow. The moisture helped.

"You lost men today?" Kevin heard the genuine worry in the tone of the Director's question.

"Yeah we lost two. One American, one British national. Both good men." Kevin didn't like to talk about losses, especially so soon after.

"I'm sure they were the best. I'm sorry for you son. But you gotta take care of that Senator, and take care of the rest of your team. Get that man the fuck out of Israel and get him home," the Director spoke quietly, filling his words with weight, and importance.

Kevin thought for a few seconds, and then finally asked the burning question, "Sir, what is happening. You didn't call me a fucking idiot for telling you I saw dead people sit up, and that strikes me a bit queer. What the fuck is going on?"

Silence again. Kevin heard the same clucking noise of the Director's tongue for a few seconds, and finally he replied in monotone, "Something has gone very wrong with the world Mr. Whitten. We're seeing credible reports from all over now about dead people doing what you saw earlier. A lot of reports Mr. Whitten."

Kevin couldn't believe it. It was probably more military-political bullshit to deny some new terror attack. Pretty soon they'd be invading Belgium or something over this. This was all just another reason to go to war, dredged up by the

Washington war machine. "Sir, are you serious?"

"Serious as the rash on my asshole son." It wasn't meant to be a joke, and it didn't come off as funny either. "It started in Africa. We don't know why yet, or what's causing it, but it seems to be radiating away from Africa. It's just starting to show up here in the States now. We're trying to get it all figured out but…" he trailed off.

"What time is it there sir?" Kevin asked the man as he looked around, surveying the slowly spreading chaos in the city. He could literally see the panic spreading as they drove at breakneck speeds through the tight city streets. Sirens everywhere, people pointing, covering their mouths, clearly scared.

"It's 0230 here in D.C." Lancaster replied. Kevin could hear him sipping at a cup of something, probably coffee or tea.

"Shit." Kevin looked over at his charge, the Senator. He was still shell shocked from the violence earlier. Kevin felt bad for him. This was easily the worst thing that the old man had ever experienced. Kevin knew that without even knowing him. This was really bad. "Thank you sir."

Lancaster swallowed his mouthful of beverage and replied, "Welcome Son. See you when you get back to the States." And he hung up. Kevin sat the satellite phone back in its cradle.

The trip to Ben Gurion airport was smooth. Once the convoy got out of the urban area the construction site was in traffic freed up and the world returned to some semblance of normal. Kevin made one more phone call to the Israeli authorities informing them of the situation. They offered police or Army escort but Kevin politely declined. This whole thing was dirty from the jump, and he didn't want help unless he could stake his life on it being legit. The only real help he was going to get in Israel were the men and women in the three SUVs with him.

His phone call to the authorities did manage to smooth out the security checkpoints for them. They were passed through with minimal harassment. The airport itself was locked down. The Israelis deal with terror regularly, and they've gotten very good at reacting to it. The airport was secured by the time they arrived, complete with tanks at the entrances, and they were escorted by airport police to the secured rear of the tarmac where the U.S. government planes were waiting. More American Marines were waiting at the plane, fully loaded for combat. They had their camo gear, full combat kit, and were armed for a real fight. Kevin thought it was strange that they had arrived at the plane and were already geared up. It seemed to him as if they'd gotten advance orders to get here. Maybe there was an extraction plan in place before the bomb went off? Kevin quickly lost the thought at the big black vehicles pulled up the plane.

The three Marines held the perimeter around the Lear jet as Kevin and his men got the Senator and his aides into the plane. Once they were loaded up he gave the all clear to the pilots, and in less than 20 minutes they went from riding in the Suburbans to gaining altitude in the jet over Tel Aviv, watching the Mediterranean Sea open up before them. It had only been maybe five hours since their meeting around the big mahogany table.

The men collapsed with fatigue. The drain left behind after the adrenaline fades is overwhelming. Kevin had blacked out from the exhaustion more than once himself, and he completely understood the men who did just that. The older guys, the ones who had been through it like Kevin sat close to one another, exchanging memories, and figuring out how they were going to make sure Alan's kid was taken care of. Kevin felt one huge pang of sadness when he thought of his friend's young daughter. She was only 6, and she would take the loss of her father hard. Try as hard as he might, he couldn't think of her name. He vowed to try and see them in person as soon as he could.

Kevin wandered the length of the plane once the turbulence subsided and they reached their astronomically high cruising altitude. The thrum of the powerful jet engines drowning out the snoring of the few men who had passed out. Kevin made his way back to the grateful Senator, who promptly thanked him and his men profusely. Kevin passed it all off as just another day at the job, but deep down inside he wondered what the hell was so important about this man. Kevin didn't know.

After he checked in with all his conscious team members he set himself down next to his two youngest men, Nate and Corey. He addressed them once they were done downing the bottles of water they got on the plane, "You men did an amazing job earlier."

They both replied with a "thank you sir," in near unison. They were a little roughed up emotionally, and they were spattered with blood from the close quarter gun battle.

"You guys okay, did anyone get hurt?" Kevin downed another bottle of the water in one fluid tip. He didn't even realize how thirsty he was.

Nate responded with a quiet chuckle, "Other than pissing myself a little, I'm good to go sir." Kevin liked him. Good sense of humor when things needed it.

Corey laughed at his Marine friend and rolled up his sleeves. Kevin saw a nasty semi-circular scratch on his forearm, "you get cut Corey?"

"Nah. One of the motherfuckers bit me."

Kevin dismissed the minor injury with a hmph, and leaned his head back into the plush first class style seats in the small Lear jet. It was only a few hours to London, then hopefully home. He quickly drifted off into the post adrenaline darkness of deep sleep.

December 13th

I have been sitting here for the better part of an hour trying to decide if I want to talk about Cassie. I have thought about twenty things I would rather talk about because that's easier. Talking about Cassie dredges up memories that cause me a lot of emotional pain, and I am having enough trouble dealing with my physical pain already. What's left of my sanity already feels paper thin, and I am scared that talking about her will make things worse. I don't know if I can deal with worse right now.

Quitters say that stuff. People who are afraid of facing the truth say that kind of nonsense. I loved her, right? Why should I mourn her so powerfully when so much of my memory of her is so pleasant? I should celebrate my relationship with her instead of mourn my one bad decision about her.

Typing that helped. It's amazing the power of writing your feelings. Okay Mr. Journal, here we go. Might need to take a few breaks to get some tissues. Brace yourself.

I met Cassie when I was working at a strip club right after my discharge. Not stripping at the club, I was working security there. It was a fairly reputable establishment in the city. She was working as a bartender there and the moment I saw her I knew I had to try and get her number. I mean it was that simple. Saw her, knew it. She and I worked off nights for weeks before her schedule changed a bit and she started working Friday nights, which was the one night of the week I worked. As I've said before, my skills with women were questionable at best so I had to work myself up the whole night to say something to her. It's funny that I have no problem at all wandering downtown into a horde of undead to face potential death, but the thought of saying something to a girl puts jelly in my knees.

Cassie was pretty, very pretty. I wouldn't have said she was hot, but she had this innocent charm that suckered

ALONE NO MORE

people in. She came off as the girl next door, the farmer's daughter, the babysitter, you name the cliché. She had auburn hair leaning towards red. More red than brown really, and I have always been a sucker for redheads. She had green eyes. Pretty ones that changed color when she got mad. Maybe they were more hazel really? I don't know, I'm sticking with green as the color. I like green.

Cassie was dressed a little slutty that night, as all the girls who worked at the club had to. The service staff wore all black every night. The waitresses wore black skirts, and the bar staff wore black slacks with tight black tank tops. She had her hair in a ponytail too, which for some reason I am a complete sucker for as well. It was almost like she was trying to get my attention. She was hitting me on all cylinders that night. Every night really.

It was a really busy night that night. I can distinctly recall having something like ten ejections of drunks, or assholes that thought there really was sex in the champagne room. There are plenty of clubs where you can get something in the private rooms, but this was not one of them. I was walking a dude out the door all wrapped up after grabbing one of the girl's asses and I happened to look sideways at the bar and caught Cassie watching me. I gave her one of my patented rolls of the eyes and she gave me an overly enthusiastic thumbs up in mock celebration. I decided right then I'd get her number before we left. Had to.

I didn't. Fail. Right as the club was closing we had a fight break out and her shift ended. I was pinning some prick against the wall waiting for the police to show when she punched out and left for the night. You want to talk about frustrated masturbation? To borrow a phrase, I beat my dick like it owed me money that night.

The next week she worked on Friday and right off the bat I walked up the bar and said hi. I'll never forget it, the first thing she said to me. I said, "hi."

Her response with a smile was, "I don't date ogres."

Fortunately I have a sense of humor, and I laughed. I

165

don't think she expected that. My reply to her was, "I was told you had sex with them though…." My sense of humor is my in with girls. I might be awkward, but I'm fucking funny.

We hit it off immediately. She was a wiseass just like me. She was a senior in college, and was finishing school in a few months. She was going to school for finance, and interning during the late afternoons a few days a week. The bartending job was paying most of her tuition and she hated it. I gave her my number, told her I was independently wealthy, had a huge dick, could last in bed for days, and had a problem with lying.

She called me the next day, and we talked on the phone for hours. I never talk on the phone, so this is a pretty substantial thing for me. We had so much in common. She hated her dad, I hated my mom. We had the same tastes in music, we both wanted to travel the world, and we both liked porn. Too good to be true. The next weekend she had dinner at my place, made by me, and she spent the night. I called her a slut for putting out on the first date, and she called me a manwhore for doing the same. I blamed my parents and their shady morals. She blamed her poor ability to recognize assholes. It was a really nice night. Comfort right off the bat. We had skipped the whole awkward "getting to know you" phase.

She moved in as soon as she finished school. Once I settled in at work here I bought my condo with the GI Bill. My mortgage was jack shit and when she moved in and got herself a full time job working in the city, we were rolling in it. We took long vacations all over the place. I get weeks off because of the school schedule and she wound up doing CPA work so off of tax season she had a lot of free time. We backpacked Europe, took a few cruises in the Caribbean, spent a week in Hong Kong, climbed ruins in Guatemala, and a bunch of cool shit in between.

I knew she was awesome after she met my mother. We went over my parent's place for Thanksgiving and we had our typical disheveled holiday. Dad was telling war stories, mom was being bitchy, Caleb and his wife were trying to contain their little son Adam, with Rebecca watching it all in horror. I was completely fucking mortified. It was the exact scenario I had dreaded my entire life. My family in all their backwards glory. In fact, that was the first time I had ever brought a girl home for a holiday. As in ever. I almost never took girls home growing up and sure as shit never took any of them home for a holiday. No fucking way. Cassie took it all in stride, smiling, being sweet, she even laughed at my dad's shitty misogynistic jokes. I can remember the way she looked sitting next to my dad at the dining room table, as all of us guys retired to the couch to watch football. She was leaning on the table, resting her chin in her palm. She had her hair in a ponytail again that day and I can remember the faintly crimson shimmer of her hair as she pretended to like all my dad's stories. I could almost envision my family life as being normal right then. It felt good. I wasn't embarrassed, and she just looked so…. Beautiful.

Our conversation in the car on the way home that day went something like this:

"I like your brother," she said.

"Yeah Caleb's cool. I like his wife too, and their kid is awesome."

"Three years old is a tough age." I think she said. I replied in the affirmative and we sat in silence for a bit. I could tell she was trying to find a way to phrase her next statement. I remember resting my hand on her leg. I always did that in the car with her. I just liked touching her. I wanted the contact.

"Your dad seems… interesting," she said awkwardly.

"My dad's a great guy. He just postures up to impress cute girls." I laughed. She laughed back. She knew I was full of shit.

"Your mom seems like a complete cunt," she said without missing a beat.

It's rare when two people connect so thoroughly in life.

167

She had it all figured out the first time, and I couldn't have been happier.

We had a great relationship. She was a redhead, so she was pretty hot tempered. Full of passion she used to describe herself as. When she loved, she loved hard. When she was angry, she was pure Scottish fury. Caber tossing and all sometimes. I think she was the only person I had ever met that could actually scare me when they were angry. Even my dad didn't scare me after I was 15 or so. Cassie did.

Cassie worked her way up the ladder in the company she worked for. When she dressed herself up she could knock 'em dead, and she was damn smart and motivated. She kicked ass at her CPA firm and made junior partner this spring. We were looking at new houses closer to the city to cut down on her commute right before the world ended. Between what we'd saved and what we could afford we were actually looking at some really nice places.

I don't know why I never married her. I've wracked my brain over and over in the long nights here trying to figure it out. I just can't come up with a real answer. Were we too busy? Was she too career oriented? Was it some form of PTSD I was in denial about? Was it some repressed bullshit mommy issue? Fucked if I know. If I could take anything back I've ever done, I'd take back not making her my wife a long time ago. If I knew the world was ending I would've told her how much I loved her, and told her I wanted her in my life forever.

Maybe that's the moral of this story? Maybe that's the lesson I'm supposed to learn out of all this death and destruction. Live each day like the world will end tomorrow. I know that sounds like a fucking Hallmark card, but it's really true now. The irony of it all sickens me now. I've almost died too many times, and ended too many lives during my 34 years on this earth to take anything for granted anymore.

Cassandra Ann MacKenzie, fury of the highlands. Cassandra Ann Ring. Cassie Ring.

God I miss her. We would've made such fun babies.
I feel numb without you.

I love you.

-Adrian

December 15th

All that talk about Cassie the other night did me some
good. I didn't stop to jot down all the times I had to wipe my
eyes while writing, otherwise that entry might've been 10
pages longer. Shit I might still be writing it. I'm such a pussy.
　Mr. Journal, it is nice to be more clearheaded today. I am
off the vicodin, and as far as I can tell, I won't be needing
them again for this wound. Time will tell I guess. I'm dealing
with the soreness through brute ignorance, and about four
ibuprofen at a whack. As long as I stay relatively still, I am
fine, it's just when I am moving about that I start to build up
the pain. My redness is almost totally in check now. It
doesn't look anywhere near as angry anymore, and the clear
fluid isn't seeping out at all. Antibiotics are a wonderful
thing, it's a shame there's a finite amount in the world now.
Very frustrating being laid up like this, but such is life. Not
my first time being hurt. Probably won't be my last.
　As you can imagine, things have been really frigging
boring. The plants are wonderful, thanks for asking. Otis is
finally leaving them alone, and he's gone back to being
friendly again. I don't remember if I said it before, but he
was sort of avoiding me right about the time the infection
got bad. I think he could smell the sickness in my leg. I know
a lot of animals can tell when other animals are sick, so that
stands to reason. Other than his constant attempts at eating
my fledgling tomatoes, he's a prince. He's been keeping me
company on the recliner most days and nights. By company

I mean he sits right on my hands when I'm trying to play Playstation or read a book. Love the guy, but shit can he be irritating.

Zero activity on campus. Well, the parts of campus I can see here from Hall E at least. I've got decent views from the windows when I hobble around on my interior patrols. All quiet on the western front. I can't imagine at this stage in the game I'll get many wandering zombies up here. The road leading up here is pretty much cleared out with the exception of whatever's left on Prospect Circle. I just can't imagine there are that many free roaming undead on that street that could be a real problem for me. The past few days the more I think about it the more likely it is that the group of undead that was banging on my door was zombies from Prospect Circle that I attracted back here. I had been making enough noise to attract them for sure. No way to know really unless I check their driver's licenses for addresses, and frankly, I don't need to know that bad to go pick through their fucking pockets.

Isolation can be a successful strategy. Write that down Mr. Journal.

So what to talk about? Well I can recant the bullshit nothingness of the 13th and 14th if you like. Ready:

Not shit happened.

Well I'm fucking exhausted. Can't speak for you Mr. Journal but I might need a break after that long winded affair. Might need to crack open one of those bottles of booze I have stored away. Could be an effective way to cut the pain in the leg.

I think not. Last thing I need is another sad drunken binge. No one likes the sad drunk. Debbie frigging downer.

I think I can recall back to the early days here and try and talk about some of the shit that's happened to me. Or shit that happened to other people that I witnessed and whatnot. I remember talking about the grocery store trip. I vaguely remember talking about how the phones were caput, but the television and radio worked for awhile. I want to say the television lasted maybe 3 or 4 days after the end, and the radio maybe 10 days. Again, there isn't much useful information to share about the media. Lots of rumor mongering, paranoia, and pointing of fingers. Even ten days after they were still unsure of whatever was going on. The internet was down almost immediately. But that stands to reason, because our internet up here on campus always fucking sucked. The side effect of being so far off the beaten path I guess. Might also explain the problem we had with phone service when the shit hit the fan. Small town phone exchange maybe got overloaded? Dunno.

It was day 12 when I decided that I should go back to Moore's Sporting Goods and try to get more guns and ammo. That was my first real trip downtown after the world farted out a potato. The zombie potato, as it were. Campus during the first 10 or 12 days was pretty quiet. Well, at least a lot more quiet then I had expected it to be. I saw about half a dozen more zombies creeping their way along outside, and that was when I started to practice using the sword. By trade I'm more of a firearms guy, so facing off one on one in open ground definitely helped me get better using the short sword I brought from home. Thank God for not skimping out and buying shitty prop replica swords. Cassie always used to give me shit about all the money I spent on shit like swords and comic books.

"Seriously Adrian, you really NEED an authentic, forged Celtic short sword? For what? Are you invading England or France this spring?"

"I like the color Cass. Besides I need a nice short sword to go along with the new Timberland boots I bought. Can't have my accessories clash babe. They have to match..."

That line got me beaten about the face at least twice. I think variants on that conversation were had at least ten times. Domestic bliss!

The worst thing that went down after the world came crashing down was the arrival of a few desperate parents. There were maybe 10 in all, and they showed up starting the day after the grocery store trip. Two, sometimes four a day for a stretch of a few days. I avoided the first couple that came on campus for fear of infection, plus one guy had a rifle, and one time the car pulled up and managed to time it just right to get attacked by one of the handful of zombies that'd wandered onto campus. The second day I just had to go down and talk to them though.

It broke my heart to see the parents crying when they couldn't find their children. The remaining parents that came to campus were the same. Heartbroken, and there wasn't shit I could do for them. Most of the kids they were looking for I had seen dead, or killed myself. Well, killed their shambling undead bodies, but you get the idea Mr. Journal. Those parents at least got some closure. It was the few parents whose kids I could not verify that were the ones lost. I don't know where their kids went, but they could be anywhere. Many cars left campus that day, and there is no way of knowing who was in what cars. Many of the kids left, there's no doubt about that.

Some of the parents were so grief stricken they attacked me. How out of your fucking mind do you have to be to go after a guy my size that's holding a shotgun? Far fucking out that's for sure. I didn't hurt anyone, but I definitely twisted some shoulders and elbows out of joint to get them to calm down. I hated having to do it, but I couldn't risk injury, and I wasn't about to be their fricking punching bag. I told them the same thing I told Abigail, that I was making the campus safe, and that they were welcome to stay, but no one took the offer.

It hurts to watch someone give up like that. To watch all their will just drain away. And make no mistake, there is a moment when it happens. I watched it half a dozen times the first week when I told those parents that their kid was dead. Sometimes they look down at the ground, sometimes they stare at you, other times the color just fades from them. They're like shadows of themselves. Black and white people in a color world. Those are the real undead we're dealing with. The people that have lost hope.

I heard a fair amount of gunfire in the distance. The first day, the day I did the majority of the cleaning out of campus I heard scattered shots. One here, one there, but nothing approaching the level of a firefight. The next few days were the same, but about a week into it, after I'd gone down to the store, there were several days of fairly heavy gunfire. Again, not exchanges of gunfire, but stretches of four or five shots here and there. I'm guessing it was people encountering zombies, or perhaps folks making a break for it after they ran out of food. Think about it Mr. Journal. How long would the food in your cupboards last you if you couldn't go shopping? Three days? Five days? Not as long as you'd think.

As I was saying about the trip to Moore's it was on July 4th. I found it odd that I would be attempting to raid a gun store on America's Independence Day. Ironic? Fitting? I'm not sure what to think about it really. I just remember it was on that day I went down there.

I left super early that day. I thought it would give me the best chance if I got in and out right after dawn. My bet was that people would be asleep at that hour, or be awake keeping watch on their fortified homes. I guess it's also the military history in my past to get up early. Oversleeping isn't my nature anymore. It hasn't been for some time.

I geared up. Pistol, knife, sword, shotgun and .22 Now I had lost my Camry in the grocery store trip, and there was no way in hell I was going to raid a gun store in a fucking Ford Focus. Not a tactical vehicle by any means. Plus If I did run over anything taller than a can of soda I risked getting the car stuck, and the last thing I wanted to do was get stuck downtown without a vehicle. This was the first and last time I opted to take a school van out. Of course in retrospect I should've taken one of the maintenance F150's, but I knew where the keys were to the vans, and back then I wasn't sure about the keys for the trucks.

We've got four of the large Dodge cargo vans. They're big

and dark blue with the school logo and shaded windows. There are three rows of seats and they have really good ground clearance. Not the best vehicle by any means, but they would work for this trip. Now I've got two of them blocking the bridge to get onto campus, so even if they aren't being used to drive around with, they're still being useful.

Now Moore's is on the opposite side of town from the school here. I had two options the way I saw it. I could drive straight through downtown and brave whatever the fuck was there, or I could skirt downtown using side roads and hopefully dodge… whatever it was that might be there. There were upsides to both ideas. Downtown is heavily populated, had a lot of businesses, and would likely be worth fighting over. Look at what happened at the grocery store already for an example of what might happen. That shit happened with a few days of it all going down. Now the side roads were mostly neighborhoods, but that meant a huge number of people. Possibly dead people. Possibly living folks.

I opted for side roads. It just seemed safer to me.

That meant driving about 5 extra miles each direction. At 20 miles an hour or so I was looking at a solid 40 minutes each way, barring unforeseen…. Dead people. I left the school all kitted up, drove down Auburn Lake Road, and hung a right onto Route 18 to head towards town. Now before I took the turn to go directly to main street, I took a side street and headed into the great unknown of…

THE SUBURBS. DUM DUM DUM. (ominous drum sound)

It was pretty fucked up. Now in a stroke of amazing arrogance I made the assumption that because I was going to the gun store, I would be returning with additional firearms related supplies. I kept the Sig handy as I drove, and whenever I saw a zombie moving towards me, I slowed down and popped it in the brainpan. Sitting here with no 9mm ammo today, I feel like an epic moron. I easily could have just driven past the damn things, or hit them with the van if I felt I had to kill them.

I forget exactly how many rounds I wasted in the van that day but I know I burned through all my magazines, which is 45 rounds. I know at one point I was reloading the magazines from my vest pocket and I know there was more shooting after that, but the numbers escape me. I guess it doesn't matter now, seeing as how I am sans 9mm. That's a shitty feeling Mr. Journal. Being out of ammo. I felt invincible back then. Well, as far as ammo is concerned. I guess I should say I felt flush. 9mm hood rich.

The side neighborhoods in town were a lot like it was up here. Houses spread out in varying densities. Most of them looked to be abandoned, but there were quite a few that were boarded up and looked Alamo-ish. Almost every single house that was fortified like that had zombies around it. I mean damn near every single one. The zombies were slowly banging on the barricaded windows and doors, trying to get inside. If anything, my trip around town pulled a bunch of those undead off of the houses. The ones I didn't shoot followed me until I left their eyesight. As it turns out, many of them followed me much further than that.

In the 15 or so miles to Moore's I would estimate that I saw about a hundred undead. Give or take 20 or so. The majority were wandering the streets, with a strong emphasis on harassing the houses that obviously still had people holed up inside of them. Well, I don't know there were people still inside the houses, but judging from the appearances of the houses, and the attention they were getting from the zombies, it seemed likely.

I didn't see a single living person until I got to Moore's itself. Moore's from a distance looked a lot calmer than the day I had last been there. Other than a really nice Yukon, a shitty pickup truck, and an Ambulance, there was nothing else in the parking lot. Moore's is in a largely residential area, so there were no businesses around to speak of. Quite a few houses of course. There was one zombie in the parking lot moving with some serious purpose when I finally parked.

The zombie was moving from my right to left and clearly following something I couldn't see behind the ambulance. I got the van parked and got out of it before the thing realized I was there. It was a fairly tall middle aged guy in life. Skinny as a rail too. All I could think of was rotting beanpole when I saw him. Lol I'm such a prick.

I hopped out of the van and drew the sword. I wanted to be quiet here as much as possible. Once the rotting beanpole saw me get out of the truck whatever it was he was following became much less interesting. I could see as plain as day in the early light his arm had been bitten really badly. His right forearm had been stripped of flesh from the elbow straight to the wrist and his hand hung limply when he came at me. I took a solid backhanded swipe at his neck and took his bad hand clean off in the process. Only a few inches of the sword wound up hitting his neck, causing a fucking rugged wound across his throat that would've killed a living person. I could see his windpipe sticking out of the hole I'd made. The impact of the sword swing sent him into the side of the van where he smashed his head on the frame. I took the moment and finished him off with a solid down stroke to the skull.

The beanpole had been cut down to size.

I had to say that. Strictly for dramatic purposes Mr. Journal. It's my moment of badass-ery. One of the few times I can say something like that and feel like I was legitimately kind of a badass. Now then, moving along…

I wiped the goop off the sword using his shirt and sheathed it. I went in with the shotgun raised. Noise be damned. If I saw a bunch of them, I wanted firepower. That's when I heard someone yell out to my rear, "Freeze!"

It had come from behind me, from the back end of the ambulance. The zombie had chased whoever this person was around the far side of the ambulance, and I hadn't seen them. They'd come around the back end of the vehicle and more or less snuck up behind me as I killed the tall dead guy.

I lowered the shotgun and raised my left hand slightly.

I said, "I'm not here to cause trouble, just wanted to see if any ammunition is left."

The guy from behind me said back, "Holy shit, Ring?" As soon as I heard him say my name I recognized the voice. It was Officer McGreevy.

I turned and I was right, it was him. He had changed out of his uniform and into a more tactical style black jumpsuit. He had an ammo and gear vest on with POLICE in big white letters velcro'd to the front and back of it. I smiled and we exchanged a hearty handshake. God it was good to see another human, especially some form of authority figure.

He looked like shit though. McGreevy was big, bigger than me, and it looked like he'd skipped quite a few meals. His black paramilitary jumpsuit was covered in swaths of dark stains, and dried on bits of… people. He looked like he'd been through a frigging ringer. He also looked really happy to see me.

We stood there in the parking lot bullshitting for maybe 15 minutes. As I recall he said he'd left here maybe an hour or two after I had and that the shop had gone to shit in a hurry. I guess the dude he'd shot there in the parking lot that day was probably a zombie after all. Good call on his part. The bad news was the kid in the passenger seat had been bitten as well and he croaked after they got him inside. He bit the paramedics, and you can see where it went from there. The dudes working at the shop took the fuck off and the Chief told McGreevy to go take care of his family. So he did.

I guess he got his family safe three towns over, and he had headed back to town to raid the police station of more heavy duty guns that day. The gun locker at the station had already been emptied though. He said it was unlocked, which told the both of us that one of the local cops had been responsible. After coming up dry there, he headed over here in the hopes that he'd find something left behind, and as you might expect, this place was empty now too.

That's when his head exploded.

And I mean exploded. Blew the fuck up. The gunshot that took the top of his skull off and showered me in bits and pieces was almost simultaneous to his death. I dove down in the general direction of my van as his headless body smashed to the ground beside me. Here one second, gone the next.

Mr. Journal have you ever seen what a high caliber projectile does to a skull? The violence of it is unreal. The skull can't take the kinetic energy of the round passing through it and shock explodes it. One of the more unpleasant things to witness, of that I can assure you.

From my stomach I could hear a faint echo of a gunshot moving through the vicinity, and I rolled onto my back to try and look around. I could see McGreevy's head was smeared all over the windshield of the ambulance which told me the shot had come from beside us, basically from the direction I was exposed to. I rolled and rolled until I was under the van and started looking that way. I still had my shotgun, and I was aiming in the general direction I thought the shooter was. It was down the same road I'd driven on when I left here "that day."

Patience is a teachable skill in combat. Sticking your head up frequently gets it shot off, and I knew whoever had shot the cop was at least a decent shot, or really fucking close. I knew if I exposed myself I stood a damn good chance of getting my own head exploded. I decided to displace and advance in the direction I thought the shooter was.

I rolled to the opposite side of the van and got to my knees. The only other cover around was the Yukon, so I bolted to it. No one shot me. However there was a shitload of movement coming from the surrounding area. I could see about four shambling undead coming my way from about a hundred yards off in various directions. I didn't have a lot of time to work with, but what's fucking new, right? If I'm not knee deep in bullshit I'm waist deep.

I did a low walk to the small raised flower garden right

at the edge of the parking lot. I did a headfirst dive into the mulch and got as low as I could right in the middle of the vegetation. I squirmed up so I could see through the plants and waited and watched. I sat there for a solid thirty seconds. I kept a close eye on the four dead guys coming my way and the closest was halfway to me when my shooter finally made himself known.

It was a fucking kid. I mean, maybe 18. Probably more like 16. He rode his goddamn bicycle right up to McGreevy's body and hopped off, he even putting out the fucking kickstand and propped the bike up carelessly in a chunk of McGreevy's fucking head.

The scrawny prick un-slung a hunting rifle off his back and took careful aim at one of the undead coming in our direction. One by one with accurate head shots he dropped the four zombies heading our way. He didn't see me from where he was. I was mostly hidden in the tall plants and flowers. He stopped after he was done shooting and did a stupid little dance to celebrate. Fucking fist pumping how badass he was. I was so fucking furious. I'm mad now just typing about it. I wanted fucking blood.

He threw back the bolt on the rifle and started to reload it. I took my chance and leapt out of the greenery, shotgun up, screaming at him. I started off with the industry standard, "Freeze, drop the gun!" but all he did was look up at me with a completely confused look. He did freeze, but he didn't drop the gun. I knew he'd gotten one round in the chamber, and as I got to about 20 feet away from him, he threw the bolt forward, and started to raise it quickly to his shoulder, pointing it at me.

I bucked him center mass with the 12 gauge twice, sending his body backwards into the ambulance like it'd been hit by a car. One of my shots hit his rifle dead center, blasting the damn thing into pieces. His hand holding the gun was vaporized by the heavy shotgun pellets. The boy slid down to the ground, resting against the white ambulance, blood spraying from an arterial wound in his neck. I remember his jaw opening and closing reflexively as he watched his own blood spray across the parking lot.

I remember screaming a lot of fucking profanity. And I mean a lot Mr. Journal. I hate shooting people, and I really hate the idea that I shot a kid. I mean I fucking despise myself for that, and I fucking KNOW I had to do it. Him or me, it's that simple. He may have thought he had the drop on me or something, but the bottom line was; I wasn't dying that day.

Him or me, right Mr. Journal?

Right?

Ah shit. I forgot how much this trip really pissed me off. It reminds me so much of the senseless fucking bullshit Kevin and I had to deal with in Baghdad. Suicide bombers, kids with AK's, donkey bodies filled with explosives. Just fucking stupid shit that we humans do to each other. Makes me think we deserved this. Almost like this is some divine bitchslap to wake us up from being complete dinks to each other. Whatever I guess.

As I was finishing up my angry tirade in the parking lot he had died and was starting to twitch and sit back up again. I kicked the fucking idiot's bike into the middle of the road with a huge boot and stomped over to his body, still slumped against the side of the ambulance. I kicked him onto his side and used the stock of the shotgun to smash his head into a pulp. I kinda regret that too. I could've just stabbed him in the head with the sword, but I wanted so *badly* to teach him a fucking lesson, even if it was after his death. I threw up on him after I realized what I'd done. I didn't mean to throw up on him either, it just hit me like a freight train when I looked at what I'd done and it came out. It hit him in the leg. Eggs. Fresh eggs too. Some of the last eggs I've eaten.

Just a complete waste on every fucking level.

The kid had a .30-06 hunting rifle, but as I said, one of my shotgun blasts totaled it. In his backpack he had 6 rounds for it, and I grabbed those. McGreevy's vest wasn't bulletproof.

It was a vest cops wear over their Kevlar. I was kind of pissed because man I would have loved to have gotten his vest. He would've been about my size too. McGreevy's service weapon was gone. He didn't even have his holster on him. I suspect he left it with his family wherever they were.

He did have a hunting rifle. Gorgeous too. Savage Model 70 in .30-06 with a Burress 2.5-10x scope. Legit sniper rifle shit. Probably McGreevy's Cadillac hunting rifle. This is like a $2,000 rifle here. McGreevy's vest was about the same thing as the vest I already had on, and I didn't feel like taking it off him. I emptied his pockets of ammunition for his rifle, and found his keys, as well as a security pass card for the municipal complex where the police station was.

Yeah. I said that. I have the keys to the police station. Why haven't I gone there yet? McGreevy said everything there worth taking was already gone. Well, there's at least one thing that I think is still there that I want. Plus the station is downtown. Like… downtown-downtown. Downtown with a capital D. But that plan is for another day, and another entry Mr. Journal.

Once I got his ammunition and his keys I headed inside and proceeded to check the interior of the gun shop.

Just as he'd said, it'd been tossed already. There was almost nothing left inside of value worth taking. The gun vaults were all wide open and empty, the ammunition shelves were cleared off, the clothes were all gone, there was almost nothing there worth taking. I snagged some extra holsters, belts, and rifle slings. Those are surprisingly useful items to have around too, I was sort of in awe they hadn't been taken.

In the far back room I found the body of old Sheriff Moore. He was the owner of the shop, and he'd been bitten in the leg. There was blood all over his foot. I could only tell it was him by his nametag. His head had been blasted open by a large caliber round. There was nothing to identify him by. His face was gone.

In his desk I found a box of .357 magnum shells, which

was cool, except I don't have a .357 magnum. If I find one though, I'm ready to rock and roll. I gave the shop a final once over and got into the van with my meager gains for the day. As I pulled out I saw another tall male zombie shuffling towards the shop, dragging a broken leg or foot as it went. I got out real quick, sighted in the Savage, and obliterated the damn thing's head at 75 yards. The rifle sounded like a cannon going off. I could even hear the birds flying away out of the trees the gun report was so loud.

And I left. The drive back got a little hairy when I crossed Main Street near my condo. I had to drive through a dozen or so undead in the road. They were making their way towards the gun shop like a mob of undead Somalians. Awful shit Mr. Journal. I ran over a few of them and drove away from the rest. They left bloody streaks on the windows that are still there to this day.

I took the same route back. That's where I saw the zombie caught in the swing again. I laughed for an hour about that. If you can't recall Mr. Journal, I've mentioned this before. There was a zombie who had walked into a swing, and kept walking far enough that the swing had gotten lodged up under its armpits. These things are so single minded it kept walking forward, straight into the swing, like it was on a treadmill. I stopped the van and watched for a bit, and it actually turned in my direction to walk towards me, still bound up in the swing. Hilarious. Stupid zombies. It's probably still stuck in that fucking swing right now.

Got back here, parked the vans on the bridge and holed up for the rest of that day. It was a shitty trip all in all. I guess you could say I saw fireworks that July 4th, although it wasn't the kind I was interested in.

Can you see now why I was a little sour on telling that story Mr. Journal? Meet Adrian Ring, mom killer, child murderer, abandoner of girlfriends.

My whole life I feel like I've always been the guy that has to go all in on 7-2 off suit.

At least I'm a good shot.

Classy fella.

-Adrian

December 17th

I think I've gotten rid of the Ninja shits. At least, I think I have. I've been wrong before though. They are…. Very sneaky. I haven't had the shits in a few days, so I'm pretty excited. It might've been the painkillers though. I know many of them cause constipation as a side effect. If that's the case, then I killed two birds with one stone. You have any fucking idea how painful and difficult it is to take a shit when your leg is fucked up? I had to crap with one leg sticking straight out in front of me, grimacing the whole time. Forget standing up afterward. Yowzas.

Something happened today that has me somewhat excited. I went outside today for the first time in a week I think. It was around noon, and it was actually pretty nice out. A pleasant 40 degrees F according to the thermometer. My leg has gotten much better and I desperately needed to get outside and get some direct sunlight and fresh air. I stood outside of Hall E, holding the door open if I needed to make a quick escape when I heard a weird, thrumming noise. It was a sound I hadn't heard since late June.

It was an airplane.

I didn't see it, but I heard it. It was distinct. I nearly danced for joy. Signs of educated, advanced survivors. Pilots who knew how to fuel a plane and fly, overhead. Holy shit I was, and still am excited about that. Full chubber.

The first thing I thought of was 9/11. Mr. Journal you might not remember this, but for almost two days they stopped all flights here in the states. No planes overhead except for military ones. It was weird, especially if you were anywhere near a major city with a big airport. I remember feeling weird back then when someone pointed out to me how quiet it was without the civilian planes. I'd forgotten how quiet it was again.

Who was in the plane? What kind of plane was it? Where was it going? Large planes don't take off without a damn good idea that they can land where they're going, which implies to me that two locations were still communicating effectively over vast distances. I'm betting my shirt it was a military plane flying from one base to another. A lot of bases use satellite comms, and as long as they have power on base, the satellites will last for a year, maybe more. Now whoever runs the orbit corrections for the comms satellites needs to stay alive for them to last though. More than likely our bases are still operational all over the world, and it was people shuffling about. Man that's exciting. Hope for stability.

So what's new with me Mr. Journal? Damn little, that's what. Yesterday I spent inside yet again and tried to stay off the leg. I can get around more or less without pain, just soreness, but the less activity I have, the faster it'll heal. I read a few books this week that I had here in the dorm from the kid's rooms, and I also experimented with canned food recipes with mixed results. I haven't had any venison in some time. I only really like it if I can grill it, and the grill is outside, so I've been skipping the meat. I've checked the meat twice, and it's holding up pretty good in my freezer room deal.

I am going to have to make a trip down to the gas station as soon as I feel comfortable moving around. Maybe I can do it tomorrow or the next day. I could have done it today I think, but on the outside chance I run into trouble, I can't risk re-injuring the leg. I've been burning through fuel for the gas generator like a motherfucker. It's been really cold, so I've had to turn up the heat a few degrees above where I had been keeping it. Also, because I've been inside all day, I haven't been turning it down a few degrees like I had been when I went out to clear houses. All in all, I'm at least halfway through big Blue already, and that's far ahead of my schedule.

If I can just fill up my gas cans I'll be good to go until my leg is fully healed. At least into January I think. I can't recall how much gas is in the Tundra, but I think it's somewhere less than a half tank. That plus the fuels cans would be terrific. It sucks being all alone when you're hurt or sick Mr. Journal. There's no one to bring me chicken soup anymore.

Much like the previous few days it's been boring here. Nothing has passed through the campus, and other than hearing the plane earlier today, there's nothing new to report. Food is good, the plants are slowly growing, Otis is his mischievous self, and my leg is getting better. 1st and ten.

More tales of the past you think? I'm getting low on stories to tell about what's already happened to me Mr. Journal. In fact, if I spend the rest of this entry talking about the remaining time between June 23rd and when I started the journal, I'll be flat out of shit to talk about. Not like I won't be doing stuff in the future, but I won't have much to talk about as it relates to the past. Is that good? I always had this notion I could talk forever about that crap. Maybe it's because I'm putting way more entries than I planned on. When I first started this I was looking at doing entries once a week. I must like your company bud.

Oh well, all good things come to an end I suppose. After my trip back to Moore's on July 4th I got pretty motherfucking paranoid. Realizing a pipsqueak teenager had blown the head off of my cop friend really put the fear of humanity into me. I holed up here in Hall E and moved back and forth between here and the cafeteria like I was on patrol in Iraq. Everywhere I was guns up, looking for trouble. I fully expected either a horde of undead, or a 10th grade class of Uzi wielding assholes to jump me at every corner. Mercifully I found no hordes of undead, or submachine gun wielding teenagers.

I started to clean the campus up after July 4th. The heat was terrible that month and the smell in the air became entirely unbearable. I would occasionally just dry heave when I got a good whiff of it, and I couldn't take much of that before I got up the motivation to deal with it. I found some good overalls in the maintenance barn, plus some work gloves and rubber gloves. I got the four wheeler and the little trailer all set up, and I started to move the corpses to the far end of campus, near the staff housing area. Shit what an awful process that was.

There were quite a few undead roaming the campus though after that. I think the sound of the four wheeler drew them out. I found a few extra kid zombies in the far rear of campus near the staff housing sometime in mid to late July. My gut tells me they were hiding there and starved. Unlike in zombie movies, most of the zombies appear pretty much as they appear in life, as opposed to these emaciated stick figures you see in movies nowadays. Why would zombies get skinny? It's not like they need to eat to maintain weight, they're fucking dead bodies. If anything, you'd imagine they'd be fat as hell after eating all the rest of us. Most of the undead I'd seen or killed looked like normal living people, just dead. And real fucking smelly.

These kids I saw were emaciated though. I think they hid from me when I cleared staff housing and wound up starving to death, or OD'ing on something. I found like 6 or 8 of them, and they got handled with relative ease. I found the archery shit about… August 3rd or so, and started to put range time in. I got to be a pretty good shot with the crappy bows, and I vowed then to use them first if possible. That reminds me, as soon as I can I really need to get back to the range, even in this cold. I haven't fired the bow in fucking forever, and with ammo as low as it is, every bullet is as precious as can be. I can get 5 or 6 shots out of every arrow if I take good care of them. I can't say that I am that comfortable bringing the bow out as a tactical weapon yet, but I desperately need to get back to practicing with it once I'm able. Maybe I'll do that tomorrow.

I lost a lot of weight back then. I should definitely mention that. The school food supplies were really substantial, but I was so frigging scared of running out of food I ate like a bird until mid September. I think I put myself on a 3 can a day diet once I went through or lost all the fresh foods. Like I said, I was out of eggs the first week of July, and I had to throw out so much produce it makes me angry to this day. Heads of lettuce by the box went. I wish I'd started growing shit in July. I'd have had the most bitching compost heap to jumpstart it. So many missed opportunities to make life easier for myself. Live and learn. Learn or die is more like it.

Most of August was spent laying low. It was brutally humid and rainy that month which really did nothing for my demeanor. The other side effect of the rain was causing all the blood and gore to run off the roads and sidewalks. I was so fucking afraid of the run off getting into my water supply I hoarded water and drank nothing but my stored supply the entire month. I still to this day don't know if the… disease or whatever it is that's causing this is transmittable. As I've said, I don't think it's a virus or a disease. It has got to be something worse. At the very least I wasn't willing to risk drinking water that had human filth in it. One of the fastest ways to die in a warzone is getting disease from dead bodies and shit. Cholera, dysentery, diphtheria, you name it.

And Mr. Journal, dead bodies poop. I know, you wouldn't think that would be the case, but all dead bodies poo. Once we die the muscles that control our bowels and sphincter call it a day, and if they have poo in the pipes, it all falls out. Campus was very unpleasant during the clean up. That also partially explains why the undead smell so fucking terrible. In addition to being rotting bodies, they've shat themselves.

Oh what a world.

Um so what happened during July and August that's worth writing about for historical integrity? Well, I stopped hearing planes fly over sometime around June 30th. I didn't see any parents after July 4th or so. Last living people I saw actually for some time. I can't recall exactly, but after killing the kid downtown, I don't think I saw another living person until I went down to the gas station in October. And even that sucked ass. Crazy ass wife pulling a gun on me.

I wonder what happened to her and the little kid? Mr. Journal if you get a lead, gimme a holler. Inquiring minds want to know.

And that's it. Random undead, asshole parents, cleaning campus…. Oh yeah, as I cleaned campus I tossed all the kid's rooms for usable stuff. A mother load of marginally useful shit. Lots of cologne and perfume, some snack foods, clothing, cd's, ipods, dead cell phones… Lots of junk. Not all junk, just lots of it.

I've made my decision, tomorrow I'll hit the range and get some archery time in. Day after that, if the leg is feeling good, I'll head down to the gas station and refill my cans and try and get big blue back up to the top. I really need to make sure my fuel supplies are good, as the roads are sure to turn to shit soon, (if they haven't already) and I don't want to get stuck a mile down the road with a stiff leg and little to no ammunition.

Mr. Journal, I bid you adieu!

-Adrian

December 18th

It has been a day of conspicuous occurrences Mr. Journal. I am pretty sure I am not alone anymore. I'll get to that in a moment.

As I said I was going to, I spent the majority of the day outside. Holy shit it's cold out. I had forgotten what it was like outside being cocooned up in Hall E for over a week now. Shit I can barely type this, my hands are so stiff, and I've been inside for hours now.

Early on, sometime around 10 in the morning I went out to the archery range. There's only a few inches of snow on the ground, so it wasn't too bad. My leg is getting better and better, and with a good dressing on it I can move around pretty good. I can't run, but I can waddle at a good magazine. I spent about an hour at the range, missing targets with amazing regularity. It's funny how fast you can forget how to do things. I wonder how long it'd take me to send a text message today?

I took three trips out to the range, heading back inside to warm myself. I didn't see any undead moving around on campus, so that was a big relief. Towards the end of my afternoon my arrogance got the best of me, and I saddled up on the four wheeler. It hurt like a bitch to bend my leg to get it on the peg, and I couldn't shift and brake worth a shit, but I did it nonetheless. I used the four wheeler to make my rounds of campus. I haven't done a real patrol outside since before I had my nuts nearly bitten off, and despite getting my nose frozen solid, it felt good to check out the whole joint.

When I was finishing my trip, I saw a wild rabbit hopping across the snow. It was a fat bastard, easily the size of Otis. He had white and grey downy fur, and came to a stop when I rounded the bend coming up from the athletics field. He and exchanged a friendly moment of quiet, and he continued his journey across the snow. That's only the third animal I've seen since I got up here. The deer, Leviathan the evil dog, and now the rabbit. Weird.

I had a late lunch, refilled the gas tank on the generator, did some basic maintenance around the Hall and then finally made the brilliant decision that I was okay to make a trip to the gas station. I can already sense the disdain Mr. Journal. Don't get all uppity on me, I've got cabin fever.

I'm fine, really. Just stiff.

I had the gas cans pretty much already gathered here at the Hall, and I knew it would be a cakewalk. The houses are all clear down there, and all I needed to do is pull up, fill the tanks and get out. If there were zombies, I'd either run over them with the Tundra, or back off and plink them in the grapefruit at distance with the .22. Easy peasy.

I was right. Nothing happened down at the station. I filled up all my gas cans as fast as I could crank the damn pump. I had to steal a folding chair out of the garage to sit down though, because it was hurting my leg something fierce to stand there bent over. Taking a knee wasn't an option either. Hurts too much to bend the leg. Feels like someone twisting corkscrews into the meat after I stand on it too long. I had to take half a vicodin about an hour ago to take the edge off of the pain.

Anyway I got all my gas cans filled and loaded into the truck bed, and got out before anything happened. I can't even describe to you the naked feeling I have without the Sig on my hip. Don't get me wrong, the .45 is great and all, but I'm really low on ammo, and frankly, I just miss the old gun. Familiarity is a big deal with weapons, and I'm scared I'll draw the .45 and forget to thumb the safety off, and that one moment of oops will get me killed. Small mistakes lately have had pretty dramatic consequences.

Luckily, I made it back with no issues. Big Blue is filled to the brim with spare still left in the cans. I figure I'm good to go for another week or so at least before I need to figure another trip out. However, I think I need to make a new trip, with a potentially horrifying destination.

I heard gunshots today. Very close gunshots. I think they were pistol shots, something like a 9mm, or maybe a .38. I can't be certain exactly where the shots came from, but I've got a good idea. I was unloading the gas cans into big Blue here at the Hall just as it was getting dark when I heard the shooting. Pretty sure it was one gun, and there were maybe 6 or 7 shots. One shot, then a pause for a second, then a couple more. That pattern happened again maybe a minute later. I fucking froze SOLID. I wasn't scared, I think I was just shocked as balls that someone was that near to me, and they were shooting at something. Remember the stages of gunshots Mr. Journal? This was a class A shot. Just gunshots in the distance.

I would put down cash money (now entirely worthless, mind you) that those shots came from the Prospect Circle area. That's maybe a mile away, and really more like half that. I haven't checked any of the houses out there yet, and I'm wondering if someone else is looting them right now, while I'm laid up here. Tomorrow afternoon I'm going to go check it out. I'm gonna gear up for World War 3 and swing down and do some recon on the cul de sac. If I see someone taking shit from those houses I'm gonna....

Shit. What am I gonna do? Kill them? Scare them off? That crap isn't really mine. I don't really have any claim to it. It still belongs to the people who used to live there I guess. Well whatever happens, I plan to find out what's up. If I have to shoot some motherfuckers, then I will. I hope I don't, but what I want, and what happens is usually pretty fucking different nowadays.

I'll throw an entry up tomorrow night when I get back.

-Adrian

The Chief

One thought ran through Chief Moore's head as he drove down the highway at nearly 90 miles an hour on June 23rd, 2010;

"The world had come undone."

The phrase repeated over and over in his head as cars pulled over for his cruiser's lights and siren. He blasted past them like they were standing still. At least some people still had sense left he thought. The high speed traffic headed in the opposite direction was bumper to bumper, and they were flying along nearly at the speed he was going. They were probably headed to the interstate to get north to escape whatever the fuck was happening. It was just a matter of time before there was a catastrophic accident on the road. All it takes is one person to drift into the other lane, or someone to brake sharply and there would be a wreck. A big one.

He didn't even know what to think as he looked over his shoulder at his little daughter sitting in the backseat next to her grandmother, his mother. He forced a smile through his worry in the rear view mirror at his little girl. He could see the anxiety on her little face. Tiny Sarah forced her own little smile out to match his. God his little girl looked just like her mother. It was uncanny.

His mom was barely keeping it together sitting next to her. Just fifteen minutes ago when he scooped them up from their day out at the Butterfly Museum he'd pulled her aside and told her there had been an incident at his father's gun store. Her husband, his dad, had been bitten by a child infected with some strange disease, and he'd died. He didn't tell her the child had been dead when he bit her husband, and he didn't tell her that his dad had been shot in the head by Phil, his father's best friend. It was the only way to stop them. To stop the dead from returning to life.

Once again the line came back to him, deep inside his head, "The world had come undone."

The dead weren't staying dead, the living was going insane with panic and no matter how Chief Moore tried to rationalize it, he came back to the same thing. The world had come undone. It was as simple as that. No other words made any sense when he thought about it.

His mother had a tissue in her hand and steadily raised it over and over to dab away the tears welling in her eyes. Her husband had always been at risk of getting killed. Before her son was Chief his father was the Chief, and getting hurt as a cop was part and parcel with the job. When he retired from the force and opened the gun store she'd thought all that danger had finally walked out of their life. Apparently not. It was somewhat fortunate that she she'd built such a thick skin over the years, all the late nights waiting for that phone call had given her some resiliency. She knew it'd set back in someday soon, maybe tomorrow she thought.

The Chief had called his wife about an hour prior and told her what was going on. Just like with his mother he didn't tell her the whole story. Chief Brian Moore went into work early every day. It was his personal oath that if you weren't early, you couldn't be on time. His morning started off shitty and had only gotten worse. He said good morning to his two dispatchers and gave his day shift guys a standard issue pep talk before they headed out. His email inbox was four inches deep with an assortment of federal and state notifications plus the fax machine had emptied its paper tray printing out incoming alerts. He refilled the fax, got his morning coffee, and sat down to go through everything that had come in.

They all cycled through a steady escalation of events. The first and oldest messages warned of strange behavior overseas. As he sat at his desk, flipping from one warning to the next, the warnings got steadily worse, and closer to home. Violence in Africa overnight turned into sickness by morning. Violence in Europe and Middle East in the morning turned into sickness by midday. Violence in midday in Asia and South America turned into sickness by afternoon. The same pattern had started here in the states at early morning.

The briefings that started to roll in at about 7am sounded like jokes. Brian actually looked at his calendar to make sure it wasn't April Fool's Day. There had been dozens of fatal car accidents, work accidents, and fairly mundane crimes all over the country resulting in mob violence shortly thereafter. Keeping with the pattern, there were outbreaks of fatal fevers in the same cities shortly afterwards. At noon the CDC issued a broadcast saying the violence seemed to be linked to the sickness, but without any samples to test, they were unsure. They were strictly speculating to government and state agencies at that point.

It escalated dramatically at 10am or so. The FBI and ATF started sending out much more serious messages and the State Police started to issue local alerts as well. They were setting up road blocks at the borders to screen for illness, and almost immediately they started to have trouble at them. The State Health Department started to send out warnings about people who had been bitten, or appearing ill. Any sickness at all should be treated as deadly serious, and the ill should be brought for medical attention immediately. The CDC and Department of Homeland Security were apparently in full panic mode. The news had absolutely lit up with footage of violence and video of hospitals overflowing with the sick, and the people who thought they were sick. The violent people looked wrong on the television. Brian couldn't think of it any other way. They walked funny, moved stilted and stiff, and attacked anything that moved with a primeval, animal instinct. It was almost like rabies. Well, if rabies killed you and brought you back to life as a lunatic cannibal he thought.

From 10am to 2pm earlier that day Chief Moore had his five patrolmen on heavy duty traffic enforcement. Brian instructed them to pull over every single vehicle exceeding the speed limit, or doing anything even remotely sketchy on the roads. He felt that if he could prevent some of the car accidents or arguments he might just be able to prevent any of the bizarre violence gripping the rest of the world. Plus, the more people his officers saw that day, the more likely they'd be to see someone acting funny, or showing signs of being sick.

At 2pm his personal cell phone rang. His father was calling, and he needed help at his gun shop. Apparently the crowd was getting a little too large for his liking, and he wanted to know if Brian could spare an officer to park in the lot and help maintain order. Without a second thought he radioed for his largest officer, Danny McGreevy to head over. Danny was a solid six foot three or so, and easily put up 2 and half bills. His bald head and dark sunglasses was usually enough to enforce the law without a gun or a badge. He sent Danny over to the shop immediately.

It wasn't 20 minutes after that when he got the call from up on high. The shit was officially in the fan and flying. The FBI and ATF considered the situation volatile enough that they felt weapons needed to be made more available to the public. They had suspended the need for background checks. All gun sales were subject to local preference. It was his call to decide who got a gun and when. Unbelievable.

At about the same time, the federal government issued several notices suggesting that many major metropolitan governments should consider martial law, and that all medical grounds should be quarantined to help prevent the spread of any dangerous pathogens. It was official; the wheels had come off the world.

He called for Danny at the gun shop so he could talk to his father about the suspension of background checks. He told his dad the story, and they decided that his father and his employees would make the call. That seemed really sensible for Brian. There was no one he trusted more in the world than his father. After he and his dad made their plan, he told Danny to put down anyone bitten, or anyone who was visibly sick or hurt. His other officers chimed in after that to make sure his orders were correct. Shoot anyone hurt and unresponsive. They couldn't risk contamination.

After he had gotten done sorting out all the worst case scenario plans in his head, he got the call over the radio about the shooting at the gun shop. Brian had been in some pretty shitty spots during his career as an officer of the law, but nothing hit him quite like hearing Danny McGreevy call out an officer involved shooting at his father's place of business. The Chief's guts twisted up in a knot and his hands got all clammy as he sat there at his desk. It took him a few minutes to shake the cobwebs out of his brain. As soon as he did he jumped into action.

Brian got in his cruiser and pulled out of the town's municipal complex right behind the ambulance that was responding to the same call. The two vehicles flew through town getting to the shop. When they were halfway to his father's store another 911 dispatch call came out saying there was a dead body laying in the parking lot of one of the condo complexes in town. Apparently a gunshot wound to the head. Brian distinctly knew when that second call came out that he no longer had the time to plan to prevent anything. Whatever it was that was covering the world in panic and violence had reached his town. They were past prevention already, and were dealing with fallout.

The events at the shop were still fuzzy for him. He actually hoped the memories never became clear. He remembered the dead man in the parking lot, and Danny explaining why he shot him. After that it got messy in his head. He remembers the little kid. Donny? Danny? Mikey? Who knows now? If the world survived until next week he'd worry about the kid's name then. He remembered the kid taking off his jacket after sharing the story of the bloodbath at the hospital he and his father had just left. The kid was bloodied under the jacket, and told the paramedics he'd been bitten. Ten seconds later the little boy began convulsing, and dropped dead.

The paramedics worked on him, and somewhere along the line he came back to life, and they got bitten. Guns were drawn, the young boy was shot, and somehow his dad was bitten during the fracas too. Brian couldn't remember much after that; just that his man McGreevy called out for additional assistance, and nothing came back over the radio. Something else bad must've been happening.

His dad knew it was over for him though. They knew the bites infected. They'd just seen the bites infect first hand, and his father knew. Brian couldn't bear to watch though, and after saying his tearful goodbyes, he left. As he closed the cruiser door and started to drive away from the gun store, he heard a single gunshot, and the Chief knew his father was dead.

Brian drove for a few miles until he was almost back at the station. He kept thinking over and over about how he would break this to his mother, and his two kids. Then Brian realized that he needed to find out where his family was. He radioed out to his officers to let them know things had finally reached town. All of them were in the middle of dealing with developing problems. Fender benders, a couple 911 calls for injuries and sickness, and one of his officers was headed to the scene of the dead body at the condo complex. The state hadn't responded to any of his dispatcher's calls for assistance regarding the body either, which meant they were up to their own eyeballs with major crimes as well.

Brian made a decision and cut his men loose. This was no longer about maintaining law and order. In less than 30 minutes he'd had five fatal shootings in a 3 mile radius. They had families to take care of, and in order for them to do that, they needed to get home, and get their kids and wives safe. He told them to wrap up what they were doing, and get the hell home.

He called his wife Stacey right after that. They didn't talk for long. He told her about what happened at the gun shop, and he told her about whatever was happening across the world. He told her this could legitimately be the end of the world, and they had to get home, and get it safe. He cried when he hung up with her. He knew this would get much worse before it got better, he just didn't realize how much worse, and how fast it would get that way.

*****

In the hour Chief Moore was out of town picking up his mother and daughter from the Butterfly Museum, things had changed for the worse. It was like a faucet that had been slowly dripping pure panic had been opened until raw unadulterated lunacy was pouring out. Cars were running red lights right in front of him, and he could see houses either already fully boarded up, or being boarded up everywhere he looked. Reminded him of the hours right before an impending hurricane along the Gulf Coast. Businesses were putting up closed signs, and every gas station had a line of cars out into the street. One hour had passed, and everyone had lost their minds.

Chief Moore stopped at the municipal center where the police station and fire department was headquartered. He hit the automatic garage opener and drove his cruiser directly inside the station's booking area. It was a godsend during shitty weather, or when the media was sitting there to be able to stay in the vehicle until it was behind closed doors. Today he was happy because it meant he could get his daughter and mother into a secured area and feel safe about leaving them in his squad car.

Brian told his mother and daughter he'd be right back, and left them in the back of his cruiser. He went to the heavy duty station door and swiped his access card on the reader. With a curt beep the locks opened, and he pulled the door open with a tug. Once he was out of the line of sight of his family, he drew his sidearm. No sense risking his life, even here in the supposed safety of the police station.

Brian went room to room and checked for signs of life. No one was there. He had no desk officers on duty today; everyone was out and about already. His two dispatchers were long since history, having left when he issued his "go home" message earlier. Half drank cups of coffee sat on their coasters on their desks right next to half eaten granola bars. There was a donut too. Brian touched the coffee cups and they were still warm to the touch. Lights all across the 911 board were lit up. On the dispatch monitors there were dozens of emergency calls coming in from the state level, and there was no one left to send out to help these people.

Sitting in the center of Danny McGreevy's desk was his already filled out Incident Report form. He must've come straight here and filled it out before he took off for the day. Brian thumbed through the few sheets of paper and nodded in agreement with how it was written. Damn fine cop.

Two hours ago his town was normal and now it had all but fallen in on itself. He holstered his handgun and rubbed his eyes. They were dry and stinging from a lack of blinking. Brian hadn't closed them out of fear he'd miss some danger in this new, weird world. Once he got the shit rubbed out of his eyes he reasserted his plan in his head and went about his business.

In the arms locker adjacent to his office he grabbed two of the station's four M4 assault rifles. He also grabbed one of the police riot shotguns and a spare Kevlar vest. One of the heavy duty gear bags got stuffed with the weapons and he tossed in six spare magazines and about a dozen boxes of ammunition. He also grabbed three of the Motorola radios his officers used to communicate with each other.

Brian dropped the bag of weapons right next to the door leading to the intake area and checked on his family. His mother was entertaining his daughter and all seemed well. He ran across the indoor garage to the opposite side, and swiped his card on the access door for the fire station side.

He tugged that door open and walked in. Immediately his foot slid out from under him on a slick spot on the linoleum floor. He reached out and grabbed the walls to prevent a horrible split that could've wrecked any chance he had for increasing the size of his family in the future.

"Jumping Jesu-" Brian looked down at the floor and saw the enormous congealed pool of blood. It had formed a thick skin but when his foot planted in it, the skin had torn and revealed the dark red grease below. He'd nearly gone down in literal bloodbath. That amount of blood meant a dead body. No one could bleed a patch that big and make it. Brian steadied himself and slid his Glock 21 out of its holster again.

He took a few slow steps down the hallway leading into the fire station's lunchroom before he announced himself, "Police! Anyone in this building needs to identify themselves immediately!"

He waited a few seconds and listened, his finger poised like a snake stretched out next to the trigger. It was a few seconds before he heard the scuffing of feet being dragged on the floor from somewhere ahead of him. It was dark in the fire house. No windows reached this interior room, and only a few small fluorescent bulbs shed any light. The noise was coming from one of the gear rooms he had intended to get inside of. He had come for medical supplies, and they were in the room the noise was coming from.

Brian barked again, "This is Chief Moore! Show me hands or you will be shot!"

No response, just a few more scuffs on the floor. His heart skipped a beat when he heard a tremendous crash to the floor from the room. The noise forced his hand, and without waiting any longer he strode into the kitchen and rounded the corner to the left to see what was happening in the room.

He took the corner tight, showing the muzzle of his .45 caliber pistol to the noise before he walked out into the open. He took a half step to the side and was immediately hit by a raw, visceral odor that made his stomach and bowels turn inside out. His brain didn't have the time to register the man standing in front of him before he was forced to dry heave. Instinctively Brian backpedaled in the nick of time as the man lunged at him. Fortunately Brian had the presence of mind to double tap his trigger finger, sending two heavy slugs into the form coming his way. The two gunshots were louder than he could've imagined in the concrete room as his back hit the hallway wall and his brain caught up to what was happening.

His two gunshots had sent the man coming at him backwards several feet into the wall of the kitchen. Brian knew immediately it was Carl, one of the lifer firemen in town. He was pushing 50, and was a solid concrete block worth of belly fat overweight, but the man was a good fireman, and knew his shit. Without even realizing what was going on Brian started talking out loud to Carl.

"Carl what the fuck man?!" And then he saw what had happened to Carl. Carl's copious Pabst Blue Ribbon fed beer belly had been slashed open somehow leaving a hole that resembled a twisted grin. From hip to hip he had ragged opening that had set free his innards. Carl was pushing himself off the wall towards Brian awkwardly as his feet stepped directly onto ropes of his own intestines. The pink and purple guts snapped and popped open under his girth and spewed all manner of food and fecal matter onto the smooth floor. Brian's whole world came to an abrupt stop as his rational mind tried to find an explanation for how Carl was still upright after not only being mysteriously gutted, but after having taken two pistol rounds directly to the sternum.

Carl's eyes were glossed over and turning a hazy white color. His lips curled back in a silent snarl and he took another awkward, crushing step on his own guts toward the Chief. Brian shook his head quickly, raised the Glock and squeezed one more round off, smashing Carl's forehead inward, and sending the contents of his skull all over the white concrete blocks behind him. His lifeless body collapsed down onto its knee's further crushing his own insides into a wretched paste.

Brian emptied the contents of his own stomach onto the table in the middle of the kitchen. He hadn't eaten much that day, but the half dozen cups of coffee came out as forceful bile, knocking paper plates and cups off the table and onto the floor. After a dozen convulsions his stomach tapped out, and he wiped his mouth on his sleeve.

The world had come undone.

He held his breath and stepped around Carl into the stockroom. He grabbed one of the bright red paramedic bags that was already stocked up and ready to go. He snagged an empty red bag off a shelf and stuffed it with as many first aid supplies as he could. There was a surprising amount of usable medical supplies, and he didn't want to risk visiting a hospital after hearing the boy's story at his father's gun store earlier that day. The little boy had lost his whole family at a hospital to this madness, and Brian didn't want to be anywhere near sick people.

Once he'd stuffed the second bag as full as he could get it, he exited the room and quietly let himself out of the fire station and into the indoor garage. His mother was standing outside the cruiser, shaking, staring at the door he'd just come through.

"Mom, are you okay?" Brian asked her as he used his keys to pop the cruiser's trunk.

"I… I heard… shooting. I thought you might've been hurt." She had that napkin again, and her eyes were flush with redness. She'd been crying again.

Brian loaded the two paramedic bags into the trunk and walked over to the police station door to retrieve the bag filled with weapons and ammo. "There was another sick person in the firehouse mom. I had to shoot them after they tried to hurt me." He tried to say it in as neutral a tone as possible. He wanted to dismiss the notion of the true danger.

"Are they dead Brian? Did you kill them?" Her voice

wavered as she asked.

Brian dropped the heavy gun bag into the trunk and stopped to think about his answer. After a long pause he finally replied to her, "Mom, I'm not sure how to answer you. I think they were already dead when I shot them, but they were still moving around." He shook his head in amazement at what he was saying.

Brian's mother cocked her head to the side, clearly not quite understanding him. But she was used to not understanding policemen. They never told the whole story, even if you asked for it. She nodded thoughtfully and conceded the debate. She was happy her son was still alive.

"Let's get moving. If we head to Stacey and I's place we can get inside and lay low while all this blows over. After a day or two we can head north in the truck and maybe hit Uncle Mike's place up. That cabin of his is pretty secluded and he has those solar panels if the electricity winds up dying out." Brian walked around to the front door of the cruiser as he talked to his mom. She opened the back door and got in, sitting next to little Sarah, who had fallen fast asleep, despite the noise from Brian's gun play.

With a twist of the wrist the cruiser's powerful interceptor engine roared to life. Brian looked into the backseat and saw his daughter's angelic little face. She was just four years old, and he desperately wanted to protect her from the horror that he knew was right outside, right around the corner. Brian hit the garage door opener and backed the cruiser out. It was clear of danger in the parking lot of the municipal building, and he spun the car around and headed out. When he exited the lot on the other side of the building he saw one of the town's ambulances parked half on the grass. He looked at the plate and did some memory retrieval.

The ambulance was likely the one Carl had been assigned to for the day. The driver's side door was wide open and Brian could see streaks of the brownish red blood leading all the way from the van straight up the sidewalk and into the fire station's front door. Carl must've been hurt somewhere else, and came back here to try and fix himself up or get help. Shitty way to go, Brian realized, bleeding out after getting gutted. Poor bastard he thought.

Brian pulled the cruiser out into the street and drove with the emergency blue lights on. He kept his finger on the tab for the siren should he need it. Cars whipped by at dangerous speeds on the side streets as he made his way towards Main Street to head to his house. He only had maybe a two mile drive, but it felt like he was driving through a terrible dream.

More houses all boarded up everywhere he looked. Those homes that were not boarded up had cars frantically being packed in their yards. People carrying out suitcases of clothes, and boxes filled with food. Picture frames, books, and lockboxes filled with important paperwork were all being taken. Brian couldn't help to wonder how the mob mentality would ruin everyone's chances at a safe escape to more rural areas. Shit, this town was pretty rural, you couldn't much more rural.

As he drove into the more commercial area of Main Street he saw a complete nightmare at the grocery store. Cars parked in total disarray, blocking all the fire lanes. He saw people running in both directions in the parking lot. People running into the store to get whatever was left, and people running out of the store with carts filled with likely stolen food. The cop inside the Chief's head had to fight an epic battle with his paternal instinct to not drive into the lot with his siren blaring to establish law and order.

But he knew it was too late for that. With just one body he'd get shot by some desperate asshole, or beaten to death by a mob of people panicking, trying to get what they thought would be their last meal. He had no support from the state police either. His only option at this point was to make his family safe, and wait for the government to sort this out. Once he had reinforcements, he'd worry about enforcing the laws on the books. Brian shook his head in utter disbelief and made the right hand turn towards his house.

He drove the two miles up the hill on Dove Street at a good magazine, keeping constant watch for the erratic drivers going in both ways. One of the cars passing him flashed their lights at him, and he slowed to a stop as they flagged him down. Brian thumbed the catch on his pistol's holster as he powered down his driver's side window. The man in the midsize sedan looked like he'd seen a ghost when Brian got close.

"Chief there's a terrible accident ahead. Head on collision between a truck and an SUV. I think some of the folks didn't make it." He shook his head the whole time back and forth; enhancing the negativity and shock he was feeling.

Brian's stomach lurched when he registered what the man said. His wife drove an SUV. "Sir you recall the makes or colors of the vehicles?" Brian asked as straight faced as he could, trying to hide his growing fear.

The driver took a deep, pained breath and thought hard before he replied, "I think the truck was a big green import, and the SUV was a Ford or something. Red I think."

Brian swallowed. His wife drove a burgundy Ford Escape. He couldn't manage any words and just nodded at the man and punched the accelerator. He hit the siren and they screamed up the rest of the hill on Dove Street until they came to the intersection where he came up on the accident. He didn't need to get close to know it was her car.

"Oh God dear…" His mother could see the vehicle ahead, and knew instantly who it belonged to. She reached up and rested her hand reassuringly on Brian's shoulder. Her touch helped calm him some, but he had a knot in his stomach made of anxiety and nothing she could do would make it go away.

Brian killed the siren and pulled his cruiser over, stopping a good 20 feet behind his wife's wrecked car. He sat with both hands on the steering wheel, building up the courage to get out of the cruiser and go look at what he had to see with his own eyes. From the backseat he heard the soft whimper that indicated his little girl Sarah was about to start crying. He turned instantly and looked at her. Her big blue eyes looked at him in confusion and fear. She had been watching him and knew he was scared. When daddy was scared, little Sarah was scared. He felt guilty that his fear had scared his daughter. He reached into the back and put a smile on his face. He reassured her and rubbed her little leg and his mother wrapped an arm around her.

"Baby girl don't be afraid. Daddy is just a little scared that someone got hurt in the accident okay?" His lip trembled into a near sob as he finished. His words helped her though. Sarah nodded emphatically in agreement. Brian thought she did it to fight away the scary feelings. Brian smiled again and gave his mother a knowing look. She knew what he had to do.

Brian turned himself around and got out of the car. He looked both ways up and down the residential street and saw it was clear. He shut the door of the cruiser and slid his handgun out of the holster. Impulsively he dropped the magazine into his hand and made sure he had at least 5 or 6 bullets in it, which he did. He clicked the magazine back into the pistol and walked slowly to the driver's side of his wife's vehicle.

When he got five feet away he could see the bumper of the giant green truck had hit the top of the hood of his wife's car, driving it backwards into the dashboard. The front crumple zones had collapsed entirely, and the driver's side door was wrenched partially off the hinges, hanging down to the ground, wide open. He could see inside the car on the grey upholstery streaks of blood. Thick, long streaks of blood that meant a bad injury had occurred. An injury to his wife Stacey.

Brain took a bit of a wide circle to approach her door. A few more steps showed him his wife was gone, which gave him a surge of hope. Perhaps she'd gotten Tommy out of the back seat and walked home? Maybe she just had a cut on her head and it bled a lot? Brian moved into the door of the SUV and heard a pleading yelp from the backseat. He'd heard it a hundred times before. It was his son Tommy.

Without a moment's hesitation the chief launched himself at the rear driver's side door and ripped it open. Inside on the child's seat was his six year old boy Tommy. Tommy was mostly asleep, or in a daze, but he was alive, and didn't look injured. Tommy was more scared at his father's desperate hugs than he was at the situation he was in. Brian went head to toe on his son checking for injuries but found none. He planted a massive kiss on his boy's forehead and looked him in the eye with more sincere love than he ever had.

"Tommy, where is your mother? Did she leave the car?" Brian asked quietly.

Tommy looked in the front seat of the SUV and Brian could see the moment of confusion as his boy realized his mommy was missing. Brian watched his boy's eyes puff up with tears. He shook his head and replied back to his dad, "I dunno dad. I don't 'member what happened." He had no idea. Brian thought he might've been knocked out by the head on collision. He looked around in the truck and saw the contents of his wife's purse strewn all about the front seat. The back trunk area of the SUV had bags and bags of food that she must've just bought at the madhouse grocery store Brian just drove by. He suddenly felt guilty for asking her to brave that store.

Brian debated what to do next and undid the straps on Tommy's car seat. He picked Tommy up and carried him back towards the cruiser. He got maybe five feet away from the car when he heard a loud thunking noise from the wreck behind him. In one fluid motion he spun and drew his Glock, aiming at the intersection of the two crushed vehicles and putting his body between the noise and his boy.

He regretted turning immediately. Sitting, pinned from the looks of it in the front seat of the big green truck was the driver. His face and neck had been torn apart in the collision and he was silently clawing at the shattered windshield at the two of them. Brian leveled the green dot on his gun's front sight at the chest of the man until he realized he needed medical attention.

"Hold on man, I'll be right there!" Brian hollered. He put the Glock away and started back towards his patrol car. His mother got out of the backseat as he approached and reached up to take little Tommy from him.

"Ma, Stacey's not in the car. She must've gotten out and walked home, or walked away. The driver needs help in the truck too. I'm gonna go help him as best I can, and then grab the groceries she bought. Stay in the car." He handed Tommy to her as he spoke, and she nodded in agreement. The grandmother and grandson got into the backseat again and the door shut. Brian popped the trunk of his car and grabbed one of the bright red paramedic bags. He jogged back around his wife's truck on the passenger side and came directly at the driver.

He stopped when he reached the two smashed hoods. Brian could see something was very, very wrong with the man. His skin was an ashen blue color, as if all the life had drained out of him. The few homicides and deaths he'd experienced immediately jumped to mind. He was brought back to the look of Carl, the firemen he'd just killed. He thought also of the little boy at his father's shop that had died, and somehow reanimated after, attacking his father.

The driver of the truck was dead. There could be no mistaking it. His throat was missing. Brian could see the torn open trachea and sundered muscles, arteries and veins. No more blood ran down his shirt, and if he was alive, he should've been spurting it across the windshield. Brian switched the paramedic bag to his left hand and pulled out his pistol again. In the back of his mind he had a dim realization that he'd drawn his weapon more times in the last few hours than he had in his entire tenure as Chief. Possibly more times than in his entire police career.

As he circled the dead driver's door he noticed bloody

hand prints on the frame of the door. They were about chest height, and were clearly red handprints belonging to a woman. He looked carefully at the crimson smudges and pieced it together. A woman, obviously bloodied, had grabbed the door of the truck and pulled it open. Maybe it was Stacey trying to help the man? Maybe Stacey had died and killed this man? Maybe she was bitten by this guy as she tried to help? Brian was just a cop though, not a psychic. He couldn't be bothered to solve this crime right now; he had bigger fish to fry. As he stared at the blood evidence the driver continued to wave his arms maniacally at him, clawing and gnashing his teeth in a silent rage.

He watched the man passively, and assessed his condition. Professionally, Brian decided this man was fucked. Completely fucked. His face, throat and chest were destroyed. The truck's dashboard was oppressively crushing both his legs. Poking out the bottom of the doorframe Brian could see a mangled, twisted leg with the foot dangling off it. The man couldn't escape the car, which was comforting. Brian stood there watching the dead driver try to get at him. Ripping and tearing at the air between them repeatedly. Eventually Brian raised his gun and put the green dot on the driver's chest, right where the heart was. He gave the pistol's trigger a gentle squeeze and sent one round into the man's chest. A fine puff of blood jumped out the hole the bullet punched in the man. His dead body flung backwards into the bench seat of the truck, and he went motionless for a moment. However, another moment later he swiveled himself upright again, and turned back towards Brian. He resumed his relentless scratching and clawing immediately. The shot had no lethal effect. Only head shots counted now.

Without even realizing it, Brian re-aimed the Glock and squeezed out one more round, sending the second heavy .45 slug barreling into the destroyed face of the driver. His skull imploded as the lead missile tore its way through the head. This time the driver flung sideways and stayed that way. Brian stared at the dead body for a long minute, eventually turning to look at the crash scene as a whole. Absently he holstered the pistol. Two items caught his attention suddenly.

First he noticed bloody footprints on the pavement that led off in the direction of his house, up Hill Street. They were small prints, one with a shoe, one without a shoe. They obviously were female. As he turned to walk back to his cruiser he noticed the second thing. The truck had clearly crossed into his wife's lane, causing the accident.

Brian suddenly felt very good about killing the driver. Even if he was already dead.

*****

Brian pulled the cruiser past the car wreck after he loaded all the groceries into the now packed trunk of his car. In the backseat his little boy Tommy was sandwiched between Sarah and Brian's mother. By now there was no hiding the anguish on his mother's face. She looked out the window at the passing trees and houses with a quivering chin. She held strong against the tears, but he could tell it was killing her on the inside.

Brian was relieved that he now had his two precious children with him. Now his worry was reserved for his wife. He made the turn onto Hill Street and idled the cruiser up the street at barely 10 miles an hour. Hill Street was a reasonably affluent neighborhood in town, and the houses there reflected it. Each was set back in a perfectly manicured lawn, with perfectly manicured hedges, and driveways edged with perfectly symmetrical artistic bricks. He hated this neighborhood with a passion, but it had good resale value, and it was safe for his kids.

He looked side to side at the houses as he passed them. Most of the houses had no visible activity. That made sense to him after all, most of the people who could afford these homes commuted into the city to their jobs, and they were likely stuck in traffic coming back from there, or dead already. He couldn't even imagine how bad the city was by now. He had a nightmare on his hands with just 8,000 people, let alone 150,000.

He leaned forward in his seat and tried to pick up the trail of bloody footprints on the pavement. After perhaps 50 feet the trail disappeared. No more blood on the feet to leave behind. He frowned and continued down the road slowly, eventually coming to a stop when he saw two bodies laying half on the sidewalk, and half on one of the manicured lawns. The house they were in front of was a massive white colonial much like his own, and from memory he recalled it belonged to a couple retired college professors. He thought their name was Douglas. Or the Dougles. Brian didn't know most of the people who obeyed the laws in his town. He did however know all the assholes firsthand. The two bodies in the road were clearly the residents of the house, whatever their last names were. Both were wearing bathrobes, and both were spilling out unacceptably large pools of blood.

Brian stopped the cruiser 20 odd feet from them and got out. He looked back at his mother and nodded at her to wait. She clutched the two kids close to her and nodded back. Brian shut the door and drew the Glock yet again. He'd gotten no more than five steps when the elderly male sat straight up with a jerk. He stared at Brian with a strange, vacant intensity. It looked almost as if he'd been possessed by pure hatred. The old man was scratched deeply and had bite wounds all over his arms and shoulders. He almost looked polka dotted from the blood soaking through his yellow bathrobe.

The old balding man got to his feet on stiff legs. Brian could see the entire back of the yellow bathrobe was soaked dark red from blood. His wrinkly skin slid across his bones and revealed the true depth of the wounds on his shoulders. Tendons, muscles, sinews and bone were all visible in various deep bite wounds. They were small bite wounds as well. Brian realized he was in a trance himself as the old man shuffled across the street at him, dragging his feet and raising his arms as if preparing to choke Brian. He raised the gun and squeezed off a couple rounds at his head, sending the man back to the hard concrete sidewalk, killing him permanently.

No sooner had the old man stopped twitching his wife began to roll around, trying to get to her feet the same as her husband. She was much worse off than her husband, and Brian was starting to lose his mind.

"What the fuck is going on?!" Brian screamed at the sky, pleading for some divine response explaining why everything had gone to shit. There was no reply from above, just bright blue sky and a few clouds floating obliviously by. His rage started to boil and he stomped across the street and emptied the pistol into his neighbor's dead body. She tossed around the sidewalk to and fro as the heavy pistol slugs tore their way through her. Eventually one of the rounds destroyed her brain and Brian's finger clicked back an empty trigger. He screamed in frustration once more and stormed back to the cruiser, replacing his empty magazine as he went.

He made eye contact with his mother and her expression scared him. She was afraid of him. His rage had struck a chord with her. All his color drained away and he stopped dead in the street, suddenly realizing he'd lost control. His mother's eyes let loose another barrage of tears and she looked away, ashamed and frightened of her son. Brian's heart broke as he came to grips with what he'd just done. He was a man of the law, not a raging, gun toting lunatic. A few deep breaths later he put the pistol away and got back in the car. Everyone sat in awkward silence as Brian gathered his thoughts a bit more. After a minute he put the car in drive and pulled out, heading towards his house.

He only had a few houses to go before he pulled into his own driveway. Stacey and he owned a big colonial with a two car garage attached. They'd gotten a great deal on it years ago when the economy started to tank and he'd been promoted to Chief. Stacey had a small inheritance from her grandparents and they'd been saving for a very long time. The mortgage was a little tough on them at first, but the house was amazing. It also helped that his dad knew just about everyone in town, so when something broke, they always got a five finger discount on getting it fixed. Being Chief of Police in a small town has some benefits Brian supposed.

He stopped the cruiser in his inclined driveway just short of the garage doors and put it in park. It took him a few more seconds to build up the nerve to talk again.

"Mom, I'm thinking Stacey came home after the accident. She might be hurt, so I'm gonna go see if she's here. I'll be back in a few minutes. Stay in the car." He spoke in a hushed monotone, trying to not get his kids riled up or scared. His mother mumbled a fearful, quiet "okay" and he got out.

For no reason he could tell he dropped his magazine out of the pistol and made sure it was full. His mind started to race and his guts started to turn as he walked across his yard on the brick walkway towards his big front door. His three front steps were more bricks arranged in a half circle. The masonry people did a wonderful job on the steps and every time he came home he marveled at how symmetrical the steps were. They were perfectly radial, level and exactly as he wanted. Brian noticed the bloody scuff marks on his brick steps.

He stopped short and examined the door. All over the front of the white oak were long streaks of blood. Full hand prints were all over the frame and door handle as well. It looked like someone had tried to beat their way in and busted their hands open in the process. The door was still shut though, and Brian noticed a few bloody swathes on his own perfectly trimmed green hedges. They looked to be heading around the garage and towards the back.

Brian followed the bloody marks on the bushes until they disappeared. He walked in front of his cruiser and glanced at it, checking again to see if everything inside was still fine. The kids looked nervous, and his mother the same, but they were fine. He gritted his teeth and scanned the street for danger. It was odd to him how quiet it was. There should've been at least a few kids riding bikes or playing in the street. But now, there was nothing. Dead silence. Even the birds seemed to be gone.

Brian swallowed hard and took the corner of the garage, heading down the narrow space between his thick hedges and the garage's siding. It was much cooler in the shade there, and he suddenly realized how warm it had been all day. He wiped away the sweat he hadn't noticed earlier with his free hand and slowly walked out into the backyard. His above ground pool filter chugged away, circulating the blue summer salvation inside itself. He had a sudden urge to dive over the side of the pool to cool himself but fought it off. The tall hedges were about his height and surrounded the perimeter of his property. His white shed sat in the far back right corner of his yard, and he walked towards that to check on his dog Scotty.

Brian suddenly realized his dog wasn't barking. Fuck, he thought. He started moving much faster towards the dog run in the back of the yard. The dog house was just around the edge of the shed he thought. He came wide and saw his precious beagle torn limb from limb. Scotty the dog was on his side, tongue hanging out of his jaw on the dirt near his doghouse. Brian dropped down to his knees as the tears started streaming down his face. His stomach convulsed with silent sobs as he tried desperately to contain his emotions over his canine buddy. He wiped the tears away and tried to find his dog's missing front legs, but they were nowhere to be found. For some reason this infuriated him, not being able to find the legs.

The emotionally wounded man let out a small sob as he sat back on his feet and stared up at the sky again. Once more he drew a sleeve across his eyes to wipe moisture away. When he looked back in the yard he saw a tear in the hedges separating his yard from his neighbor's. Whatever had killed Scotty barreled through his hedge fence and onto his neighbor's property. Brian grunted and got up from the ground, stroking his dead pet's head as he moved with ferocity towards the giant hole in his bushes. He turned sideways and slid his large frame through the hole, scraping his hands and face on the rough branches. He got most of his body into his neighbor's yard when he saw a distant figure move at the edge of his field of vision. An adult figure had walked around the end of his hedge fence near the street, and back into his driveway. They were no more than 15 feet from his cruiser, and his two children.

Brian panicked. He threw his body back through the fence recklessly and into his yard again. At full speed he leapt over Scotty's rigid carcass and hurtled past his pool to slip through the space next to his garage again. Dimly he could hear a thumping noise coming from the driveway as he got closer. Within seconds Brian burst around the corner of the garage and right into his own personal nightmare.

Standing next to his cruiser, slowly and methodically raining blows down on the back seat windows was his wife. Or what used to be his wife. Her tiny frame was bent funny in the middle of her torso, like her ribs or spine was shattered. He could see in her profile that her face had been devastated in the accident. Her lips hung off her face in tatters and her nose had been smashed almost flat. It was a morbid mockery of the mother of his two children. And it was trying to get in the cruiser at them. He noticed with sickness that one of her shoes was missing.

Brian had no emotion left to feel bad for her. He was still furious over his dog's death, and as he watched his mother scream in fear at his dead wife he was empty. All he had left inside him was anger.

"Stacey! Get away from the kids!" He screamed at the top of his lungs. His wife stopped her hammering on the glass and snapped sideways to face him. When he saw her full in the face he knew it wasn't her any longer. Her eyes were yellowish and hazy. They had lost all their life, lurching to and fro in her eye sockets as she stumbled her way towards him. She lost her balance and sidestepped a few times before she balanced and continued forward. Brian looked over Stacey's shoulder at his mother and made eye contact. His mom pulled the two kids into her and shielded them. Brian looked back at his wife and started to slowly back up, moving into the tight alley of the garage and hedges.

Together the living husband and dead wife moved into the backyard. Brian had his teeth clenched as he watched the lady he loved hungrily pursue him. She didn't have enough strength or coordination to close the gap between the two of them, and for that he was thankful. Once he was fully into the yard and had ten feet of space he stopped backing up. She kept moving forward.

"I'm sorry baby."

One squeeze of his trigger finger later Brian Moore was a widower.

*****

Brian got the patrol car into the garage and ushered his two children and mother into the house. He asked his mom to get them something to eat and drink while he poured himself a double of a really nice single malt Scotch. He sat in the living room and stared at the giant flat screen hanging above the fireplace mantle. He didn't even turn it on. He already knew what he'd see, assuming the television was even still working. He sipped the warm Scotch and tried to assemble a plan.

He grabbed his cell phone out of his pocket and dialed McGreevy's number. It came back with the all circuits busy message. Not good at all. He tried two more of his officers and the result was the same. All lines busy. He sat the glass of Scotch down and tried to send a text message to another one of his guys, but it hung up on the sending screen. He tossed the phone on the couch next to him and laughed. Two hours. Two hours ago he had everything under control, and now everything had come undone.

The whole world unraveled in two hours in his town. He hung his head and thought some more. He reached up to his collar and thumbed his radio. "Any officers still have their radios on?"

Silence for a few seconds, then a reply, "Chief is that you? This is Harper."

Brian smiled, happy to hear that at least one of his officers was still nearby and alive. "Hey Al. You okay? You and Martha all set?" Brian sipped his Scotch again, savoring the smooth smoky finish.

"Shit yeah Chief. We just got ourselves set up at Martha's work." Al Harper sounded pretty confident to Brian, and that intrigued him. "How are you and Stacey? The kids okay? I heard about your dad sir, I'm real sorry."

Brian thought about his answer before he thumbed the radio. He couldn't think of a professional way to say it, so he just blurted it out, "Stacey's dead. She killed a guy in a truck, and then killed my dog. She was trying to kill my kids Al. I shot her."

No response came back from Al. Brian laughed again at the whole situation and tipped the glass of Scotch up until it all slid down his throat. He let the burn in his throat and belly distract him from the day's events. After a few seconds Al finally replied, "Shit Brian."

"Yeah Al…. Shit." Brian reached back and hurled the empty Scotch glass into his flat screen television. It embedded in the black screen like a hockey puck. Two thousand bucks down the drain.

"Chief what're you gonna do? Stay at your house until this blows over? You know you should come here, stay with us. There's a lot of us here already, and we could use you," Al pleaded to his boss.

"Where are you guys? Martha's work? Where does she work?" Brian couldn't remember. Maybe the Scotch was hitting him a little hard.

"She works at STIG. The solar panel company downtown. They're in the industrial complex off Tucker

Drive. They've got a cafeteria here that's all stocked, and they've got power from the panels they make. It's a green company, they can last for months and months with no power. We've got probably 200 people here already." Al sounded genuinely excited, and it started to persuade Brian.

"That's what? Eight miles from Hill Street?" Brian stood up and inspected the shattered television screen. He was starting to feel like an idiot for smashing it.

"Yeah Chief, probably seven or eight miles. You know, Brian…" He paused, "We could use you. These people will listen to you here."

And with that, Brian was sold.

*****

After talking it over with his mother, they decided that moving to the solar panel plant was a safe plan. Even if all they did was stay there for a few days it would give them plenty of safety until the world settled down. Brian was betting that after a week or two, everyone would come to their senses and the federal government would figure out what the fuck was going on. Once that happened, they could go home, and start the process of starting anew.

Brian asked his mother to keep the kids entertained while he packed up the stuff they needed. The cruiser's trunk was already filled with shit from earlier, so he moved everything into his truck. He had the bag of weapons from the arms locker, the two bags of medical supplies plus all the food Stacey had bought before she... Before she died.

Brian got it all moved into the truck and started on the house. The first things he grabbed were the mattresses off the bed. They'd need something to sleep on, and he didn't want to deal with the floor. He grabbed suitcases and filled them with clothes for everyone. Brian snagged the kid's backpacks and loaded them for bear with toys and kid oriented supplies. Diapers for Sarah, ass wipes, and anti-rash creams. He loaded all the food in the fridge and cupboards as well and took all the things he thought they might need. Stuff like batteries, toilet paper, bleach, and a few flashlights. Down in his basement he took his hunting guns and all his ammunition as well. No sense leaving it there. In the master bedroom upstairs he got the gun box out and took the .38 from it. In the garage he grabbed his coach's little league baseball bag filled with bats, as well as his wood splitting axe.

After taking everything he could think they'd need it was just about getting to dusk. He didn't look at his watch, but he thought it was maybe 7pm when they finally backed out of the garage, and into the street. It had been about two hours or so.

The Hill Street neighborhood he called home was still dead quiet. A couple of the houses had lights on inside but that meant nothing. Lots of people left lights on all day. The four people were packed into the front bench seat of the truck as Brian backed out of his driveway and closed the garage door with the remote. He gave the big truck some gas, and they were off.

Traffic was much more sedate. There were fewer vehicles moving, but they were still speeding and driving recklessly. Brian fought the urge to chase them down and jump down their throats. Those people were probably just as scared and desperate as he was. He could understand and identify.

He sped the truck down Main Street and onto the state route that he'd taken to get back to town earlier when he'd gotten Sarah and his mom. He didn't go all the way to the Museum though, but about halfway. He saw the sign for the industrial park and turned off onto the road that led to the solar panel plant. The road had a solid half dozen large industrial buildings before reaching the park itself. The Auburn River Valley Industrial Complex had 25 tenants in various businesses. He headed to the first large parking lot, the home of STIG, Solar Technology Innovations Group.

STIG was the town's largest employer. Between their three shifts at least a thousand people got their paychecks there. The building was a glossy black three story edifice of solar panels, concrete, and steel. It was artistic, if not a bit sterile. Standing in front of the main glass doors he could see two of his Officers, Al Harper and Jason Chambers. Al was a veteran of nearly ten years, and Jason had just finished his second year review with Brian. He was young, but a good cop. They were good people, and he was glad to see them. They both stood watching Brian weave his truck through the packed parking lot to the front walkway closest to the main door.

The two cops walked down to meet him as he pulled up. They rested their weapons on their hips as he powered down his windows. For the first time all day he felt a genuine grin come up on his face. He squashed it down when a flash of his wife's torn face hit his mind's eye. Al kept his grin as Brian stopped the truck.

"Glad you could make it Chief." Al rested his forearm on the mirror of the truck. Jason kept an eye out for danger.

"Wish I had one more with me, if you know what I mean." Brian's words were pained.

Al reached a hairy arm into the truck window and gripped Brian's wrist in a reassuring grasp. "Pull around back to the loading docks. We'll get your shit inside." He patted Brian's arm and backed away, motioning for him to "move along" as cops often do when there's nothing to be seen there. Brian got a laugh out of it.

He nodded, "Yes sir officer." Al grinned again and turned to head back into the main glass doors of the STIG corporate HQ.

Brian spun the truck around to the back end of the building and saw the three loading docks. He backed the truck up as he saw the doors lift up. There were a few dozen men and women there ready to help. He parked the truck and his mother got out leading Tommy along. Someone opened the heavy duty rear door to the plant floor and they started up the steps to go inside. Brian gathered his things out of the truck as his little girl watched on. Once he had everything he thought he wanted, he grabbed the one thing out of the truck he actually needed, his girl Sarah. She knew something was wrong, but she let slip a little squeal of delight when he tossed her into his arms. He made a wide circle of the parking lot, taking in the dusk air and assessing the area. Far off in the distance, in another parking lot in the complex he watched a rigid form move their way. In the fading light he could just make out a man wearing coveralls that were drenched in blood.

Brian watched the man stagger at a snail's pace towards them. Finally he heard someone coming up from the plant behind him, and he turned to see who it was. Jason, his young officer had walked up next to him and was watching the injured or dead man approach.

"Think he's a... you know, a goner Chief?" Jason narrowed his eyes to try and get a better look at the man.

Brian did the same, but finally decided it didn't matter. He took a sideways glance at the AR-15 carbine Jason was holding. "Jason, if he keeps coming, dead or alive, you shoot him in the head. He'll be nothing but trouble for us either way we look at it."

Jason's only response was to swallow hard. Jason hadn't fired his weapon in the line of duty yet, and hopefully would never. If the world really had come undone like Brian thought, technically his career was over anyway. No worries about job related accidents anymore he thought. Brian patted him on the shoulder and turned toward the building and walked inside. Brian gave his beautiful little girl a kiss on the temple.

Just as one of the plant workers was pulling the door shut behind him Brian heard a single sharp crack from Jason's rifle.

One less dead body to worry about.

The heavy metal door slammed shut behind the father and daughter.

December 20th

Things have become… A little more interesting here at Auburn Lake. I tracked down the source of the gunfire the other day, and you're gonna shit a brick when you hear what it was.

I sincerely apologize to you Mr. Journal for not putting in an entry last night. I didn't really get back here until late, and I was exhausted so I crashed. Yesterday I decided that I'd do some long(ish) distance recon with the Savage's scope. I got my leg dressing on good and proper and geared up for a gun battle. I took the Tundra out at about 10am and headed to the crossing of Auburn Lake Road and Prospect Circle. I parked the truck out of the sight of the houses on the road, and walked the 15 yards or so into the tree line where I could set up a good spot to observe Prospect with the rifle.

One of the things they teach you in sniper school is the observation power of the sniper team. Frequently shooter-spotter teams would be sent out just to observe the enemy. Watch, learn, and take detailed notes. Never underestimate the power of information they used to tell us. I found a good flat spot just inside the tree line and got myself into a good prone position. Lying on my belly I could see in all directions and with the crunching of the snow a zombie couldn't sneak up on me. Thank God for that I guess.

I stayed there for about 2 hours, freezing my ever loving junk solid. But, I didn't see shit. I observed all of the visible houses for a good amount of time and didn't see any movement, living or otherwise. I also noticed that there were no tracks in the snow on the road. We haven't had any accumulation in a couple days, so if there were people moving around up there on Prospect, they didn't drive in, or out. That told me the shooter either entered on foot, came from off the road, or they arrived before the last snowfall, and had stayed on the street somewhere ever since.

I wasn't sure that was good news or bad news at the time. I exfil'd back to the truck after getting to my feet, and drove halfway down Prospect to the beginning of the cul de sac. In all due honesty, getting up off the ground nearly broke me. My leg had gone stiff as a board and just would NOT bend. I had to do this awkward push up slash limbo slash situp thing to get on my feet. Sucks to be me.

I parked the truck right in the road and used the hood to set the rifle up so I could observe. I watched the remaining houses on the loop for about 15 minutes before I saw evidence of the shooting. There was one house at the bottom of the loop that was a pre-fab home, but it had some extra work done on it. There was a very well done wraparound porch, as well as some extra dormers on the roof for windows to the upstairs.

In the yard, at the bottom of the half dozen steps leading up to the porch screen door there were three dead bodies. Up close later I saw it was two adults and a young teenager. The dead bodies were lying on their backs, all feet first toward the house steps. There were large swaths of ichors behind their bodies, and a few small frozen over puddles near their heads. When I took a damn close look at the house, I saw that the porch door had been barricaded from the inside with some boards. It was done very geometrically, and I wouldn't have noticed it if I wasn't looking for it.

In fact, all along the screened in porch there were 2x4's nailed or screwed up. They were pretty strategically placed at about hip level, and with the fact that the porch was raised up, they were at just the right level to prevent the undead from getting up on the porch. Someone had gone to great lengths to secure that house in an unassuming manner, and whoever it was knew a good deal about carpentry. I secretly hoped it was either Bob Villa, or Jesus. Both would be useful carpenters to have in the neighborhood.

The dead giveaway for signs of life was the chimney slowly seeping some smoke out. Not a lot mind you, just a trickle. I watched the frigid winter breeze gently blow it directly away from campus, which explains why I'd never smelled it. The wind coming across the lake cuts right through campus, and was taking the smoke directly away from Hall E. I should've known.

I couldn't see any lights inside the house, but it was about noon or so, so that made sense. I wasn't sure what to do. Obviously whoever was in the house had shot those people or zombies in the yard. Judging by how they were dressed, I was pretty sure they were zombies. T-shirts and shorts for the most part, which fits for when the shit hit the fan. Likely they were remnants either in a house that got out of the house, or they'd wandered over here since June. Wonder why they weren't frozen solid?

It does basically prove that something inside the zombie bodies is generating some kind of warmth if that's the case. Otherwise, they'd be fucking undead popsicles. ZomPops!

Anyway.

So someone was inside, and I kinda wanted to say hi. I got off the hood and pulled the truck forward into the cul de sac, stopping opposite the house with the dead people in the yard. I'd guess at about 75 feet away. I left the truck running, and just like all of my house clearings, I honked the horn repeatedly while standing outside. I held the rifle in my left hand, clearly showing I wasn't a threat, and I stood there. I think I hit the horn four times, waited a few seconds, then four times again. Just as I was about to hit the horn for the third cycle I saw the house door open, and a dark figure shuffle out onto the porch.

As unthreateningly as possible, I waved at whoever it was and hollered out a hello. I could see they had a handgun of some form, but they weren't pointing it at me, and I could pretty clearly see they were trying to get a look at me. The way the sun was hitting the house combined with the darkness of the porch I couldn't make out a ton, but you can read body language pretty good. That's when he yelled at me.

"Cut the shit with the horn you fucking idiot!" It was an

old man's voice. Strong, a little haggard though.

I walked in front of the truck and cut the gap between the two of by about a third before I yelled back. I think I said, "Hey, sorry, just wanted you to know I was alive and wasn't trying to shoot you." Or something like that.

He yelled back, "People who aren't trying to shoot people don't carry guns with them!"

Okay that's valid. Good point right? My witty response was this, "I expected you to try and shoot me. You've got some evidence that you like shooting people in your yard here." And I pointed over at the dead bodies I thought he'd shot.

"They were dead already. I just reminded them of it." And he wagged the pistol in his hand at the bodies. It looked like another Colt M1911 like the .45 I've got. I later found out I was right.

"Seems reasonable. Hey I'm Adrian. I live over at the school. I heard your shooting yesterday and wanted to make sure everything was okay over here. Wish I'd known you were here before." Pretty sure that's what I said.

'Yeah I heard ya over there, hammering nails and shit all summer. Shooting more of the dead folk, right?" I still couldn't see him all that good. I could tell he was about five and a half feet tall. A little hunched, but he looked spry. Plus he'd been standing all this time on the porch in what looked like just a flannel shirt, so he seemed pretty tough for an old guy.

"Yeah, trying to get the place safe. It's rugged now. I've got power and heat, plenty of food to trade too if you've got barter. I can always use a hand too if you're interested in moving over." That was probably retarded to say right? I haven't even shook hands with this guy and I'm asking him to move in. I'm a hopeless romantic. An eternal optimist.

"What kind of food you got?" That piqued his interest. He came right up to the screen finally and I got a good look at him. He was about five and a half feet, skinny. His skin was leathery and covered in scattered dark liver spots, but his eyes were bright, and he was totally with it. His head was almost completely bald aside from a white streak going around the back from ear to ear. I could almost make out a gleam off the top through the screen. He looked mid seventies probably. I instantly wanted to call him grampa.

I rattled off four or five different kinds of food I knew I had a lot of. Green beans, corn, peas, and for some reason canned beats. God I have a ton of those. No one took any from the grocery store apparently and on my trip back I got a shitload. I think I heard his drool plopping on the porch when I said I'd gotten a deer and still had cured venison.

"Well young man, my name is Gilbert. And if you would be willing to trade for some of your food, I'd be interested in doing business." He was happy to see me. I could hear it in his voice. I was so happy to see him too. This was the longest I'd spoken to anyone in months. Longest I'd been around someone without gunfire in months. To be honest I was waiting for his head to blow up. Seems to be a catchy condition around me.

"Well, what've you got?" I asked him. That stumped him. I could see him thinking long and hard about it and eventually his response was this:

"Shoot, I don't have hardly nothing."

I cried on the inside. I really was hoping this guy had something I could get off of him. I finally asked him this, "Is that a Colt .45 you got there?"

"Ayup." And he looked at it pretty lovingly.

"Well, I've got one myself here, but I'm just about on E with the ammo for it. If you've got spare, I'd be pretty happy with that." Man I was reaching. Really hoped that guy had some ammunition for me.

"Well hell, I have some spare for this thing. I don't think I'll be needing a lot of bullets in the near future if I starve to death will I?" This guy was filled with valid points. He was a font of common sense for chrissakes.

"Well, I think I got a box of 50 I can trade ya. What'll you pony up for that?"

I could've thrown him to the ground and made sweet love to him on the spot. Is that technically necrophilia? I mean, at what point are you so old having sex with you is like fucking a dead body? There has to be a standard somewhere. I restrained myself and tried to hide my enthusiasm. My my my my my pokerface. Muh muh muh muh. (Mr. Journal if you get the reference, please forgive me.)

I chewed my lip some and figured on a counter offer. Here's what I came back at him with, "Alright Gilbert how does this sound? In the interest of opening up a new friendship, and to show you my appreciation and to do right by you, I will give you 2 cans each of corn, green beans, beets, baked beans, plus a can of peaches, and a can of asparagus. Plus, because I'm a nice guy, I'll toss you a quarter rack of venison ribs?" Seemed generous to me.

His reply confused me, "What do you do for a living?"

Uh what? Like, what the fuck kind of question is that after the world ends? I told him this, "I don't really have a job at the moment. I guess you could call me an exterminator at the moment. But before all this bullshit happened I worked at the school as a dorm supervisor. Before that I was Army. Infantry."

Get this, he says this back, "I knew it. You got soldier on your face. How's this for an offer, you bring all that back here, plus another quarter rack of ribs, and a few extra cans of stuff, and I'll cook us a dinner?"

I don't know why, but I didn't even think about it. I think my well thought out response was, "Alright, be right back." We waved, I got in the truck, and headed back to the campus to gather up his food. Guess what I put it in?

A banana box. The banana box. I still have it though, I didn't let him keep it.

It took me the better part of an hour to get everything packed up. I grabbed all I offered to him plus the extra stuff. I grabbed a can of cranberry relish too, mostly because I was craving something tart. I love tart things. Like sour patch kids, shit I would chop them up and snort them if I didn't think it'd melt my fucking brain.

Anyway, I think I got back to the cul de sac around 1:30 or so. I parked in his driveway and headed over to the porch. I left the shotgun in the truck. I had dropped the Savage off in Hall E when I got the food. No sense dragging it around if I didn't need it. When I got to the steps, he came out and undid his barricade. It was pretty ingenious actually. He had these metal L brackets set up to hold the 2x4's and some nifty wooden shims to hold the boards from falling out or getting dislodged. Took him maybe 20 seconds to undo, and half that to get set back up. Over his windows he had sheets of heavy duty plexiglass. I'd seen it on a lot of farm windows up here and had totally forgotten about it. Clever old dude. The sheets were screwed in securely, and even if undead got on the porch, it'd take a dozen of 'em to smash the plexiglass.

He let me in and immediately I knew we were gonna get along. His house was new, obviously, but it had a sweet old people's house feel. His walls were covered with old pictures. Lots of them were of him in uniform, old Army pictures. It looked like early Vietnam War era. That put him at about 70. I could see from a few pictures that he'd gotten to the rank of Captain, which I thought was pretty damn cool. I'm sure he was filled with neat Army stories.

His house was remarkably warm. Just off the kitchen was the dining room very open concept with vaulted ceilings. The back of the house must've had a huge sloped roof because there were four huge skylights in the angled ceiling. Squat in the center of the two rooms was a giant woodstove, obviously taken from an older house. He pointed at me and said it'd come from his first home, just outside the city.

I won't type everything he said, or we did. It'd take me ten pages at least. I'll give you the Reader's Digest version. His name was Gilbert Donohue. He was ex Army, apparently was one of the first Green Berets, and was a widower. Well, he was a widower before the end. His wife had died unexpectedly of lymphoma about 12 years ago and he'd used some of the money from her life insurance to move out here. This was supposed to be their dream home.

He left the army and went to work running his wife's family restaurant with her. They worked together over the years, and eventually grew the place into a small chain of something like 10 restaurants. They served Italian food. I'd heard of the places, but never eaten at them. He was really proud of what he and his wife had achieved. That's why he offered to cook. He'd cooked in almost all of the restaurants at one point or another. I tell you what. The food was good, and he had shit to work with.

They never had kids. I got the impression that one of them was unable. It seemed like something he was sad about too, so I didn't press the issue. He was at his house, this house when the world shit the bed. He was doing what retired military men do; obsess over details that aren't important. Mow the lawn, trim the hedges, rake the nonexistent leaves etc. He used to listen to NPR constantly like me, and he heard the news, and immediately went into lockdown mode. I guess he had the house already rigged up like this. Something about having his house broken into right before his wife died. Who said paranoia is always a bad thing?

He said the majority of the neighborhood emptied that day, or the day after. Some folks came back, packed up, and took off. He thought only one family tried to stay, and he was pretty sure they starved to death. He claims he offered them food, but the mother in the family was so scared of contamination they spurned him. Those were the bodies in his yard. Apparently every time he went out to cut down a small tree for wood they'd try a jailbreak from inside their house to get at him. The other day they'd succeeded in finally busting a window and falling out. He got himself back into the house as fast as possible but didn't make it in time. He wound up having to shoot them. Those were the first zombies he'd seen in person, up close.

Gilbert said he stockpiled food up here because that's just the way he was. He said he still had a decent amount of stuff, mostly spam I guess, so this was a nice slice of variety. I told him if he had more bullets, I had plenty of food to trade. He seemed sorrowful when I said that. I think he's low on ammo too.

I told him about most of my exploits. The gun store trip, downtown areas, and the grocery store. I told him about the young couple with the kid, and cleaning out the campus. He seemed genuinely impressed by all I'd done. He mentioned he saw my limp and I told him about the dog. He laughed. I laughed too. It was nice to laugh at myself. He even asked to look at the wound, and I showed him. He said he knew good first aid and that it looked good. He even had spare bandages to get it wrapped up again.

I like this guy. He reminds me of my dad.

We had a few cups of instant coffee made on the woodstove, and then he cooked the venison on it too. Pan seared venison ribs that he seasoned with spices he had on hand. Gilbert also warmed up the cans of stuff we had, and even showed me how to make this pretty sweet green bean casserole with simple seasonings and dried milk. Learn something new every day.

We easily sat there bullshitting for about six hours easily. He said his car was functional. (it was a small Dodge pickup) He also said he had plenty of food and water to last, but he could really use some batteries, and more variety of canned stuff. He said he had a handful more bullets he could offer up later on. I told him any would be good.

After me convincing him it was necessary, he agreed that I should clear the other houses on his street. He had left them alone because he wasn't really able to clear them at his age. He was on the fence about it for two reasons; he felt it was stealing, and he thought it was dangerous. I convinced him that those people (the homeowners) were either dead or never coming back, and that we needed the food and supplies to ensure we'd survive. Plus I told him I'd split any food I found with him 50/50. He conceded to my logic and thanked me for being young. Haha. We agreed that I'd visit him every three or four days and we'd check in with each other. I told him he was welcome do the same. He put the box of shells in my hand and we shook, and I was off.

He looked good. Tired, a little lonely, but really good. It was amazing to talk to someone and not have a weapon pointed at me or them.

I was wiped when I got back. I wound up falling asleep on the recliner. Today I spent lounging around the house, letting my leg healed up some more. Moving around in the woods and heading to the gas station the other day was a little painful, and I didn't really need to accomplish anything today. I wound up making more of that green bean casserole for myself, and it was good, but not as good as Gilbert's.

It was nice to get 50 more rounds of ammo.

It's fucking awesome to find a neighbor.

-Adrian

December 22nd

Good day to you Mr. Journal. How are you? Oh, what joyous news! You're not real and I'm asking questions to my laptop computer screen! Some days I feel wacky, some days I don't. Right now, I'm a little wacky.

I've had a good run of things the last couple days and I'm feeling relatively positive about life in general. As you might remember the other day I met my neighbor Gilbert, and we didn't shoot at each other. Now there's reason for celebration. First people I've encountered since I saw... Abigail that didn't shoot at me, get shot at by me, or got killed near me. How fucked up is that? People man I tell ya. Dangerous animals.

So today is Wednesday, and the weather was decent. I

fired up the grill outside and cooked up some venison. I cracked open a couple cans of vegetables and ate a good meal. After I gave Gilbert some of my food I realized just how much food I actually have. I felt like I was still eating small meals, so I've decided to eat a little bit more, especially now that the weather has gone to shit. Generally speaking of course, today is decent.

Anyway, yesterday I was feeling really energetic, and my leg felt like a million bucks, so I decided I'd head to Prospect and start clearing out the houses on the cul de sac where Gilbert lives. It seemed like the neighborly thing to do, plus I was pretty sure he would back me up if I need the help. I headed down there pretty damn early as I usually do, and honked my horn at Gilbert's place. He came out pretty quickly, and I hollered up to him that I was going to clear out the house the zombies he killed came from. I figured it was most likely to be empty, and thus easy for me to break back into the job on.

He thought I was crazy, but said he'd sit on the porch and watch, and if I should need help, to come running. Back up. I have back up. That was all I could think. So fucking happy.

The houses on his cul de sac are a mixture of ranches and the raised ranches that are like 1.5 floors, but not quite 2 stories. All were pre fab style, but very nice. This was a pretty expensive area to live in before the world collapsed. The first house I did was a raised ranch. White plastic siding, with generic white garage attached by simple white breezeway. Seemed cut and dried and bland as shit.

Annnnnnnd it was. Weirdly enough. There was the window on the side of the house that was broken that the zombies fell out of, which was handy. I stood at the window and hollered and screamed, and nothing came out. When I went inside there was an overall funky smell, but the odor wasn't overpowering. It was the after taint of the presence of the three zombies.

I cleared the house painfully slowly. Meticulously. I

skipped no details, and overlooked nothing. I got a little nervous when I did the upstairs. Actually I was a lot nervous. I was petrified of finding another dog upstairs, and to be honest, if I found something I had to run from, I was not going to be able to run down the stairs. I would fall down them for sure, but running? Not fucking happening.

I swallowed my fear as best I could, and cleared out the house. Signs of desperation were all over it. Guessing by their dress they died pretty early on, likely in September when it was still warm. There was absolutely no food left in the house. I found bones in the kitchen sink that looked like they belonged to a dog. The bones were picked fucking clean as hell too, so these people must've been hungry as a motherfucker to eat their damn family pet.

Although, that's one less dog that can bite me. Win some lose some I 'spose.

I popped outside and gave Gilbert the thumbs up once the house was clear, and he headed back into his place. Their basement was also empty of food, but they had some relatively generic non edible stuff that I snagged. They were out of most of the consumables. Toilet paper, toothpaste, deodorant, soap, candles, all that jazz. Taking their appliances didn't make much sense, as I've got all that shit at home, and Gilbert doesn't have electricity. They did have another decent flashlight for me, although all of their batteries were gone. No guns or ammo in the house, nor any liquor, beer, or anything worth trading.

To be honest, the only thing that came out of that house of any value was clothing. I haven't been taking much in the way of clothes out of these people's houses and I think that's been a mistake. I can use the clothes as trade bait down the road, or as fabric for rags or sewing or something. Plus there was no fucking way I was leaving that place basically empty handed. I didn't want Gilbert to see me waste my time clearing my first house.

So I got clothing. And a few other items of neatness, like a cordless drill, a decent finishing saw, and a few skilsaw blades. Shrug. I guess it wasn't a total waste.

I decided I'd clear the house to the right of that one after. That was the house right directly next to Gilbert's place, and I felt it was also likely to be empty. Plus I wanted to try and find something to show him for all my work. He was sort of against the whole house clearing idea anyway, and I wanted desperately to sell him on the idea with something badass.

I didn't tell him I was doing the second house, I just moved the Tundra over into the next driveway and honked like I normally do. I remember hearing him open his door, but I didn't say anything to him. The second house was a ranch, and was smaller than the first place, so it went quickly.

Not without some drama though. When I did the exterior walk around the back door was wide open. For security reasons I shut the door. The door entered the kitchen from a pretty nice back deck. I didn't think anything of it, but that's pretty typical of me right? Devil's in the details as the saying goes.

I saw nothing in the windows, and as Gilbert said, it looked empty. I entered via the front door, which I had to kick open. I hollered again in the doorway, but nothing answered. As I was clearing the front living room area, I heard a low growl, and damn near filled my drawers. I swung the shotgun around towards the kitchen, directly at the spot the back door was at, and standing there, backed up into the corner was a red fox. Not a big one, but it was the better part of my shin in height, just a few inches shorter than my knee.

Standing behind the red fox were three pups. Fox babies. And I had shut their only means of exit. Luckily the front door was still open, and really fucking slowly I backed out that door, and went around to the back. When I got there, the mother red fox was still sort of protecting the pups, so I rapped on the back window in the door, and they all bolted. I could kinda see them go out the front door, so I ran around and watched them cross the cul de sac and disappear over the back of a small rise in one of the houses yards.

Weird huh? I haven't seen much of any wildlife, and to find wildlife in winter, just weird. More on how weird this is at the end. And this is gonna knock your sox clean fucking off Mr. Journal. Like.. flying away through the air knocked off.

Anyway, once I got the mother and the pups out of the house it was cleared out safely and slowly. I was taking a lot of time to do it right. Rushing hurts my leg anyway, and there are only just a few houses left to clear, so there's really no rush. This house was much more profitable.

I found about 20 cans of food in the cupboards as well as some other long lasting food items. Uncooked pasta lasts a long ass time if dry, and these guys loved pasta. They also had about 8 jars of spaghetti sauce, which was pretty frigging clutch with all that pasta. They were frozen solid, but I think that's a good thing. They also had a really nice supply of spices, and after my dinner date with Gilbert I can appreciate some of the different spices now. I had no idea I liked curry until he sprinkled some on the venison. These guys had a little thing of it, and that made me happy.

As for other shit, it was pretty barren. No garage so there were no garage-ish items to be found anywhere. No worries I guess. They had a lot of clothing, which was good I guess, and they also had batteries. I'm not sure if they're good still, but I grabbed them anyway. I vaguely recalled Gilbert saying he needed some anyway.

I got out of the house and got everything into the truck. I carried over half the pasta and half of the jars of spaghetti to Gilbert's place. I also grabbed half of the batteries I found.

The old guy was fucking stoked for the spaghetti. I thought it was his turn to throw me down and make sweet love to me, but he restrained himself, and instead just tried to shake my hand until it almost fell off. Affectionately he told me I was "full of piss and vinegar."

Not sure what that means, but it seemed like it was good based on his facial expression at the time. I'm guessing it means I'm awesome or something. Yep, gonna roll with that.

He opted to only take 2 boxes of spaghetti, and two jars of sauce. He said he didn't need more than that, and I was more than happy to keep the difference. I told him about the spices I found and he seemed pretty happy with that haul as well. I offered some of them to him, and he said to keep them. He said the spices would be good to use, or good to trade. Makes sense. I remember spice trade being a big part of world history class. It stands to good reason that when people run out of canned shit to eat, they're going to want spices for the food we kill or grow. That's of course assuming that I find people willing to trade, instead of shooting my ass and taking my shit.

Fucking people man I tell you!

So that was yesterday. I got back in just after dark, and did a quick patrol in the Tundra around the campus. It was all clear. I stored all the clothing in Hall A. It's just down the way from Hall E, and I don't need to keep it warm or anything. If anyone breaks into there and steals the clothes, I probably won't even get angry. Frankly I just need to make sure Hall E doesn't get any more crowded than it is. It's already full of shit I've brought here and I am running out of space. I am starting to feel like that crazy hoarder that lived on Jones Road. I keep everything I find lol. If I start keeping the tinfoil lids to yogurt containers I'm fucked. Speaking of yogurt... That sounds delicious. I am jonesing hardcore for dairy shit. I would beat some ass for ice cream.

I was really tired yesterday after I got back in, and I crashed early. I had to take a handful of ibuprofen because my leg was sore as shit, but today when I woke up I felt good. I really think the positive attitude helps a lot. It might also be the larger meals I've started to eat. I wonder how much of my healing has been dictated by shitty diet? Incidentally, I made spaghetti for breakfast.

Today after I ate my pisketty I went back to Gilbert's cul de sac and started clearing more houses. I went up to his place and honked again to let him know I was in the area.

He waved, and said he'd watch from his porch again. Nice fella that Mr. Donohue.

On his cul de sac there are 5 houses, and then 2 houses on the road leading down to it. I already cleared two yesterday, and I don't need to clear his, so that leaves four houses going into today remaining.

The last two houses on his cul de sac are raised ranches. I got them both cleared out just as the sun went down. I won't bore you with the mundane details, but both houses were empty of foxes, dogs, cats, (living or dead) living people, dead people, and those that are sort of in between living and dead that like to bite living people.

I found a mediocre haul of food. Few cans of Chunky soup, some plain soups, more green beans and corn, a couple boxes of rice, a handful of granola bars, and a couple boxes of macaroni and cheese. Decent, but nothing to write home about.

Stuff wise it was actually a pretty good haul. I found another 5 gallon gas tank, already filled with gas, and another really nice chainsaw. I don't know what I need 2 chainsaws for, but if one breaks, or if someone needs one, I've got spare now. I also found an ass ton of paper goods. An 8 pack of paper towel, and a 16 pack of toilet paper, and it was the good stuff, so that was a score. No chapped ass for Adrian. The first house had a decently stocked liquor cabinet, and I took everything out of that in a suitcase. The second house also had a gigantic linen closet filled with all kinds of vitamin supplements. They also had a small indoor workout area that had a treadmill, elliptical machine, and a stationary bike. I've got that stuff in the gym already at the school, but again, it's good to know it's here if I need it.

I swung by Gilbert's place and we split the food right down the middle. He offered to let me keep all the food if I gave him all the liquor, and told him hell no. I'd split it, but frankly I was a little scared he'd drink himself to death with all the brandy I found. He seemed let down, but I told him to grow up, and he laughed. He did take all the damn brandy though. I guess that's cool.

So I got in at about dark again. Did yet another patrol in the Tundra and called it a night. Here I sit, talking to you Mr. Journal. Me and my buddy.

I'm feeling positive today. Got some decent stuff the last couple days, I've got a new neighbor, the weather was mild today, and I saw that red fox.

Oh shit yeah. Almost forgot to mention. Funny too, I've got the fucking wildlife book right in front of me here on the table.

So out of curiosity when I got back earlier today I went over to the library and found a wildlife book so I could figure out what kind of fox I saw. It was some kind of red fox. I don't recall the exact coloration, but from the pictures in the book, it was a red fox. According to said book the mother fox takes care of the young for about 3 weeks until they're able to regulate their body temperature.

Sounds good right? Nothing too weird so far.

Here's the mindfuck of the day: Red Foxes have their litters in Spring.

It's almost Christmas. That mother should not have pups. They are at least 3 months early according to this book. What does that mean? Did she just… randomly find a male in heat the same as her four or five months ahead of schedule? That seems really fucking unlikely.

And why the sudden appearance of more animals now? Usually I see fewer animals during the winter, but now it seems like I'm seeing more of them? Maybe it's just that I'm fucking loony and I have no idea what's going on, and I'm making something out of nothing. I don't know though. This has weird written all over it.

It makes some sense to me that the animals would come near me here, because I've killed all the zombies, and destroyed a lot of the bodies that were left behind. Maybe they can sense the air is cleaner or safer here. Maybe I'm the pied piper of the apocalypse? Having all the animals follow my 12 gauge pipe as I go to and fro?

This is cool, but at the same time, it doesn't sit well with me. I feel like I'm missing something, some obvious piece of the puzzle that I should be seeing, but I'm not. That feeling drives me nuts.

Anyway, I guess it's moot to kill myself about it. If it was meant to be, it was meant to be. I'll figure it out in good time I'm sure. Or I won't, and I'll have frustration for the remainder of my life on this burnt to shit world.

Join me next time Mr. Journal, where our intrepid hero continues to clear houses of the undead, and prepares to set up his safe houses downtown, to hopefully draw new residents into his NerdCave!

BAM! POW!

-Adrian

December 24th

My life is filled with ups and downs. On one hand, things basically couldn't be much worse for me. This is going to sound really stupid. This might be the best Christmas I've ever had. And I really mean that. Even though my life has fallen apart, the world has shit the bed, I'm missing the love of my life, and I have a stiff leg due to attack by land shark.

I don't know. I just feel really good about things today. I feel like things are finally turning the corner. I think it's because of Gilbert. I'm living not only for myself, but for him as well. I'm invested you know? When I wake up I worry about something other than me. I enjoy seeing him and helping him out. There's tangible reward when I give him something he needs, or we trade and both of us come out better after. It's interaction without insanity in a world gone mad.

I love it. I genuinely fucking love it.

I'm missing Cassie kinda hardcore tonight. We always used to do our Christmas on xmas eve rather than xmas day. On Christmas day we'd drive all over creation to our family's places to exchange gifts with them. We'd alternate which years we had dinner where, and despite all my bitching about spending Christmas driving in the car, I miss it today. I wish I had some gifts to give her.

I'm not crying though. Maybe I'm out of tears, maybe I've gone numb, maybe I'm just happy with the way things are going and that's outweighing my negative emotions. I'm rolling with it though. I feel good and it's been a long time since I felt good about things. A really long time it seems.

Let me recount the last couple days for you Mr. Journal, and you'll see why I'm happy tonight. Actually I'm gonna put some Christmas music on first.

Done. I found some Christmas cds in one of the houses I raided awhile back. Didn't seem important at the time enough to mention in an entry as "hardcore loot" but I took em anyway. I didn't have any Christmas music on my laptop, and I figured I might as well grab some.

Yesterday I went back to the last two houses on Prospect. These were the two homes furthest from the cul de sac, and closest to the main road of Auburn Lake. Gilbert's home was only barely visible down and around the slight bend of the loop. I didn't tell him I was house clearing. My leg felt pretty awesome again yesterday, so I was feeling good to go. One house was on each side of the road, almost directly opposite one another. Both were flat ranches, and one had a huge shed behind it. I checked that one first, and it wound up being the only house I did yesterday.

The house itself was empty of anything dangerous, but there was a dead guy in the tub. He had put a gun in his mouth and sent his brains out the back of his head. The gun itself was a Smith and Wesson .357 magnum revolver, which is pretty fucking nice. It's far too heavy for casual use I think, but as a backup should I get low, it'll do quite nicely. Later on during my house searching I found a locked gun box as well. He had the key in his pocket, and after breaking my back getting his keys out, the gun box had two packages of ammo, one full, the other half full or so. After counting it was 70 rounds of ammo, plus the 5 in the revolver. His car keys were on the ring as well, and they matched the big Chevy truck in the driveway. Major score.

The rest of the inside of his house had meh stuff. He had some food, nothing remarkable in quality or quantity. He had a small collection of batteries, which was nice, and he had a good amount of hygiene and cleaning stuff. You could tell from the decorations this was a single man's home too. Ugly pictures of deer and bears and stupid posters on the walls. No curtains, mismatched furniture, and he didn't own any sweaters. That's a dead giveaway. Women always make us get sweaters. WTF is up with that anyway? What's wrong with a sweatshirt?

So the house was a bust other than the pistol. However, the dude's giant shed was a goldmine. Whoever this dude was, he had a fetish for woodwork. In various stages of done-ness in the shed were at least a dozen bookcases of really impressive quality. A few were waist height, a few head height. I immediately decided to take them back to the school for the books I'd accumulated so far. I figured at the very least the way I'm trying to hoard information for the future they'll be handy later on.

More to the point, this dude was a serious motherfucking woodworker, and he had raw stock out the butthole. I actually didn't bother counting all of it, because there was too much of it. I had to make three trips back to campus with just the wood. I had an entire truck bed filled with 2x4s, then one with just 4x8 sheets of plywood, then another truck bed filled with other finer stuff for finish work. He had all different kinds of wood in all different kinds of raw sizes. That's a major score for the fortification efforts for this spring.

As you'd imagine, he also had the tools. I had another truck run back to campus just for his tools, and I still left his table saw. The fucking thing was ENORMOUS. Easily dwarfed the woodstove I still want to move back here. However, he had a few smaller ones as well as skilsaws, jigsaws, routers, a sawsall, and screws, nails, hammers, rasps, and even a lathe, but I left that there. It's too heavy to move.

I dragged all those loads straight to the gym and left it all in the gym lobby. We have a woodshop, but frankly, this shit is waaaay better than the crap we had. Turns out there aren't many nerds interested in woodshop, hence the craptacular tools. Now if you need a chess board....

This was a substantial find for me yesterday. The really surprising thing about yesterday was the fact that even after moving all that shit outside, and being uber paranoid about getting jumped as I did it, my leg felt pretty good this morning when I got up. I mean sore still, but that's to be expected. However, I was expecting like... a 7 out of 10 for pain, and only had a strong 5. Four ibuprofen later and I'm golden.

After I got done moving all the shit back I went and split the food I found with Gilbert, and told him about the tools. He was happy for me, and I asked him if he could show me how best to work with them, and he said he'd be delighted. I'm thinking maybe instead of using the second generator I found to get the heat going in another hall, I might use it to power my new woodshop so I can get some fortifications going. I might do that in early January depending on how things go.

I didn't tell Gilbert about the gun I found, or the dead body. For some reason I kinda feel like the ammo is too important to tell him about. If he thinks I'm low, then he might be more likely to trade me his ammo out of sympathy, or for security reasons. Of course if he thinks I'm low, he might rake me over the coals. I dunno. Maybe that's a mistake. I guess I can always tell him about it later. Though for some reason I really don't want to LIE to him. Forget to tell him shit, sure, but a straight up lie seems really bad to me.

Maybe it's because deep down inside I don't want the one relationship I have with the one human being that I know to have lies involved. I think the only way I can be a better person and feel better about all the shit I've done wrong is if really try to do things the right way. I don't know. Wish I knew. No regrets about not revealing the gun though. I think I did the right thing on that.

So today I opened up with a fat ass breakfast. I had some of the cereal I have still in the bag in the box with some of the dry milk I reconstituted. Yay fruity pebbles! Not filling though, so I had a can of pear slices, and then a granola bar. It feels good to be stuffed. I can't recall many days since June when I felt that way.

I only had the last house to clear, and I decided I'd do that. Kinda crappy thing was snow. When I was headed down you could see it in the sky, and it fell all damn day today. I think we've got about 4 inches outside right now, and it looks like it'll keep going for awhile. Might get a foot if it goes all night. At least I'll have a white Christmas.

So in the snow I cleared the last house. This one has drama so bear witness Mr. Journal. This ranch was right across the street from the house with the huge woodshed. There was a car driven into the yard that up until today I hadn't noticed. The compact car was driven into the side of house, and from the looks of it, had rolled back some, and was parked in a pretty normal spot. I noticed the damage to the house when I was doing my exterior check.

A dusting of snow was covering pretty much everything so I didn't see any footprints or anything. All the house windows were wide open, and the back door was open, with just the screen door there. I wound up entering through that. The house was set up with the kitchen, dining room and living room running into one another, and then a single centered hallway heading down the length of the house. It had vaulted ceilings, and actually would've been a damn fine house.

245

I cleared the open area of the common rooms, and noticed some serious wreckage as I went. There were knocked over chairs, shit smashed off some shelves, a few pretty substantial dark brown crusty bloodstains on the carpets, and most importantly, the distinct odor of the dead. I stopped at the edge of the hallway and listened, and could hear a faint thumping noise coming from one of the rooms.

I went into panic mode for a few seconds, then got myself calm. Of the four doors off the hallway three were open, and only the one thumping was closed. I checked and cleared the three open rooms with the .45. Yeah Mr. Journal, I should mention that I'm using that for clearing right now. I still am a little nervous about the shotgun recoil with the sore leg, and seeing as how I've lost a step, it's a lot easier to move and shoot with the smaller pistol. Anyways....

Without the shotgun, I couldn't blast a hole in the door like I have been. So I went outside and checked the windows, and all of them were too damn high to see in. I limped across the street and found the woodworker's stepladder, and brought it back. Clever me, I set it up outside and used it to get a look in the window for the room with the closed door.

The room was pretty dark, but I could see a female body face down on the floor, scratching and pushing against the bottom of the door. There was another body laying all half upside down next to the bed in the middle of the room, but it wasn't moving. I took a few seconds as I got the .45 out and realized they were definitely dead. The woman's right leg was shattered. I could plainly see she had one foot twisted almost all the way the wrong way, and the bone was sticking out of the side. The color of her skin down near the wound was pretty fucking clearly gangrenous. Skin tone of the undead is almost a bluish yellow color. Sort of like someone with jaundice freezing to death. Her leg was filthy green and brown with crusty yellow pus streaks.

It looked to me like she'd gotten her leg broken, and subsequently died of an infection. I got one word for you Mr.

Journal. Antibiotics. Fucking A. The window was open, and I put the sights of the .45 on the back of her head, and pulled the trigger. Her head popped open like a crushed egg and she fell silent and still after a twitch or two. No more movement anywhere.

I got down off the ladder and headed back around front and reloaded the .45. I opened the front door and started searching when I heard a car moving in the snow outside. I drew the gun and looked out the window, and saw Gilbert outside, shuffling through the snow towards the house. He started yelling my name when he got ten feet or so from the door, and I hollered back. I went outside and told him what happened.

He looked like he had a heart attack. He heard the shot and came running, figured I was in trouble. I told him I was okay, and there had been a zombie. He smacked me on the shoulder and told me I was, "a fucking head case" for not telling him I was clearing houses. He said never to do that again, and to tell him so he could be on alert. I apologized, and he and I went through the house together.

I could tell at first he was uncomfortable going through other people's shit, but once he found something neat, it was like watching my dad pillage a yard sale. "Holy shit, you see this? They only want a nickel for it!" Gilbert found so much crap I've left in other places that he thought was amazing. For example, salt shakers. I've left a hundred salt shakers behind, but he pointed out that salt is a terrific seasoning as well has having other practical uses, and eventually, we were gonna run out. Every speck of salt was valuable. He wound up taking pretty much everything back to his house in the trunk of his Buick.

When I finally got back to the rear bedroom and pushed her body out of the way of the door, I could make some sense of what happened. It looked like she had been hurt. Her leg was broken. She was dressed pretty nicely, in a business casual slacks kind of way. One of her high heels was missing, and I found it lodged in the eye of the body that was upside down and half on the bed. I'm guessing her leg got broken in the car accident outside, she made it in here, and somehow for some reason she had to kill the other guy with her shoe. That told me she must've sat here, starving, getting infected, since the end of the world. It must've been a horrid way to die. Very slowly, and painfully. I felt bad because if I'd have known she was in here, I could've saved her, or at least helped ease her suffering. If only right?

When we got out of there all I had to show for it was half of a pretty decent food split with Gilbert. We'd found a damn good stash of energy drinks, which I got all of. They also had a lot of coffee and soda, mostly diet stuff, but whatever, I'll drink anything at this point.

I said adios to Gilbert, and thanked him for his help. I think he was excited to have gotten out of the house and joined me on my adventure. Spry guy for a dude his age. I like having him around.

So I got back here pretty early. With only one house, Gilbert's house, and a moderate haul to boot it was a short day. I tended my plants, listened to some music, stretched the leg out, made sure the generator was filled, and made some dinner. I boiled some of the spaghetti I found and opened a can of asparagus. Added some spaghetti sauce, warmed the asparagus and mixed it in, and it wasn't bad at all. Reasonably nutritious and tasted pretty good to boot.

I'm going to spend the rest of tonight in a similar and enjoyable fashion. Tomorrow I am staying in all day, and I want a nice quiet Christmas day. Oh wait. I need to give something to Gilbert for Christmas. It's the only sensible thing to do. What can I give the guy? Ooh. Tough call.

Hm. What do you get the guy that you know next to nothing about? Food? That seems generic. A cook book seems insulting. Gift certificates have lost their allure given the state of the world. I know. I'll gather him some firewood from campus and bring it over to him tomorrow midday. I'll sleep until I'm done tonight, then head out and gather some wood for him. I know he's been struggling to keep himself in wood.

That makes me feel happy. Mr. Journal if I don't put in an entry tomorrow, Merry Christmas to you. Despite everything, I think this will be a good Christmas for me.

-Adrian

December 25th

Merry fucking Christmas.

I killed some people today.

But I've got more neighbors now. I just wish they didn't live in Hall E with me. Although it was nice to see a familiar face today. More details soon Mr. Journal.

-Adrian

December 27th

Sorry it took so long for me to get an entry in here Mr. Journal. It's been a bit of a whirlwind here and frankly, dealing with what's going on is far more important than typing it down for posterity. I want to record history, but I need to get past the events before I can find time to write them down.

I am typing this from my bedroom, which has become my sanctuary now that I have been overrun with the frailest, skinniest, and most grateful family in the history of mankind. Christmas day, right around dark I heard banging down on the front main door of Hall E. I was sitting in the living room in the recliner and I'd just put the movie The Ref on. I fucking love that movie by the way. Denis Leary is the fucking man.

I snapped my head around and through the window plain as day I could see movement over at the door. I snapped up the .22 and the maglite and got myself to my feet, and shined the light out to see how many zombies there were. Lo and motherfucking behold, I hit Abigail right in the face with the beam of light. She was waving her arms up at the window at me and I could hear her yelling my name. I nearly shit myself with excitement. I couldn't see how many people she had with her, but I bolted down to the front door and opened the inner door. You remember Abigail Mr. Journal? The young girl I sort of rescued from the staff office building after the world shat the collective bed?

Now I kept the outer door shut in the event something was up, but she came to the window and told me they'd come here to stay, and that they were freezing, hungry, and were happy to see me alive. I think she said oh my God ten times. I only waited maybe 30 seconds to think about it, and I let them in.

There was mom, dad, little brother, and Abigail. I've got opinions on each of them I'll share below afterwards.

I let them in and I'm pretty sure Abigail sodomized me with her hug. I mean straight up rape. She grabbed me like I was the only person left in the world. She was freezing. Her parents were crying the whole damn time I was getting them into the kitchen, and the little brother was staring at my rifle with a mixture of horror and admiration. I got them into the kitchen and got them sat around the table. The dad had a double barrel shotgun, but as soon as he got inside he popped the barrels open and emptied it. I felt pretty uneasy at first, but he sat it on the counter a few feet away from where he sat. That gesture made me feel a lot better.

Mr. Journal they are so skinny. I mean… almost at the point of distended Ethiopian belly hungry. I got them all some water, and cracked open one of my multiple cans of tomato juice. I wanted to get them hydrated with something nutritious before I fed them anything. I metered the juice into them about a shot glass's worth at a time while they told me about their trip to get here. Pretty smooth from the sounds of it. I guess they got jumped by a lumberjack zombie near here and after a struggle, they put it down. I made all of them strip down to minimal clothing after that to make sure there were no bites. Not taking that risk. They were fine.

The mother had a pretty bitching sore on her foot though, and I got her the first aid kit so she could start taking care of it. I think it was a blister from all the walking they did. After about an hour or so of them telling me how bad their life has been since June, I decided I'd feed them. Usually you don't want to stuff someone who has been starving. Typically they'll just throw the shit back up because their stomachs are not used to digesting anymore. I wanted to feed them something bland and easy to digest. I warmed up a can of green beans for them to split, and after that I gave them some hot oatmeal with a little bit of brown sugar on it. Really small amounts too, maybe the size of a deck of cards.

As they ate Charles, Abigail's dad, told me all about the group of assholes that had taken over their town. Apparently a bunch of the powers that be had set up shop in the local high school, and had instituted a form of martial law. Ex cops, National Guard dicks, city politicians, etc. Well, they ran around doing whatever they wanted, took everything, and anyone that couldn't contribute was left to die. This whole family had nothing to put on the table other than slave labor, and Charles said he was scared to death they'd rape his daughter and wife. He busted out crying when he said that, and I almost lost my shit with him. Been emotional lately.

They thought they had avoided being seen when they left town. The whole family packed into the same wagon that Abigail left with in June, but they ran out of gas. They found the truck I had tried to go to the gas station with back in October, and as you'd expect, the thing turned right over for them. My luck right? It dies on me, but starts for them. Of course I did put that whole thing of dry gas into it after the fact, and I'm sure it cleaned out whatever it was that was fucking up the engine. Water in the fuel line or something? Fucked if I know. Chuck said he parked the truck at the edge of the bridge on the other side of the vans. He tossed me the keys and I heard another bang bang on the door.

Instantly I could see a tremendous amount of panic on their faces. I mean shit, even I felt my heart jump straight up into my goddamn neck. Two people knocking on my door in the same day? That rarely happened to me when the world was normal, let alone since the dead started being so active.

I motioned for them to sit still, and I definitely motioned for Chuck to keep his double barrel on the counter. I moved to the upstairs as fast as I could and went into one of the bedrooms I'm not really using. I crawled pretty painfully across the floor and peeked down to the door. Standing at the door was three fairly large men. I could clearly see they had guns, and they were scanning the area with them, looking for threats. I got the immediate impression that the two in the back knew what was going on with their guns. They were either hunters, or cops, or ex military. They just had that look. The dude banging on the door looked reasonably normal. Skinny, kinda tall, was wearing a knit cap, and I could see the glint of round eyeglasses on his face from the lights coming from inside. He didn't have a long gun that I could see.

I lowered my head and sat down and thought. I could see Abigail crouching low in the doorway. She was smart, staying low. They couldn't see her. She crawled towards me and whispered as I heard the guy downstairs start to yell out hello or something.

Abby whispered something to me like, "Those are people from the high school."

Fuck me, right? I wasn't sure what to do. Plus I was suddenly remembering I had left the shotgun and the .45 in the living room downstairs, not 15 feet from three total strangers, one of which was a goddamn teenager. Responsible of me, right? Fml. I started to think this was all just a clever way to separate me from my guns so the family could let these guys in, and then I'd have fuck all I could do about it.

The skinny fuck was banging real hard by then and yelling out something like, "We know you're in there, we just want to talk!" Like Gilbert said, people don't talk with guns. I decided to risk it. I had to trust somebody, and if they were going to fuck me over, they were going to fuck me over. I asked Abby to go get my shotgun and run it upstairs to me and to get her dad too. They both came up and Chuck had his shotgun ready to roll. I told him to get down to the front door and stay real low. If I started shooting, then he should open the inner door, then the outer door, and blast them too. He took off with no hesitation.

I told Abigail to get her mom and her brother down into the basement where the generator was. It was safe, solid, and secure down there from errant fire should shit hit the fan. She left me with the shotgun and crawled out. Very slowly I reached up and undid the window lock, and slid it up about three inches. Luckily the new dorm windows open quietly.

I got into a firing position kneeling, hiding behind the corner of the window. I had the very edge of the barrel on the inside of the window frame so it wasn't visible to them. It hurt my leg like I can't even explain, but I had to do it for good cover and a good firing position. Discomfort is better than being shot. I waited to about the count of 20 to make sure Charles was ready, and then I hollered out. Here's the conversation as I recall it;

"Stop banging please, we can hear you." And he stopped and backed up, looking for where my voice came from.

"Who's there? Where are you?" He had a pretty deep voice for a skinny dude wearing a beige trench coat. I could see a bulge at his hip, which told me he had a pistol. He didn't draw it, but his hand dropped down to the bulge and hovered there. He wasn't a tool, I could tell by his body language, but he still wasn't like the other guys. The two dudes in the rear brought their guns up to my rough location pretty quickly, which was a little disconcerting.

"My name is Adrian, who are you sir?" That was me.

"I am Sean, I'm one of the council members from Westfield down the way. We followed some people here and wanted to touch base to see if we could establish a relationship. This is quite the place you have here Mr. Adrian." He did this queer grandiose kiss ass motion as he said the last part. I could FEEL the politician coming off of him. Mr. Sean had gone instantly on the Adrian Ring shit list.

"Thank you. It's currently private property. We are not interested in establishing any trade relationships at this hour. If you'd like to return in a couple days, we can meet somewhere and talk then." I said WE because I wanted him to think there were several of us.

"How many people are here?" He asked.

"We've got about thirty at the moment." And there goes my whole thing about lying to people. Remember that whole diatribe about honesty, and relationships? That lasted.

"I don't think you can fit thirty people in that building Mr. Adrian." I did not like his tone.

"I don't think you know as much about our situation here as you think you know Sean. And I suggest you and your men come back later if you want to talk like civilized people. We've had some bad experiences with people who are desperate, and I'd hate to feel threatened and have all these guns go off by accident." Low. Threatening. He stiffened at the statement, I could tell he didn't like being threatened before he said what he said back to me.

"I don't like your tone Adrian." Same low, threatening tone I gave him.

"Sorry to hear that. Make your decision Sean, leave now and come back later, or I've been told I'm supposed to shoot you guys where you stand." I didn't want him thinking I was in charge. The two dudes behind him lowered their guns and looked over at him. My leg was SCREAMING in pain, and one way or the other something had to give shortly or I was going to stand up, ruining most of my cover.

They stood there for a solid minute, and I could see the gears turning in the Sean dude's head. I think he was debating asking them to open up on me, but the bottom line was he had no idea who I was, or how many guns actually were pointed at him. He started nodding slowly and I could see him smile. I wish I could've seen his eyes, but all I could see was circles of light where his glasses were.

"Alright Mr. Adrian, perhaps you're right and this is a bit dangerous for everyone. How about we return tomorrow at 3pm and we meet on your bridge, where those vans are parked?" He thumbed over his shoulder towards the general area of the bridge.

I waited a second, then said, "Hold on, lemme ask." Then I waited another minute, and responded, "That's fine. If you want to trade, we have extra wood we can trade, and we have a few extra cans of grapefruit juice."

He nodded, I think he read through my bluff, "Sounds good my friend. We can probably scrape up some batteries if you need them. We also have a few spare crank radios that don't need batteries if you need one."

Generous counter offer to my crap offer. Smelled fishy. "Sounds fair. We can definitely work something out tomorrow at 3 on the bridge."

"Sorry for your troubles man, we'll be back tomorrow." He waved, and the three of them were off.

I stood up and wiped the sweat off my brow. My leg was throbbing in red hot agony and I shook it out as I heard Abby come into the room behind me again. She and I talked about what the fuck we were gonna do as I headed downstairs. I also scolded her for leaving the basement. When we got down to the kitchen, her mother was *pissed* at her too.

Charles was sitting at the table cradling the shotgun and he looked nervous as fuck. He was so skinny the absurdity of him even shooting a shotgun was hilarious. He'd snap like a twig. Once we were all down there I belted on the .45 again and got the vest with my shells handy. I turned off some of the lights and we sat down and talked about the situation. They were all equally adamant that this was a bad idea, and I agreed. I wanted them out though, and that got them gone. Or so I thought.

I was sitting there thinking about how we would handle tomorrow when Otis made his first appearance. He was a sort of skittish guy, and whenever Cassie and I had company he'd always hide for an hour until he realized it was safe. I said "Hey buddy!" Then I reached down to stroke his back and I heard a gun go off outside. One of the windows smashed apart in the living room and I felt something hit my head. Within half a second my left eye clouded red with blood and I dove to the floor. There was a second gunshot and a hole the size of my fist appeared in the wood I have halfway up the windows on the first floor. From the floor I knew where the shots were coming from. All of the new people had hit the deck and I made sure they were fine.

Patty, (the mom) saw me and she went white. Apparently I was fucked up pretty good. I'll tell you about that later Mr. Journal. I said "stay low" quietly to them and Otis bolted up the stairs, hair standing up straight as an arrow. I got the vest on somehow while laying on the floor, and I low crawled around the bottom floor as fast as I could with the pain in my leg and made it for the side door. That door had the porch that I'd taken the stairs off of and barricaded. It'd be good cover, and it was around the side so I could slip out more than likely and flank them.

I got to my feet at the door and peeked out the inner door into the foyer area. That area was clear so I went out and peeked in the second door. I couldn't see anyone outside, so I popped the door open quickly and stepped back inside, trying to bait out a shot. No one fired, so I peeked out at knee height and looked around. It killed my leg, but I didn't see anyone.

I let myself out silently and hugged the outside wall. The left side of my forehead was starting to throb pretty good by that point. The snow was starting to fall again, and it definitely helped to muffle the noise. I peeked around the corner slowly, and saw the two goons crouched about 25 yards from the house. I already had the gauge ready to go, so I drew a bead on them, wiped the blood out of my left eye and unloaded three quick rounds at them.

In movies people get shot with a shotgun and they fucking FLY backwards. They go through windows, into walls, over cars... That shit doesn't really happen. When people get shot they usually just double over in pain and go down, or they just fall straight down. There's no huge impact that sends them flying. Unless they're hit with a massive bullet from up close, and even then it's not like the movies.

Both of these assholes doubled over and went down. Direct hit! I sunk their Battleship! Bitches. Common sense escaped me though, and after I threw three shells back in the shotgun I got myself over the railing and dropped down to the ground. Yowzas. Talk about stupid. Felt like I drove a railroad spike into my thigh. My leg was weak as fuck, giving out on me every other step.

I hobbled around as sneakily as I could and came up to the guys. Just as I got to them I saw headlights turn on at the bridge, and a large vehicle spin out in the snow backing away. My guess was Sean making his escape after his failed assassination attempt. I had to wipe the blood out of my left eye again too. Anyway.

The two dudes were down in the snow and one of them was fucking done for. Some of the shotgun pellets had gone right through his neck and he was pumping out blood like a goddamn fountain. By the time I addressed the two of them he was already fading fast. The other guy was rolling around next to his dying buddy as I swung around to get a good look at them. They were wearing something like Dickies pants, and had heavy coats on. Both of them had pretty full beards going on, which is sensible seeing as how shaving is a bitch without electricity or hot water, plus its winter.

The dude rolling around was moaning in pain and I finally told him to freeze. He jerked when he heard me say something. I don't think he realized I was that close. As soon as he froze, he looked over his shoulder at me and reached for his gun. I yelled stop, but he kept going for it, and without missing a beat I shot him on the ground where he lay. Is it strange to say I intentionally shot him in the face? I knew he'd come back as a zombie if I didn't do it. The other guy was dead, and I knew he'd be up and moving around in less than a minute. I hollered inside for the sword, and the little kid Randy brought it out to me. He watched as I stabbed the blade into the eye of the body.

I didn't want him to watch, but if this is reality now, he needs to see it firsthand. We can't hesitate when there's a body around. Hesitation breeds more bodies. His age needs to be seen as an advantage, not a hindrance. He's young enough that the habits can hopefully be instilled into him without too much trouble.

I grabbed up their guns and searched them for ammo and stuff. They had ammo, I'll go over all that later. Once I got back inside Patty immediately took over and sat me down. She took my first aid kit and went to work on my eye. Well, my eyebrow really. She used the tweezers in the kit to pull a shard of glass out of my upper eyebrow the size of my pinky. Strangely enough, once it was out, it felt better, but it bled like a bitch. We ruined one of the dishtowels trying to staunch it. She got some butterfly bandages on me and I washed my face in the sink. I excused myself and redid the bandage on my leg too. My leg wounds are mostly healed, but the scabs broke loose on the deeper bite wounds and I was bleeding some. I cleaned it off, got a new dressing on, got about six Advil down and went back out.

I had no sooner sat down at the table when the third

banging came on the door. I was like seriously God? Really divine presence of an as yet unnamed religion that I don't care about? What. The. Fuck?

Abby was right near the window, and she peeked through the hole in the wood the dead dudes outside had just put in my barrier. She said, "It's some crazy looking old bald guy." Words of relief.

Fucking A Gilbert. I let him in and told him what was up in the foyer area. He shit himself when he saw me, but he was guardedly excited when I told him more people had shown up. I brought him inside and that was the first time all of us were together. It was weird, but cool.

We cleaned up the kitchen of the wood, glass, and my blood, and Chuck got a trash bag over the busted window for the night. I already swapped out a window from Hall D yesterday, so that's dealt with. After that we all sat around in silence. Gilbert got the story of their trip here and what had just happened out of us, and the look on his face pretty much summed it up nicely. Sour face.

Chuck, Gilbert and I all decided that based on what we knew, and what had happened, the likelihood of them returning was almost inevitable. Chuck had heard of some pretty rancid stories from these guys, and if the Sean guy got back and told them about what happened, and what he thought we might have for supplies… It seemed like a foregone conclusion they'd make an attempt to either get revenge, or raid us and take everything I've worked so hard to gather.

Everyone stayed here Christmas night. Even Gilbert. I crashed in the living room on the recliner, and Gilbert slept sitting near me on the shitty dorm couch here. The entire Williams family crashed in one of the rooms with double bunk beds upstairs. Gilbert and I more or less took shifts keeping watch, but we both blacked out midway through the night. Old soldiers. We can sleep anywhere I think. We woke up and instituted our makeshift defense plan.

After we got rid of the two bodies outside, we made a

plan yesterday to stake out the bridge all day and that's what we did. Chuck took my spare pump shotgun and Gilbert sat in his Buick just around the corner on Prospect so he could see anything coming our way. I set up another sniper position in the woods on a small rise and had full visibility at a hundred yards. Abby and Randy brought hot apple juice and coffee out to us all day to keep us warm. I had a shitty blanket on the ground below me, and another one on top of me, and with the hot juice and coffee, it wasn't that bad. Kind of a mild day outside yesterday. Although it did start to snow right at dark. And I mean really fucking snow. Blizzard style bullshit.

Patty was a godsend to have in the Dorm. She was a fucking awful cook, but she gladly whipped up food for us all day, trying to keep us fed and warm. By the end of yesterday the whole family had their color coming back, and their cheeks were already filling out. Funny what getting a little food into you does for your demeanor and health. We kept it low key last night. I let Randy fire up the Playstation and the rest of us hung out chit chatting about all the stories of what happened "that day." More on their stories in another entry.

Last night we took shifts again, but it was Charles and Patty instead of Gilbert and I. Gilbert said he'd camp out in his car as long as I gave him gas to keep it running and warm. I gladly gave him two of the five gallon cans. This morning we set out with the same plan. Gilbert wound up coming back to the campus for breakfast, which was more cereal made with dry milk. He seemed more than elated to mow down some raisin bran with the chalky milk. It's nice to see so many people smile, especially after just getting done killing people. Sigh. Weird world.

So today we set out with the same plan. Charles and I hidden in the trees waiting for visitors, the kids keeping us in food and fluids, Patty running the Hall like a field general, and Gilbert out on Prospect as our rear guard if it got ugly. So much tension.

It didn't get ugly though. It was colder today too, and it snowed like a bitch last night and most of today so it was fucking miserable. The hot drinks helped, but the wind was whipping up good, and it just sucked. We got about nine inches of snow overnight, and more during the day so moving around was a bastard. We camped out in our ambush positions until I couldn't feel my hands anymore. I think we headed back right before the sun went down. We spent the evening here in Hall E eating a dinner Gilbert made for us. He asked to get back into the venison, and I was hungry, and it seemed fitting. We all dug into everything he made pretty hardcore. Most of the evening was us adults sitting around the table wringing our hands. We did it half for warmth, and half because we were all nervous, waiting for the assholes to come back in force.

Gilbert said he had a plan though, and he would look into it early in the morning. He thought they'd come early in the morning though, so we hit the rack ahead of schedule. Abby and Randy are taking watch downstairs with Chuck asleep on the couch. Gilbert went back to his place to work on his master plan. Right now I'm upstairs in my room with all my guns and the laptop. This is the first spare time I've gotten really. I ought to be asleep right now, but I'm stoked to finally get all this written down and off my chest.

What a clusterfuck.

I'm happy that people are here. They seem pretty cool too. Appreciative of me, and nice too. Abby's cool, Patty seems a little anal retentive, but I guess she's an accountant, and that's part and parcel with that line of work. Chuck seems… frazzled. He seems really fucking smart though, but I think he's been so strung out with worry for so long he needs time to get his head back together. He's almost got that PTSD look and feel to him, so I need to keep an eye on him. I thought there'd be a power struggle between him and I, but honestly, I think he's relieved to not make decisions. It's a burden I'm sure he's borne too long. The teenage brother Randy seems a little shell shocked. I can sense he's rambunctious though, and teenage boys can be a lot of fun, and a lot of trouble. However, he seems reasonably cool (if a bit awkward and strange) so far, and that's nice. As I said I like Abby. She was a cool student here before the world deep sixed, and nothing has changed. She's calm, cool, and I think after some time around me here she'll become an excellent decision maker.

I haven't gotten Gilbert's take on all this in private yet, so I have no idea what he thinks about the situation. He seems really happy to have the people around though, and I think he's really happy to be helping. Plus this is right down his area of expertise. Captains in the Green Berets run units of Green Berets, and they do the entire mission planning. I think he's having fond flashbacks with all this ambush nonsense.

Frankly, the more I think about it, I'm still waiting for the other shoe to drop. All these new faces here, all this tension, plus weapons all over the place. For whatever frigging reason I trust Gilbert, and I am pretty sure Abby is good to go, but I'm still not sure about Chuck, Patty, and Randy. Chuck seems like a loose cannon (maybe because I'm threatened by another man), Patty is a mother in a world that's out to get both her children, and Randy is a 12 year old boy, which is trouble waiting to happen.

Which brings me back to... Tomorrow we're doing the same thing. That'll be three straight days of sitting in wait, ready to be attacked. I'm used to the tension from my Army days, but Chuck seems pretty worn thin. I don't think he can take many more days of this before we need to pull him off the line, and if something happens, I'll just have to deal with it myself. I'm curious to hear what Gilbert's plan is. He and Charles are both convinced we won't be attacked for days now because of the snow, but we can't risk not being ready for them. Charles says the roads were bad enough with just three or four inches of snow, and with nine inches or better over the entire valley, it'll be impassable except to the largest trucks.

All I can think about is the fact that Charles said they had a lot of trucks, and if just one of those motherfuckers knows how to run a plow… Like I said, we just can't risk it. I just hope Gilbert's plan comes into play and is actually helpful. Maybe he's got some old claymore mines kicking around in his basement. My left testicle for a crate of claymores. Going once... going twice...

Oh, those two oafs who I plugged with the gauge dropped yet another 12 gauge shotgun, and a bolt action.300 magnum hunting rifle. The dude with the scatter gun had 18 shells, and there were 14 rounds of the .300 mag. It's a good rifle, but the Savage is better imho. Plus that thing doesn't have a good scope. At the very least, it's nice to accumulate more guns. I can do basic weapons maintenance, but it's not like gun parts are currently growing on trees.

So yeah. That's where we are. Tomorrow we do the same again, and I suspect we continue to do the same until we decide to go after them, or they finally come after us. Chuck thinks they'll come soon. Especially if Sean saw through the window how much food I have in here. There are copious amounts of cans clearly piled in plain view. He thinks they might have 200 people in their high school, and that's a lot of desperate mouths to feed.

I don't want a war. But I will see every last one of those motherfuckers rot before I give up what is mine.

They better bring a motherfucking army.

-Adrian

Can't wait for more?

Turn the page for a special preview of

The Kinless Trilogy
- Book One -
The Wrath of the Orphans
by Chris Philbrook

Available now in print and Kindle format.

"WE'RE ALMOST OUT OF TIME. We
need to move faster!" The young man said, panic ripe in his
voice. He carried a small woman in his thin arms. Her head
hung limp, and the arm not pinned against the man's chest
swung to and fro lifelessly. She was dead.

Ahead of him ran his younger sister. They'd just entered
the fringe of the small village their farm was on the outside
of. New Picknell. Quiet and safe New Picknell. As the son
carried the dead body of his mother at a jog, the smaller
sister searched out for the single home that would contain
their salvation. The home of New Picknell's lone Apostle
resident.

"Catherine!" The daughter yelled, her voice cracking
from the emotion she'd been expending since her mother's
death. "Catherine we need you!" They would have to cross
the entire town to get to the small farm Catherine's family
lived in. Theirs was a good sized home still inside the town's
edge, still protected from solitude and the wilds of Elmoryn.

A woman stood up from her seat at a washboard, letting
the wet laundry slide down into the metal basin. She saw the
siblings running as fast as they could manage, and her face
went pale. She reached down beside the washbasin and
produced a mallet. Her lungs inflated to holler a warning,
"Dead body in the city! Dead body in the city!" After
screaming her warning she clutched the mallet to her chest.
Her anxiety decreasing, she retreated to the safety of her
home, where she shut the door, and barred it.

As the frightened pair ran through the small village the
doors of homes either slammed shut, or swung open with an

adult standing in the frame. Everyone was armed, and stared at the body in the boy's arms. They feared it. They feared what it could become. They feared what it would become if their journey took too long.

"Catherine! Catherine!" The daughter screamed again, losing what was left of her already bruised voice. Other voices joined her, sharing the tremendous urgency. The screams of "Catherine!" were nearly deafening by the time they reached the dirt street that ended at the wooden fence that marked the edge of the family farm they had been seeking.

"Catherine please, come quick!" The son yelled, his arms failing. He had been carrying his dead mother for almost an hour at nearly a sprint, and his young body was well past its limit.

His voice pierced the home and a black haired woman opened the door. Her face was calm, reserved, and full of a timeless poise that instantly spread relief to all those in a panic outside her home's fence. As she stepped outside her door and walked down the finely laid stone path to the sturdy gate she moved with purpose, and confidence. Her trip ended just as the daughter and son reached the gate. The Apostle flipped the latch on the gate and pulled it open, motioning for the son to bring the dead body to a stone bench that was curiously placed just off the stone walkway. Its purpose was not for sitting.

"How long has she been gone Nickolas?" Catherine asked calmly, gathering the fabric of her long cream colored dress to her hip. The garment flowed in the warm, late summer breeze. The stink of the dead body hadn't yet come, and inside the yard the only scent was that of freshly cut grass.

The young man, Nickolas, panted as he put his mother's body down on the polished granite slab. She looked very small and almost stately as he arranged her arms at her side. "I don't know. She was hit by a rotting timber in our barn. It fell on her from the hayloft and struck her dead. We found

268

her and came running as fast as we could. The trip here alone was an hour. She could've been dead for a few hours more."

"Where is your father?" Catherine asked in a slow and steady cadence, inspecting the dead body with tender care. She had done this many times, and this was her way.

This time, the daughter replied, her voice almost entirely gone now, "He left early yesterday to bring a small harvest to the rails. He won't be back until tomorrow at the earliest." She coughed a dry cough and shed a thick tear down her cheek.

Catherine winced, "That's a shame. He will be heartbroken, as I'm sure you both are." She put a reassuring hand on the shoulders of the siblings. From the other side of the fence the town's residents that were brave enough to watch had formed a line against the thick wood separating Catherine's property from the town proper. Pitchforks, shovels, hammers, and even a few swords and axes were in their hands. They stared intently at the body on the granite surface just a few feet away.

From the front door of her home a brother and sister duo not unlike the ones that had just delivered their dead mother's body walked out into the yard. The twins were tall, thin, and had hair black like their mother. They both shared clear eyes of a striking blue. They looked on from the step of the home with calm concern.

Catherine reached out and took the hands of the siblings that were now half orphaned. "Everyone gathered here please give the spirit of the recently departed Julianne a few moments of silence while I free her soul from the bonds of flesh that bind her."

Everyone went silent, and Catherine began the service, her hands still clutching to the brother and sister.

Head lowered, her silken voice reached out beyond the veil of death, "All life is fragile. Today we learn that lesson yet again. The life of Julianne has reached its end, and despite the injustice of her being taken away from the world

269

of the living, her legacy does not end today."

Catherine looked up at the body, ensuring it was still on the slab before continuing, "Julianne's immortal spirit is still within her, and in this moment we shall set her soul free from the body she had in life. She will roam these plains, and these hills forever, lending support to her friends and families and their descendents for all time. She shall hear the praise and adoration of the living as if she were still here. She shall lend Apostles a bit of her very essence, allowing us to perform The Way, and give mystical boons to those we can. In life she gave love and security, but in death she gives so much more, and she will do this forever."

Catherine let go of the sibling's hands as they slowly wept. They'd seen the Blessing of Soul's rest done before, and to complete the ritual, Catherine needed both of her hands. The mother of three reached into a small pocket on the front of her dress and produced a handmade cloth bag. She retrieved a tiny vial of scented oil, and sprinkled a minute amount of herbs down the length of Julianne's dead body. The herbs and the oil were essential components to the blessing Catherine was performing. They physically and tangibly bound her will to the act, and enabled her to use the Apostle's version of The Way, or Elmoryn's magic. Catherine's magic was fueled by her latent talent to access the hundreds of thousands of ancestor spirits roaming the land. In a few moments, Julianne would join them.

When the proper number of oil drops had been applied, and the right amount of herbs placed on the right points of the body, Catherine placed her hands on Julianne's body. The intimate connection of Apostle and body signaled the final moments of the blessing. Catherine reached out of her own body and soul, and into the body of the deceased woman. It was not unlike opening a metaphysical cage, and setting free a bird kept within. Her hands never moved, but behind her closed eyes she felt Julianne's body shudder briefly as her spirit was set free. Her soul would not rot and fester in her body. She would not become the undead everyone gathered feared.

She took her warm fingers from the now cooling body and reached her full height. The young girl still wept, but when Catherine embraced her, she calmed quickly, feeling the relief the blessing had given them. The crowd gathered gave a quiet round of clapping as the tension faded from the afternoon. They filtered out quickly, letting the family grieve in privacy.

"Thank you," Nickolas said.

Catherine smiled warmly, "You are very welcome. We can store the body until your father arrives, give you time to gather wood for her pyre." Cremated bodies couldn't be animated by rogue Necromancers, no matter how unlikely the chance of that happening was. Tradition was tradition after all, and since The Great Plague almost eradicated all human life from the face of Elmoryn three hundred years ago, all bodies were cremated.

"Thank you."

"You're welcome. I'll have Malwynn and Umaryn help with your mother's body. In the meantime, head over to Jalen and Naomi's over there, and let them know what's happened. They'll take care of you until your father returns."

"Thank you Catherine. My mother would thank you as well," Nick said softly, taking his little sister under his arm.

"With any luck I'll cross paths with her spirit, and she can thank me herself. I'm glad you made it here in time."

Nickolas could only nod. The thought of not making it to the Apostle in time was too much to contemplate.

- About The Author -

CHRIS PHILBROOK is the creator and author of *Adrian's Undead Diary* as well as the popular webfiction series *Elmoryn* and *Tesser: A Dragon Among Us*.

Chris calls the wonderful state of New Hampshire his home. He is an avid reader, writer, role player, miniatures game player, video game player, and part time athlete, as well as a member of the Horror Writers Association. If you weren't impressed enough, he also works full time while writing for Elmoryn as well as the world of Adrian's Undead Diary and his newest project, Tesser; A Dragon Among Us.

- Find More Online -

Visit **adriansundeaddiary.com** to access additional content. Learn more about Adrian's world, contact the author, join discussions with other readers, view maps from the story, and receive the latest news about AUD.

Check out Chris Philbrook's official website **thechrisphilbrook.com** to keep tabs on his many exciting projects, or follow Chris on Facebook at **www.facebook.com/ChrisPhilbrookAuthor** for special announcements.

Read more by author Chris Philbrook in *The Kinless Trilogy*. Explore Elmoryn, a world of dark fantasy where death is not the end. The story begins in *Book One: The Wrath of the Orphans*, available in print, Kindle, and online. Visit **elmoryn.com** to learn more about Elmoryn, view concept art, and much more.

Follow Chris Philbrook's latest epic series as it unfolds in *Tesser: A Dragon Among Us*. Meet Tesser, the Dragon. He who walks in any form, and flies the skies free of fear. He has slept for millennia, but now he has awoken in a world ruled by human hands, where science has overshadowed even the glory of old magic. Follow Tesser as he seeks to understand why he slept for so long, and where all the magic has gone. Visit **adragonamongus.com** to learn more.

Can't get enough of AUD?

Visit the School Store at **adriansundeaddiary.com** for stickers, hats, and a wide variety of awesome shirts!

27483593R00161

Made in the USA
Lexington, KY
11 November 2013